With a ... came d...
he...

The Bedouins had never experienced a sonic boom before—the kind a missile traveling at Mach 6 would make after it passed. They started heading faster toward whatever it was that had hit the ground.

Fouad was scared by the sudden noise and commotion, but his clan's wealth was represented in no small part by those sheep and they were his responsibility. The young man started after the sheep.

Abdulla had his hands suddenly occupied with trying to control a panicking camel. He hauled back on the reins to stop its frightened run across the desert. When Abdulla looked back, he saw a strange pink cloud rising up from the spot where the thud had come from.

As the cloud drifted along toward Fouad and the sheep, the sand it touched blackened instantly. A thornbush shriveled and shrank as the cloud passed. And as the first sheep contacted the edge of the cloud, it fell to the ground, kicking and struggling. Within seconds, the sheep was still in death, its wool blackening and crisping.

Abdulla screamed a warning at Fouad, but the young man stood frozen in shock. The boy was just too far away, Abdulla wouldn't reach him before the cloud did.

And he didn't notice how close he was getting to the lethal pink gas himself . . .

Other books by S. M. Gunn

SEALS SUB RESCUE: OPERATION ENDURANCE

SEALS

SUB STRIKE

OPERATION OCEAN WATCH

S.M. GUNN

AVON BOOKS
An Imprint of HarperCollinsPublishers

AVON BOOKS
An Imprint of HarperCollins*Publishers*
10 East 53rd Street
New York, New York 10022-5299

Copyright © 2003 by Bill Fawcett & Associates
ISBN: 0-06-009548-2
www.avonbooks.com

First Avon Books paperback printing: March 2003

Avon Trademark Reg. U.S. Pat. Off. and in Other Countries, Marca Registrada, Hecho en U.S.A.
HarperCollins® is a registered trademark of HarperCollins Publishers Inc.

Printed in the U.S.A.

10 9 8 7 6 5 4 3 2 1

SEALS

SUB STRIKE

OPERATION OCEAN WATCH

CHAPTER 1

★ ★ ★ ★

The desert was old, so much so that it seemed beyond age. Timelessness blew across the sands and
gravel plains with the wind that moved the grains
of sand together. The grinding sand created dust,
and the dust lay thick. The sand had seen Noah's
flood, felt the footsteps of Alexander the Great, the
marches of the Roman legions, the sandals of
Christ, the hoofbeats of the Crusaders, the treads
of British tanks, and the thud of German bombs. It
was the desert, and it took no notice in the affairs
of what moved across its sands.

April 1987
1247 ZULU
33° 31' North, 43° 12' East
Southern bank of the Wadi Haurān
Al Anbar Governorate, Western Iraq

The scene on the undulating gravel plain was one
that had remained almost unchanged for hundreds,
if not thousands, of years. A family group, a clan,
of Bedouin nomads were moving with their flocks

and herds through the desert. Even in the turmoil-riddled Mideast, flocks were moved from grazing land to grazing land, and borders were crossed for trading livestock. Jordan was a place where the healthy camels accompanying this particular Bedouin clan would be more appreciated than in the bazaars and souks—or marketplaces—of Iraq.

The patriarch of this particular Bedouin clan was Abdulla Waheed. The members of the clan were few; only ten people traveled with the handful of camels and dozens of sheep and goats. But the pride of the Bedouins ran strong in the family, and nowhere stronger than in the veins of Abdulla, whose eyes had been looking out over these sands for more than seventy years.

Few things could impress the old desert dweller. He had seen soldiers clash and cannons roar—but that power was nothing compared to the terror of a desert sandstorm. At night the clear skies and myriad stars showed why Arabia had been the birthplace of astronomy in the Western world. The makings of man were inconsequential compared to the marvels of Allah's creation.

The Waheed clan had been traveling these desert lands since the days of Muhammad, Allah's blessings on his name. And if Allah so willed, the clan would continue to travel with their flocks and herds for several hundred years yet to come.

The furrows of the heavily lined face of the old Bedouin deepened as he quietly smiled to himself. It was good to be free in the desert. As his eyes glanced over to where his youngest son was driving the herd along, the smile in Abdulla's face widened in pleasure. It was good to have sons, even if the ways of the Bedouin might be fading into the past.

The modern age was going to come, no matter what it seemed. Only the desert remained the same. His brother had long ago left the desert life of the nomad and settled in to take up date farming and establish another branch of the clan. The fact that he was in one place meant that his sons could be educated in the schools of the towns and cities, but Abdulla considered that a small payment for the cost of giving up the freedom of the desert.

Saddam Hussein might be the leader of Iraq, but he had also been raised a Tikrit city dweller who had no real grasp of the desert life that had existed for millennia. But he did do some good for everyone in the country, even the Bedouins who had settled down. Saddam's own upbringing had been hard. His stepfather had forced the future president to work the farm and flocks rather than attend school and get an education. Saddam now wanted his people to have the opportunities that had been denied him when he was younger. His many changes to Iraq included making schools, and even universities, available to all—or so he said.

The smile passed from Abdulla Waheed's face, leaving only a hardened line of the lips and eyes behind it. Abdulla had more than just his youngest son, but Fouad was the only son he had left in the clan at the time. The voracious appetite of Hussein's army had taken several of them. The old Bedouin could only pray that Allah looked over his sons as they served. The war with Iran had been raging for years. It could easily happen that the army came for the youngest male Waheed before many more years passed.

In the old man's opinion, it was far better to face the clean harshness and trials of the desert than to fight in another land. The Persians—he still thought of the Iranians as such, just as his father and grandfather had—were little more than rug merchants. What did they have that the Iraqis needed?

His brother's eldest son had no need to serve in the military. He had not only completed school, he had gone on and become some kind of doctor. That kept him from military service. But no Bedouin of the Waheed clan had ever taken up such work. Even a farmer spent the day under the sun of Allah, all praise be on His name. But a doctor! He must work inside with the women! Not a proper place at all.

But there was no need to think of such things now. Even the freedoms of the desert were tempered by its heat, sand, and gravel. They were traveling southwest, along an ancient trading route to the markets of Jordan. The Wadi Haurãn off to their right was dry and would seem to have seen little if any of the winter rains of just a few months earlier. But only a few kilometers ahead—in fact eight, though the measurement of distance meant little to the Bedouin Arab—were the ruins of Muhaiwir. The village had been in ruins for ages, but there was drinkable water in the old wells nearby.

Abdulla knew that Muhaiwir would be a good place to stop and camp for the evening. There should be sufficient fodder for the herd, and the camels could of course feed on whatever grew. There would be further water a day's travel to the southwest, an underground pipeline with a pumping station along the path of the Wadi Haurān. And then there was Rutba, farther to the southeast. But other Bedouins traveling through the area had said that something was going on in the stony waste near the water source.

Iraqi construction and military units had been seen along the highway that traveled between Baghdad and Amman in Jordan. In the desert half a day northwest of Rutba, the Iraqi military had driven some of the Bedouin clans from the trading paths they had traveled for generations.

Allah, all praise be upon His name, put these trials in front of man for him to prove himself worthy of paradise. But He also allowed a man to go around a serpent laying on the trail in front of him. It would be better for the clan to take the western trail after they left Muhaiwir. There was no need to force a confrontation with the military. Let the desert have them. They were—

With a sudden crashing thud, something came down from the sky and smashed into the desert only a few hundred meters to the north. The camels honked and brayed, bolting in the opposite direction. As the herds scattered, there was a thunderous crashing boom echoing across the cloudless sky, increasing the panic of the sheep and goats.

In spite of the modern military forces in Iraq, Jordan, and Syria all about them, the Bedouins had never experienced a sonic boom before—the kind of boom a missile traveling at Mach 6 would make after it had passed.

The herds ran faster, but were heading straight toward whatever it was that had hit the ground. Fouad was scared by the sudden noise and commotion, but his clan's wealth was represented in no small part by those sheep, and they were his responsibility. The young man started after them, hoping to stop them before they ran too far.

Abdulla had his hands suddenly occupied with trying to control a panicking camel. He hauled back on the reins and pulled the creature's head to the side to finally stop its panicked run across the desert. When he looked back, he could see that the clan was trying to stop the animals' flight. And Fouad was still running up to the front of the sheep.

What Abdulla also saw was a strange pink cloud rising from the spot from which the thud had come. Whatever this beast from the sky was, Abdulla thought, Shaitan himself must have sent it. And what was that cursed pink cloud doing?

As the cloud drifted along toward Fouad and the panicked sheep, the sand it touched blackened instantly. A thornbush shriveled and shrank as the cloud passed. And as the first sheep contacted the edge of the cloud, it fell to the ground, kicking and struggling. Within seconds it was still in death, its wool blackening and crisping.

Abdulla screamed a warning at Fouad, but the

young man stood gazing in shock at what he had just seen happen to his sheep. The boy was too far away, and Abdulla knew he wouldn't reach him before the cloud did. But he didn't notice how close he was getting to the lethal pink gas himself.

A small black dot appeared in the sky to the south. The dot quickly grew and transformed into the wasplike shape of an Aerospatiale SA 319B Alouette III helicopter. On the sides of the tan-colored bird were the markings of the Iraqi Air Force. As the aircraft approached the area where the bodies could be seen, it turned and began to circle the area.

The man seated to the left of the pilot looked out from the cockpit at the scene below. His dark blue coverall-type uniform showed that he was assigned to one of the "special weapons" units of the Iraqi military. The devices on the shoulder boards and collar of the uniform were the three stars of a naqib—a captain with the insignia of the Iraqi Air Force.

With binoculars to his eyes, Captain Adnan al-Majid examined the scene of horror below him with the clinical detachment of a soldier. Bodies of several people could be made out among the carcasses of a number of animals. Whoever they had been, it was just their fate to be in the very wrong place at the worst possible time.

The concern of the Iraqi officer was for the additional difficulty this made of his immediate mission. His thoughts for those dead on the ground

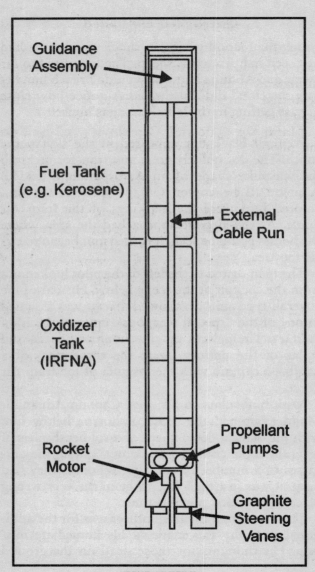

SCUD MISSILE

were fleeting and of less concern than he would have for a good meal. In the helicopter, he had measuring and marking equipment, but not the kind of protective gear he would prefer to have available right then.

"Tariq, set us down," Captain al-Majid said to the pilot. "Set us down upwind and well away from the burned area. Those fuel fumes will have dissipated by now, but the ground could still be contaminated."

"Muktar," the captain said into his headset to the man in the back of the helicopter, "you're going to get out here and stand guard. That damned missile had a lot more fuel in it than we were prepared for. We have to go back for some protective gear before we can examine the impact site."

The helicopter swooped down low and settled easily onto the hard-packed gravel. The ever-present dust of the desert swirled and roiled away from the downwash of the helicopter blades. As Muktar unbuckled his safety belt and prepared to open the door to the cabin, Captain al-Majid turned to the backseat and shouted over the noise of the engines.

"Muktar," he said, "you make sure no one approaches the site until I return from the base. The recovery truck will probably get here before then, and I don't want any accidents. If anyone comes back for those bodies, you make sure they do not take anything away."

Muktar answered with a quick "Yes sir" as he grabbed up his AKMS-47, where it had been secured for the flight.

Captain al-Majid turned to the pilot as soon as Muktar had secured the cabin door and moved away from the helicopter. "Back to the base," he said. "This damned thing hit more than ten kilometers from where it was supposed to, and I want to examine it before anyone tries to move it."

Nodding, the pilot twisted the throttle in his hand while pulling up on the collective lever to which it was attached. With a screaming roar from its turbine engine, the helicopter lifted off in a swirl of dust. The pilot quickly climbed up and away from the dust, turning back toward the south and the direction from which they had come. Below them the youngest and oldest males of the Waheed Bedouin clan lay unseeing on the ground, the dust and sand stirred up by the helicopter now settling down around them.

September 1987
1400 ZULU
Ministry of Industry and Military Industrialization Headquarters
Baghdad, Iraq

The entire military procurement system for Iraq was controlled in the 1980s by a single organization, the Ministry of Industry and Military Industrialization. Iraq was in the middle of a war with Iran, and the development of the armed forces, as well as supplying them with materials, weapons, and ammunition, made MIMI one of the most important and powerful ministries in Iraq. The desire of Iraq's president, Saddam Hussein, to arm his country with missiles, weapons of mass destruction, and especially a nuclear weapon, gave MIMI even more status.

The collapse of the world's oil prices in 1986, and the military victories of the massed armies of Iran, cut heavily into the economy of Iraq. But with over forty percent of the country's budget going to military procurement, literally billions of dollars were under the control of MIMI and the man who headed the ministry—Abdul Talfaq.

The son of President Hussein's mother's brother made Abdul Talfaq a member of Saddam's own family. This allowed him to be put in a position of trust within Iraq. But it was Talfaq's own abilities that made him a close confidant of Saddam.

In addition to being in charge of MIMI, Talfaq was also the head of the Iraqi Secret Service Organization. The SSO had the direct responsibility of protecting Saddam Hussein. It also oversaw the operations of all of the Iraqi intelligence organizations. As the head of such an empire, Abdul Talfaq wielded great power and influence in Iraq, and he liked showing it.

Some of the offices of MIMI in Baghdad were opulent, which fitted their location on the banks of the Tigris River, on the grounds of the Presidential Palace off Kindi Street. Abdul Talfaq had a reputation for bestowing largesse freely. People and officials who pleased him, or his uncle, often found themselves in possession of a new Mercedes-Benz or fancy home. But the dark side of the Hussein connection also moved just below the surface.

Abdul Talfaq was a physically strong man, as befitted the second most powerful man in Iraq. When a rage overtook Talfaq from the failure of an underling, he was well known for beating men senseless with his fists. At a military camp near Taji, north of Baghdad, the SSO had a torture and interrogation center. It was rumored that Talfaq would conduct his own special interrogation on those who failed him, so they could learn not to displease him in the future.

The men gathered in the posh surroundings of a conference room at MIMI headquarters were not worried about a possible failure—or at least they weren't too worried. At the meeting, they would be presenting Talfaq, and MIMI, with the results of their latest tests of a new missile for Iraq.

Project 144 was to be the development of a missile with much greater range than those Iraq had been able to purchase from their allies in the Soviet Union. And a longer range missile would have a direct effect on Iraq's war with Iran.

A number of engineers, officers, and technicians surrounded a long polished teak table in the posh conference room. All of the high-backed antique chairs around the rich brown wood table were filled except for the one immediately to the right of the head of the table. Around the room the lower part of the cream-colored walls were of white marble, while the upper part was covered with paintings and ancient tapestries. But the attention of each man at the table was centered on the squat black-haired individual who sat at its head.

Abdul Talfaq focused his attention on the air force officer in charge of the recovery of the test missiles. His reports indicated that the new designs could have the range that was demanded by military necessity. Captain Adnan al-Majid knew he was in the spotlight, and there was nothing he could do about it.

"And there was a problem with the first tests back in April?" Talfaq asked.

The soft tone with which he asked the question did little to mask the menace radiating from the person behind the voice. But Captain al-Majid knew that Talfaq had read the reports that were stacked up on the table in front of him. A straight answer was all that could save, or damn, him at this meeting.

"Not a problem exactly sir," he answered. "The first missile went off course and impacted some distance away from the expected target. The range we achieved indicated that the design was on the right track, we just needed to increase the accuracy of the system."

"And for some reason that first missile had a live chemical warhead?" Talfaq asked with a raised eyebrow.

"A live warhead?" al-Majid asked in a puzzled tone. "No, sir. It was carrying only a concrete weight in the nose. The weight was balanced to replace what a real warhead would be, that was all."

"But the report reads that there were casualties at the test site," Talfaq went on.

"Oh, those, sir," al-Majid said, with some relief

slipping into his voice. "There were some Bedouins in the area of the missile impact. There wasn't any kind of warhead in the system. But a lot of the unused fuel remained in the tanks and they burst on impact. To keep the range of the missile down enough to keep it in the test area, the burn of the engine was much shorter than normal. When the missile impacted, it sprayed TMI85 and AK27I over the hot sands.

"TMI85 is simply a formulation of kerosene. But AK27I is a Soviet formulation of inhibited red fuming nitric acid and additives. It makes a very lethal cloud when it vaporizes. That's what killed the Bedouins and a number of their livestock."

"And you don't think the survivors would be a serious security risk?" Talfaq said in a more menacing tone than he had used earlier. "Not having an eye for security strikes me as a flaw in a military officer."

Now, al-Majid felt the sweat start breaking out on him as it had when he was in the western Iraqi desert. "I don't think any survivors would be much of a risk, sir," Majid continued.

"You don't?"

"No, sir, for the simple reason that we couldn't spot any survivors. And we flew over the area before we landed. The cloud of acid would kill anyone or anything that contacted it almost instantly. I seriously doubt that those Bedouins ever even knew what had killed them. The bodies were pretty severely burned when we found them, and they died very fast."

"It is a good thing that my security people agree with your estimate of the situation," Talfaq said with a smile and a more relaxed posture.

Relief flooded through Captain al-Majid's system at Talfaq's words and reaction.

"I understand the tests last month went much better?" Talfaq asked.

"Yes, sir," Dr. Hamza al-Banna, one of the chief designers for the new missile, answered. "The modifications we added to the design have extended the range of the Soviet R-17—what the West calls the Scud B—more than double what it was originally.

"Our first test flight back in April," the doctor continued, "gave us an extended range of 450 kilometers. The original missile only gave us a 280 to 300 kilometer range. The new design we launched last month gives us a range increase to 650 kilometers. Though this is at a cost in payload weight, the new missile can still deliver a substantial load of high explosives, between 300 and 350 kilograms."

"The new missiles may have to carry something other than high explosives," a new voice added from the far end of the conference room, "but that project isn't your concern."

Striding into the room from the silently opened door beyond him was Saddam Hussein himself. The medium-height, thick-bodied ruler of Iraq took in the entire room with his eyes as he strode to the table. Behind him, armed Republican Guards took up positions on either side of the door. Even in their absolute stillness the two guards showed more life than shined out of the round face with the brush mustache, topped by a thatch of oiled black hair.

The military men around the table immediately leaped from their seats and snapped to attention. The civilians got to their feet only slightly slower than their military counterparts. Abdul Talfaq got up the slowest of all, a wide smile on his face at the discomfiture of the others.

As Saddam took his place at the head of the table, Talfaq moved and sat down to his right. Saddam indicated that the others should take their seats, and he looked at the doctor who had been speaking and asked, "As I understand it, there's a problem with the accuracy of the new missiles?"

"Uh, no, sir," the doctor stammered, momentarily flustered. He gained control of himself and continued, "There is presently a tendency for the new design to vibrate heavily in flight. That will possibly cause a breakup of the missile, but we believe that the problem will be solved very quickly. We expect the CEP of the new design—"

"The CEP?" Talfaq questioned quietly. He knew that Saddam hated to be reminded of any possible ignorance on his part, and that even he could suffer if Saddam flew into a rage.

"Oh yes, sir," Dr. al-Banna said, explaining quickly. "The CEP is the Circular Error Probability. That's the area where we would expect fifty percent of the missiles to land. The CEP of the new design is estimated to be 500 meters at maximum range."

"Half a kilometer!" Saddam said loudly. "And only half the missiles would be expected to hit that?

If I hunted as well as you scientists made your weapons, I wouldn't have a trophy to my name.

"But no matter," Saddam said in a calmer voice. "Your work for the greater good of Iraq will not go unnoticed."

Talfaq was the only man in the room who knew Saddam's outburst was an act to demonstrate his control over the people around the table. Saddam was a master at using the stick and carrot approach in controlling people under him. The loud voice and the fear it induced was the stick. Soon it would be time for the carrot.

"A destructive enough warhead will not need great accuracy to destroy a target," Saddam continued. "But that will be a problem for others to deal with. I want you men to perfect your design and get this new missile into production as soon as possible. I have decided to name your new weapon after the Shi'a martyr Imam Hussein. I want the al-Hussein missile to be ready to rain down on the heads of our enemies within the year.

"From what I have been told," Saddam went on, "your new missile uses parts from other ones to complete your design?"

"That's true, Alza'Im," Abdul Talfaq said, using the latest term for Saddam—the leader—printed in the Iraqi papers. "They can make two of the new al-Hussein missiles from three of the older R-17 designs. The fuel tanks of the new missile are lengthened with sections from the old models."

"Yes, yes," Saddam said with a curt wave of his

hand. "I'm sure these wise men around this table realize that they will be consuming weapons that could otherwise be used in the defense of Iraq to create the al-Hussein. It does seem a possible waste to me."

Another wave of fear went around the room as the men at the table thought they were about to see another outburst from the most powerful man in Iraq. Talfaq suspected Saddam was now going to use the carrot part of his motivation system. As he saw the benevolent smile cross the Iraqi leader's face, Talfaq knew he had been correct.

"But I'm sure the people of Iraq will have their trust in you men upheld." Saddam said as he got to his feet.

The rest of the men around the table stood immediately as their leader rose.

"I will leave you to the direction of my most trusted aide," Saddam said as he nodded to Talfaq.

When the Iraqi leader left the room, a Republican Guard officer returned and placed a small box next to each of the men sitting at the table. Then, without a word, he turned and left.

The men looked at Talfaq, and he indicated that they should open the boxes. Inside each one was a set of car keys. By the insignia on the key ring, they were to one of the new model Mercedes-Benz cars that were known to be parked in ranks in the palace garages.

"You each have a gift from President Hussein," Talfaq said to the stunned men around the table. "The guards outside will show you to the cars outside. I will expect regular reports on the progress of Project 144. Good day."

With that, the stocky man left the table and moved to a side door that led to his private office area.

For a moment the men around the table stood and looked at one another, most of them holding the keys to their new cars. Some of them wondered just how different things would have been if Saddam and Talfaq hadn't liked the results of their project so far. Just what would the small boxes have held then?

CHAPTER 2

★ ★ ★ ★

The Iraqi biological weapons research center was housed in a new facility. Though the bioweapons program had existed for years, it languished as a poorly funded, low priority project until Iraq suffered defeats on the battlefield with Iran. Then the search for all kinds of new weapons became urgent, leading to the conclusion that a functional, deliverable biological weapon would have the same effect as a small nuclear device. The Iraqi high command, and Saddam Hussein, invested in facilities and personnel for a bioweapons program. But the prestige of the program depended on its delivery of a weapon—something it hadn't done by the end of the war with Iran.

Biological weapons were tricky and difficult to work with. Using them meant aiming a disease or natural toxin—a poison—at a given target. Though diseases had been a scourge of mankind over the millennia, nature had her own way of spreading them. The few biological organisms that could be developed as weapons were a lot harder to manipulate than the metal and explosives of a common munition. They were living organisms, or their products. And they didn't respond well to being produced in bulk, stored, or packed into a warhead, bomb, or shell.

Concerning the effectiveness of a final product, Saddam had been told that a single warhead for a Scud missile could carry enough sarin nerve gas to contaminate an area of more than 230 square kilometers. But botulinum toxin was almost three million times more deadly than sarin. Under ideal conditions, that same Scud warhead filled with botulinum toxin could cover 3,700 square kilometers, an area sixteen times greater than that covered by the sarin warhead.

Nerve gas killed in seconds, minutes at the most. Botulinum toxin could debilitate troops exposed to it in a few hours. It could kill them starting at twelve hours after exposure. And the symptoms of botulinum toxin were not uncommon, so by the time they were noticed, it would be too late to treat the victim.

A botulinum toxin bomb incapacitated and killed quickly enough to be used as a tactical weapon. Commanders in the field could use weapons carrying such a payload to break up troop concentrations, contaminate supply dumps, and generally destroy the enemy. But biological weapons also offered a strategic value.

The anthrax disease could kill within two to four days, and the symptoms of an anthrax infection were not recognized for what they were by most doctors in the world. Furthermore, the spores that

spread anthrax were persistent. They could contaminate a huge area for years, decades, unless destroyed by very difficult means. And the same
warhead that carried botulinum toxin would contaminate a much larger area if loaded with anthrax.

These were the kind of weapons that Saddam
Hussein very much wanted. But he wanted them
delivered in a usable form, as the scientists de-
scribed it to him. Saddam hated germs and had a
personal fear of being infected or poisoned. He
couldn't imagine that anyone else wouldn't share
such a fear. And that fear made his fascination with
a biological weapon all the greater.

Such fear was a weapon itself, and Saddam believed he needed all of the weapons he could get.
Iraq had been in a state of war with Iran, its neigh-
bor to the east, since late September 1980. Instead
of a quick, decisive set of battles, Iraq was bogged
down in a ground war—one it was losing. Saddam
wanted weapons capable of destruction on a massive scale. If he couldn't have a nuclear bomb, he
would settle for the chemical and biological
weapons of mass destruction that killed people and
left material alone. The Iraqi army was not facing
what they had expected—a disorganized mob with
poor leadership. Instead, the Iraqi military was
fighting thousands of fanatics who had no fear of
dying if it meant eliminating even one Iraqi.

Iran had been swept by a wave of Islamic Fundamentalism that threatened to engulf the entire Arab
world. The religious revolution that put the Ayatollah Khomeini in power in Iran had gutted the Ira-

nian military of experienced officers. Anyone suspected of having loyalties to the earlier ruling
regime in Iran was quickly thrown in prison by the
Pasdaran—Khomeini's Revolutionary Guard.

The Pasdaran were a corps made up of the faith-
ful. What they lacked in specific military skills they
made up in loyalty and religious fervor. Even the
Pasdaran leadership consisted of religious mullahs,
men with little or no military experience at all.
Thus, the Iranian military was led by junior officers, at best, and the religious mob of the Pasdaran
looked their shoulders, which led Saddam Hussein
to believe that his well-armed and organized army
could roll over the Iranians. In one major action,
Saddam felt he could capture a larger area of the
Persian Gulf and eliminate the danger of Khomeini
exporting his Islamic revolution into Iraq.

Iraq's army of over 190,000 men, 2,200 tanks,
and 450 aircraft were ready when relations between Iraq and Iran deteriorated past the point of
repair by the spring of 1980. The leadership and
command in Baghdad sent the military into Iran,
and soon learned that the Iranian Air Force was
still a strong force to be reckoned with.

When it looked like the Iraqis would overrun a
major air base, the Iranian president released pilots
from jail. Even though the pilots were suspected of
still being loyal to the previous regime, Iran needed
their skills. And their skills greater than that of the
Iraqis.

By November 1980 the last major capture of
Iranian territory by the Iraqi forces was complete.

From that point on the war went against the Iraqis. The Pasdarans proved to be a formidable foe, not because of any military skill on their part, but simply because they were more than willing to die if it meant helping to defeat the Iraqis.

The Pasdaran forces were soon augmented by 100,000 Basij, or People's Militia, volunteers. The Iranian forces, committed to driving out the Iraqi invaders, were known to carry their own shrouds into battle with them. They welcomed martyrdom and fought bravely.

In 1981, Iran introduced their human wave assault strategy, in which thousands of volunteers would charge the Iraqi lines. The Iraqis were not willing to accept the same level of casualties as their foes. And the Iranian Air Force, though limited in the number of planes was, successful in attacking Iraqi targets.

By 1982 new offensives by the Iranians had begun to seriously drive the Iraqi lines back. Entering Iraq itself, the Iranian forces continued to use their human wave attacks. Thousands of volunteers, ranging in age from nine years old to well over fifty, swept into the Iraqi lines. Paths were cleared for the few Iranian tanks by the simple expedient of mobs of people setting off the mines before the tanks reached them. In spite of horrendous losses, the Iranians forced the Iraqis back.

In 1983 over 6,000 Iranians were killed in a single battle, with almost no gains at all by the Iranian forces. The Iranian human waves were broken by Iraqi armor and mechanized units, but not without high losses among the Iraqis as well. Tens of thousands of children were noted as being in the human waves thrown against the Iraqis in 1984. But those sacrifices were mostly in vain.

The Iraqis did find the weapons to defeat the human wave attacks, with limited risk to their own forces. Thanks to his engineers and chemists, Saddam had his initial *aslibatal dammar el shamal*—weapons of mass destruction. Mustard gas, which caused severe burns and blistering of the skin, as well as death, was the first Iraqi chemical weapon to be used in combat.

Iraq employed chemical weapons against Iran early in the hostilities between the two countries, and as the Iraqis became more sophisticated in making, loading, and using them in the field, they employed them more often. Rockets, aerial bombs, aircraft spray tanks, and artillery shells were loaded with mustard and nerve gases and sent out onto the battlefield. Tens of thousands of the Iranian forces who charged the Iraqi lines were felled by chemicals.

Baghdad and Tehran are a little over 700 kilometers apart, but Baghdad is less that 125 kilometers from the border with Iran, while Tehran is almost 600 kilometers within Iran. Both countries obtained whatever weapons they could from outside suppliers, and both ended up with supplies of Scud ballistic missiles manufactured in the Soviet Union or North Korea.

The NATO designation of the Soviet R-17 missile is the Scud B. Similar in design to the German

V2 of World War II, the Scud B has a maximum range of around 300 kilometers. With both sides having the same weapon during the war, Saddam Hussein soon discovered that the Iranians could shell Baghdad with the 1,000 kilogram high explosives of the Scud warhead, while Tehran was well out of reach for retaliation.

In 1982, Iraq fired the first Scud missile into Iran. Over the next six years of the war, Iraq fired 172 Scuds into Iran, while Iran fired forty missiles into Iraq. In 1988, Iraqi technicians, aided by advisors from the Soviet Union and other countries, had changed the design of the Scud missile, more than doubling its range.

On February 29, 1988, seventeen Iraqi missiles rained down on Tehran—what would come to be known as the "War of the Cities" had begun. Before it was over, Iraq had fired a total of 189 Scud missiles into Tehran, and the Iranians retaliated with seventy-seven missiles of their own. The accuracy of the Iraqi Scud variant was poor, but the volume of missiles that the Iraqi military industrial engine had been able to produce helped overcome that inaccuracy.

Saddam Hussein freely used mustard gas and nerve agents as part of his new offensive launched in March 1988. Though his technicians were not able to successfully mount an effective chemical warhead to the new al-Hussein missile, the missiles helped break down the morale of the Iranian people. All that could be heard around Tehran as the missiles passed overhead was an eerie howl. Then the supersonic missiles would come down and explode, and only after the warhead had detonated would people around the impact site hear the sonic boom of its travel.

The human wave attacks by the Iranian zealots had proved crushing against the Iraqis. No matter how many bullets were fired, shells launched, or bombs dropped, the Iranians accepted the losses and kept coming on. But the chemical weapons, the nerve and mustard gases, broke the back of the human wave attacks. The final straw for Iran had been the impacting of missiles on Tehran itself. It seemed that the mullahs and ayatollahs were willing and able to exhort thousands of their followers to their deaths, but when the risk was to their own mortality, the situation changed.

With the flow of the war changing in Iraq's favor, Iran saw there was little that could be done to reverse the situation. In four major battles in 1988, between April and August, the Iraqis routed or defeated the Iranian forces. Iran finally accepted UN Security Council Resolution 598 in August 1988. The cease-fire took effect on August 20, and eight long years of war were finally over. The Ayatollah Khomeini died on June 3, 1989, and the threat of the Islamic Revolution spreading out over the Persian Gulf states lost some of its urgency.

CHAPTER 3

★ ★ ★ ★

1989
0425 ZULU
Exit 120, I-395 Northbound
Alexandria, Virginia

Lieutenant Greg Rockham drove his '85 Silverado Suburban northbound up Interstate 395 past Alexandria, Virginia. One thing about traveling 395 into D.C., Rockham thought, it didn't seem to matter what time of day you were heading in. You always hit some kind of rush hour. It was nice of the Special Warfare Command people to schedule a meeting at 1000 hours, rather than earlier, so everyone could hit the heavy traffic. But Rockham wanted to be sure to get to the meeting early, so he had planned to be at the Pentagon by 0900 EST.

"No good deed goes unpunished," Rockham said out loud as he stepped on the accelerator to get around a slow sedan with Kentucky plates. He was right in the middle of the morning traffic crush. Just trying to read the proper turnoff signs was hard enough; the scattering of tourists to the nation's capital certainly didn't help the traffic flow.

Finally reaching the turnoff he needed, Rockham headed around the Pentagon to the north parking area. The guys back at SEAL Team Four who had spent time in D.C. had told him that it was easier to just park away from the Pentagon and walk up to it rather than search for a closer parking space in the south lot. And by the looks of the parking areas, they had been right.

A quick trot by the very fit SEAL officer put him at the river entrance to the Pentagon in just a few minutes. His cushion of time was being eaten up fast. A flash of his ID to the guard at the doorway, and he was inside the huge five-sided building—the nerve center of the military might of the United States.

That sounded pretty grand, but it seemed that the whole building had been built to withstand an invasion. Not that it would be that hard for a determined enemy to get inside the building—no, that would just draw the unwary into a trap. The trap was the labyrinth layout of the interior of the WWII-era structure.

Not including the basement, the Pentagon basically had five floors. Each of the floors was divided into concentric rings around the central courtyard of the building. The rings were labeled A to E from the center of the building out. Ten corridors, like the radiating spokes of a wheel and numbered one to ten, interconnected the rings. To further confuse things, the Pentagon basement had two additional rings, F and G. Knowing how to get around the Pentagon without asking directions was almost an art form.

But his old platoon chief had taught the SEAL officer well. "Remember the six P's, Rock," Chief Monday had said. "Prior planning prevents piss-poor performance."

So Lieutenant Rockham had put that six P mantra into play two days earlier, when he received the orders to report to the Pentagon, and had taken detailed directions from Ed Shepherd, a friend of his who was the intel officer at SpecWarGroup Two. Ed had pulled a tour of duty at a staff position at the Pentagon, and he knew the layout well. What Rockham had to find was the way to Room 3D526. According to Ed, that meant the room was on the third floor, D ring, off Corridor 5, Room 26. Sounded easy enough. Yeah, right.

The interior of the building was confusing, to say the least. Legend had it that there were still people wandering the corridors who had died decades before—not even their ghosts could find the way out.

Now Rockham walked at a quick pace through the Pentagon, down Corridor 9 to its end at the A ring. Stairs gave him access to the third floor. Then it was around to the right on the A ring, almost halfway around the building, until he came across Corridor 5. Now it was back out toward the outer wall of the Pentagon, until he came to the D ring.

Access to where he had been ordered to report was restricted. The Marine sergeant sitting at the desk at that section of the ring blocked Rockham's further progress. It took an examination of Rockham's ID against a list on a clipboard to get the SEAL officer down the ring. Room 26 wasn't hard to find; the young Marine standing guard outside the doorway was a good landmark.

The Marine guard on duty looked young, tall, fit, and spotlessly dressed in his uniform. He was practically a clone of the Marine sergeant at the desk not a hundred feet away. The guard's "high and tight" haircut was trimmed with only a short bit of his brown hair showing above the almost bald sides of his head. For all of his showpiece appearance, Rockham imagined that the holstered M9 Beretta at the man's side was just as spotless, and ready for duty, as the Marine was himself.

"Sir," the Marine said as he stepped in front of the door at Rockham's approach, "would you please wait here."

Greg was all of ten minutes early; so much for hitting the head and then getting a cup of coffee from the cafeteria he had passed. He hadn't expected this much security, even at the Pentagon. But the SEAL stood, as he'd been asked to, while the young Marine knocked and then opened the door.

The Marine leaned forward and spoke to someone in a quiet voice. In a few seconds he straightened and closed the door. "They'll be calling for you in just a moment, sir," he said, turning to Rockham.

Greg didn't have to cool his heels more than a few minutes before a Navy yeoman came to the door. CHIEF YEOMAN BARNHART, according to his uniform insignia, came out and asked Rockham to enter.

It turned out 3D526 was a conference room, or perhaps some kind of briefing room, to Rockham's glance. At the long table that took up the center of the room were nine people, all but two of them in uniform. The yeoman chief sat at a desk just to the side of the door Rockham had entered. On the far walls were maps of the world and various close-ups of areas unfamiliar to Rockham. Across the long conference table were scattered file folders, note-pads, and the occasional coffee cup.

By all rights the room should have been sinking slowly from the weight of all the gold braid he saw around the table, Rockham thought. Quite a bit of rank to face as a lieutenant. Mostly flag-rank officers, five admirals, two captains, a man in a gray business suit with his head down as he read papers, and a honey-blond civilian woman who was very familiar to him.

Drawing himself to attention, Greg spoke to the rear admiral (upper half), the highest ranking man in the room, who was sitting at the head of the table. The admiral was someone Rockham recognized immediately as being the vice commander of the United States Special Operations Command (USSOCOM). He was the Navy man in command of all of the Navy's Special Operations Forces, the SEAL Teams, SDV Teams, and the Special Boat Units, and he was the highest ranking SEAL in the Navy. Whatever was going to happen in this room, they certainly had brought out the big guns for it.

"Lieutenant Greg Rockham reporting as ordered, sir," Rockham said.

"At ease, Lieutenant," Admiral Cromarty said. "Take a seat, please."

As Rockham sat down, he came to eye level with the civilian in the business suit. Now he recognized Peter Danzig, the CIA case officer who had been with him and his platoon almost a year ago. Their mission then had been to rescue a Soviet defector, and Operation Endurance had quickly turned into a mini-invasion of Soviet territory for Rockham and his SEALs. Was this meeting some kind of further debriefing on that op? Because Sharon Taylor had also been aboard the submarine during that op, and she was sitting right there next to Danzig.

"Okay, Lieutenant Rockham," Admiral Cromarty said, "I understand introductions to our two representatives of the Intelligence community here won't be necessary."

"No sir, Admiral," Rockham said, "I remember Mr. Danzig and Miss Taylor very well."

Sharon Taylor put on a wry smile at the "Miss" designation from Rockham. Admiral Cromarty looked down at an open file on the table in front of him and continued.

"You're presently undergoing a tour of duty as the operations officer at SEAL Team Four, as I read things," Admiral Cromarty said as he looked up from the table directly at Rockham.

"Yes sir," was the only answer that came to Rockham's mind.

"By the look of things, you'll be going on from

there to a shore tour, probably on the Staff at Special Warfare Group Two," Cromarty continued.

"Yes sir," Rockham said again.

"We may be going to change that, Lieutenant," Cromarty said. "You have been brought here because of your unique qualifications, as well as your special operational experience." Cromarty paused.

"When I saw Mr. Danzig and Miss Taylor here, sir," Rockham said, "I suspected that something was going on in relation to just where I received that special operational experience."

"You can be certain of that, Lieutenant," Cromarty said. "But probably not in the way you think. Out of the whole Navy, there's only four officers with some of your unique qualifications.

"The United States is going to be meeting a very different class of enemy soon, Lieutenant. And some of us think that meeting will take place much sooner than others plan. This enemy is going to be one you and your SEALs have faced before. There isn't anything new about Naval Special Warfare taking on terrorists wherever and whenever they find them. What those of us around this table are concerned with is just how some of those terrorist groups will be armed, and how the Navy will deal with them.

"Your mission last year went far to prove that the Soviet Union has a very well-developed and sophisticated biological warfare establishment. There's more than a few rogue states and major organizations that the Soviets have used as surrogate forces in the past. It doesn't take much of a stretch of the imagination to consider that some of those surrogates would be able to field a weapon of mass destruction.

"Whether biological, chemical, or even nuclear, there are terrorist groups who wouldn't hesitate to use such a weapon to further their own aims. If those aims happened to match up with those of the Soviet Union, they could possibly obtain such a weapon.

"Even if they can't get such a thing from the Soviets, who have enough problems of their own right now with a collapsing economy and a defeat in Afghanistan, there are more than a few governments that are working hard to develop such weapons. Libya, North Korea, Iraq, Iran, and a few others who don't think that much of us, have ongoing chemical, nuclear, and biological weapons programs.

"Run-of-the-mill terrorists are something the SEALs have dealt with. But there's a new class of terrorist coming up in the world who's a different kind of animal. This terrorist is educated, smart, fanatical—and he could be armed with weapons of mass destruction."

A subdued murmur went around the conference table. A few of the assembled officers moved in their chairs, and others turned their heads to get a better look at the young SEAL officer sitting at the opposite end of the table. But if they were hoping to see some outward sign or reaction from Rockham, they were disappointed. His gray eyes remained locked on Admiral Cromarty, Rockham's attention focused on the admiral.

"Part of what we're looking for," Cromarty

went on, "is to establish a special detachment of men trained and equipped to deal with just such terrorists. Of all the people in Navy Special Warfare today, only a few are particularly qualified to be in our planned special detachment. Most of those men are the ones you led on that mission last year, Rockham."

"And how is that sir?" Rockham asked, puzzled.

"According to Dr. Taylor here," the admiral nodded to Sharon Taylor, "all of your SEALs are presently immunized against anthrax and other biological weapons."

"We did undergo a long series of shots and tests, Admiral," Rockham agreed. "But that should hardly make us special. The entire crew of the *Archerfish* had the same thing done to them."

"No," Cromarty disagreed. "It seems that it takes almost a full year for the whole series of shots to immunize a person against anthrax. It just isn't a common immunization in the service—yet. All of our intelligence indicates that anthrax is one of the more popular biological agents to be weaponized. And you and your SEALs have all completed the entire series of shots. Like it or not, Lieutenant, right now you're the man on the spot.

"What we want you to do, Lieutenant," Cromarty said, "is to build what we are calling a 'Navy Special Materials Detachment.' It will be a composite unit, but the core will be the SEALs you pick from the Special Warfare community. For the time being, the list of possible candidates for the detachment is necessarily short. You only have the choice of the men from your old platoon, and those from the SEAL delivery vehicle and dry deck shelter units who were also assigned to your operation. Bringing in new people will have to be kept at a minimum since they won't have the time to build the same level of immunity you and your men enjoy.

"Each member of the detachment must volunteer, including yourself. As the mission dictates, you will have specialists from the rest of the military—as well as intelligence, scientific, and industrial communities, assigned as needed. But the ultimate success or failure of the detachment will rest on the shoulders of yourself and the SEALs you lead.

"You will be outfitted and trained to handle any contingency and you and your men will have to learn the special counterterrorist training and skills they've developed down at SEAL Team Six. There will also be courses of training in biological and chemical weapons in the mix. It's going to be a high-speed and very demanding curriculum, Lieutenant.

"It will do us no good at all to have the very best technicians available if we can't put them on the target and give them the time they need to do their work. That's going to be the primary mission for you and your detachment—to gain access to the target, secure the area, and control the situation. The SEALs already have a well-earned reputation for working in any environment on the planet. You proved that yourself in the Arctic last year. So we're going to put you in the most hostile environment any of us can imagine—right next to a possibly live biological or chemical weapon.

"Now for the bad news," Cromarty said with a smile. "The Joint Chiefs and I want this detachment to be operational in under a year—six months would be my preference. Your commanding officers have assured me that you are a man who likes challenges, Lieutenant. And both Mr. Danzig and Dr. Taylor were very impressed last year with your ability to think on your feet.

"Now there's a carrot attached to this stick I'm waving around, Lieutenant," Cromarty continued. "You can probably expect to make lieutenant commander a bit ahead of your contemporaries if you're successful at this assignment. On the negative side, you'll be dealing with some of the most lethal weapons on the planet. Screw up just once and we'll probably be planting you with full honors next door at Arlington Cemetery.

"This is going to be a very difficult assignment, the kind that can make or break a young naval officer's career. Every mission you undertake will be classified. Damned few people will ever know if you were successful on an operation. Fail just once, and thousands may die along with you. But you get to build and lead a unit that you handpick every member of. Not many young officers in the Navy have been given that opportunity. So, Lieutenant, do you want the job?"

"You have your first volunteer, Admiral," Rockham said simply.

CHAPTER 4
★ ★ ★ ★

After going over organizational charts, mission parameters, logistics, and a myriad of other details for several days, Greg Rockham had contacted the first three people to help make up his new unit. Senior Chief Boatswain's Mate Frank Monday would again be his platoon chief. Mike Ferber would be the platoon's leading petty officer. And Lieutenant (junior grade) Shaun Daugherty would be his assistant platoon leader. The designations might change as the unit developed, but these would be the men he had to build on. Having spoken to each of them in private, the men had immediately volunteered.

Now, in the privacy of his home, Rockham was discussing with his "command staff" the difficult question of manning the new unit. His wife Sharon had seen to it that there were sandwiches for the SEALs and that the refrigerator in the den was fully stocked. She was used to the fact that her husband had a career whose details she couldn't be privy to. This was very hard on some SEAL marriages, but the Rockhams had worked past the difficulties of official secrecy.

Sharon had taken the Rockham's six-year old son, Matt, to a friend's house for the evening. The boy loved these little adventures, and the SEAL wives' community had their own network to deal with the demands of their husbands' jobs. So Greg Rockham was alone in the house with his fellow SEALs, where he could detail out the organization of their new unit.

He was standing. Chief Monday sat in the easy chair, a beer in his hand. And Daugherty and Ferber were at opposite ends of the couch, a stack of files, memos, and orders between them.

"Sizewise, we'll be an enlarged platoon," Rockham was saying, "eighteen men instead of sixteen. That will give us two squads with four two-man shooter pairs each. The ninth man in each squad will handle the boat or vehicle and team up with any special personnel we may have attached for a mission. So even if we had everyone from the old platoon, we'd still need more men. A couple of the people can come out of SDV Team Two, as long as we pick them from the men who were with us last year. But I think we'll still be short some manpower."

"The only one I know of from the old platoon who isn't available is Ken Fleming," Monday said. "He had to leave the service after busting up his knee on a practice jump. Now he's started up a restaurant and catering service on Shore Drive here in Virginia Beach. He came in to some family money and started up the business he always wanted.

"Limbaugh was going to get out and finish his degree, finally hang out his shingle and call himself a doctor. But he's still in for the time being and is pretty much a go-getter. Ask him, and I think he'll jump at the chance to come on board.

"Wilkes might be a different story. He's married with four kids. From the training schedule we'll be looking at, he'll be lucky to see home during daylight more than a few hours a month—if that. Then again, his kids are all girls and he might want to volunteer just to be with guys for a change."

"Well," Rockham said, as he paced across the room, "there's one on the list of people BuPers gave me that we have to think about."

"And just who did the Bureau of Personnel pull out of their hat?" Shaun Daugherty asked.

"Sid Mainhart," Rockham replied. "He was a torpedoman second class on board the *Archerfish* when we did our little party last year. Seems we left something of an impression on the man. He reenlisted soon after that cruise was over and volunteered for BUD/S."

"So he made it through?" Daugherty asked.

"You might say that," Rockham said. "He graduated as Honor Man of his class. And the class voted him the Fire in the Gut award. Seems there wasn't much the instructors could do to stop the guy. The guys I've talked to at the schoolhouse say he was a real stud."

"Has he even finished probation yet?" Monday asked, a serious expression on his face.

"Nope," Rockham said. "He's been assigned to Team Five in Coronado and still has a couple of months to go before he earns his Trident. But he's had the full regimen of shots, same as all the rest of us. It would be taking a chance bringing someone that green into the unit, but at least he hasn't had the time to develop any bad habits yet. And he did prove himself pretty well in BUD/S. I'm going to leave the final call on him to you, Chief."

"Well," Monday said thoughtfully, "it is deep water to just throw a new man into. But if he's one of the people BuPers says we can take, we should at least look him over. What do you think, Mike?"

Ferber, who'd so far been silent during the exchange, had been an instructor at the Basic Underwater Demolition/SEAL training center in Coronado only a few years earlier. He had been pronounced Instructor of the Year during his tour at BUD/S, so his opinion on the subject of Sid Mainhart held considerable weight to the other SEALs in the room.

"Honor Man for his class," Ferber said from where he sat at the opposite end of the couch from Daugherty. "That's no small thing, though I know that each one of us were in the last really hard class."

The SEALs smiled at the old joke.

"But I can tell you," Ferber continued, "that the

instructor staff at the schoolhouse has maintained the quality of the graduates. If Mainhart graduated at the top of his class, he's got something on the ball. The fact that he earned the Fire in the Gut award means he has the drive to back up his physical and mental abilities. I'd say give him a try."

"If we can't fill out the manpower we need from the old crews, we'll definitely look the man up," Rockham agreed. "If I have to, I'll fly out to Coronado and conduct an interview with Mainhart out there. You'll come with me, Mike, and see if any of your old contacts at BUD/S have anything specific to say.

"I'm going to be conducting interviews over at SDVT Two next week to see if some of those who were with us want to come over," Rockham went on. "Their records all look good." He indicated a stack of personnel files on the coffee table in front of Chief Monday. "There's a couple who would be an asset to the unit. I can't find Sam Paulson anywhere, though."

"There can't be that many ensigns over at SDVT Two," Daugherty said.

"There isn't," Rockham replied. "He's just out on assignment somewhere and it's hush-hush. I would have thought with the priorities we have with this new unit I could have found him. But it was a no-go. So you and I are the only officers aboard, Shaun."

"That's going to eat heavily into our training time with the men, won't it, Greg?" Shaun asked. "With only two officers, we'll be doing a lot of the admin work when we should be getting our own qualifications up."

"That's why they give us the big bucks, Shaun," Rockham said.

All four of the men in the room had a laugh at that thought.

"But you have a point," Rockham went on. "Administratively, we'll be assigned to Group Two as another Special Warfare Detachment. Our primary support will be from SEAL Team Two, and that includes some of our paperwork requirements. That should help take some of the pressure off. As far as the chain of command goes, we take our directive straight from the Joint Special Operations Command. We've got one step from them to USSO-COM and then directly to the Joint Chiefs of Staff."

"That isn't something I agree with, Rock," Monday said. "My experience is that special units tend to stand out more than they blend in. And if we're supposed to keep a low profile, that's going to make it all the harder. That kind of thing can cause friction between the men and the other Teams. It's a big community, but there's damned few hot operations to go out on. If only a handful of operators get the lion's share of the ops, that's not going to sit well with the teams that've trained just as long as we have, if not longer.

"It happened between SEAL Team Six and the rest of the East Coast Teams when Six was getting all of the hot ops. It could just as easily happen to us. These 'special' units with their own chain of command can cause more friction than good."

"That's the situation as we've been handed it, Chief," Rockham said. "I know Team Six went through some of the same things back when they were first starting up. But a lot of our training is going to be away from Little Creek, so that should help things out. Those are our orders."

"Aye, sir," Monday said. "And we will carry them out."

The four men in the room then gave some attention to their drinks. Each man considered his own thoughts about just what the future would be holding for them. There wasn't a whole lot more to say—but there was going to be a lot to do.

0430 ZULU
Building B417
U.S. Naval Amphibious Base
Little Creek, Virginia

A little over two weeks since that first meeting of Naval Special Materials Detachment One, all of the men Lieutenant Rockham had wanted to find for the new unit were on site and ready to begin work. Except for one man, all of last year's Fourth Platoon of SEAL Team Two were present. The missing man, Ken Fleming, had indeed started a business after he left the Navy only some six months earlier. But it didn't look like he'd be forgotten anytime soon. Fleming's, a new eatery on Shore Drive in Virginia Beach, looked like it would be the off-duty hangout for the new unit.

The new building the detachment had been assigned wasn't much larger than two garages stuck together. But it was what the base had immediately available. It seemed that whenever a new SEAL Team, or even the old UDTs, were started, they all began their operations from some old shack that the Navy found for them. But the men would make do. The Teams always did.

The eighteen men crowded into the room were sitting on a variety of seats, boxes, one of the two available desks, and on the floor. Greg Rockham stood behind the other desk as he looked out at his men. A strange mix of thoughts went through the SEAL officer's mind. These were the men he had operated with, gone into harm's way with. And they would follow him—they had proved that. He had a surge of pride that these men were his to lead, and concern that he would be putting them back into danger. But he knew that was the job they had all signed up for. Not only had each of these men volunteered for the Navy, they had volunteered for BUD/S. And now they were volunteering for an unknown unit. Just what the hell was wrong with everyone in the room? he wondered. Including himself.

"Okay, settle down, guys," Rockham said, beginning the first briefing. "Welcome to your new home."

"Some home," a voice piped up. "I've seen larger shipping containers."

"Ah, I see that Kurkowski made it here," Rockham said as a chuckle went through the group.

"Maybe if you dropped some of that lard ass you

drag around, there'd be more room in here," Wayne Alexander said.

Wayne was roughly the size and shape of a large fireplug, and built just about as hard. Kurkowski was larger than the shorter man, but not a hell of a lot stronger. In the whole room there were perhaps a few ounces of extra fat on all of the men—maybe not even that.

"Belay that," growled Chief Monday. The men quickly settled down, their jovial humor replaced by a more serious tone.

"Yes, and I missed you all too," said Rockham. "So much so that when I was offered the chance to be the CO of this new detachment, I just had to have you all with me.

"And that's not just an expression. That wonderful series of shots we all had to take after our last mission together not only immunized us against what we found on the ice, it also gave us all a very special qualification."

Some of the men unconsciously rubbed their arms at the mention of all the injections they had received over the last year. During the course of the operation, which should have been nothing more than a pickup of a defector at sea, they had all been protected against a possible exposure to a biological weapon they recovered and returned to the States for study. At Rockham's mention of a special qualification, they all froze and gave the SEAL lieutenant their undivided attention.

"I thought that little bit of news might interest you all," Rockham said with a smile. "As I have been told, everything we went through from the medics all those months was also planned for the possibility of this unit.

"We're going to make up the Naval Special Materials Detachment, the NSMD. For the time being, we'll be the only one in the Navy. We'll be called in when there's a terrorist or tactical incident involving a weapon of mass destruction on or near a maritime environment. Nuclear, biological, or chemical weapons—all of the bad guys want them. If the bad guys have it, we're going to be the people who take it away from them.

"Our particular area of responsibility is going to be biological and chemical weapons, for the time being. Explosive Ordnance Disposal will still be handling any nuclear weapons threats. But it could easily fall to us to secure a site to allow EOD to come in and do their job. But the majority of our missions will come because of a threat of bugs or gas."

A murmur went through the men as the specifics of what they were going to do settled in on them.

"To make sure we're up to the task, the next year is going to be taken up with some very high-speed training. Did I say a year? Let's say six months instead. We're going to be taking down ships, aircraft, and buildings. Our methods will include jumping, swimming, climbing, driving, and just walking. We will shoot, scoot, and blow things up. On top of that, we will be learning how to best seal off an area, secure a contaminated site, and handle some of the nastiest things on the planet. That's going to give us all the very best possible chance of getting sick, poisoned, or just glowing in the dark."

With that, Rockham folded his arms and sat down on the edge of his desk.

"Bugs and gas?" Kurkowski spoke up.

"Yup," Rockham said, "and lots of 'em."

"Yeah, but NSMD," Kurkowski went on. "We're the smud? That sounds like something you'd find on the bottom of an old boat."

"I will take up your complaint with the CNO the next time I see him Kurkowski," Rockham said referring to the Chief of Naval Operations, as a small roll of laughter went through the room.

"But on the serious side," Rockham said as silence settled over the group, "once we've mustered in today, we start preparing. Training is going to be a constant thing. We'll be lucky to see our families once a month. JSOC expects us to be operational in a year, but Admiral Cromarty would like to see us ready in more like six months. And I expect to make the admiral happy.

"If you have any doubts about what we're going to do, voice them now. If the kind of thing we're going to be working with bothers you, you can go back to your Teams without any problems at all. Bugs and gas scare the hell out of a lot of people, myself included. There's no shame in not wanting to play with Satan's toys.

"But know this: once you've signed in on the muster list, that's it, we start. You're all going to be plank owners of a very new kind of unit. We're going to be learning as we go, and I expect you all to help each other.

"Most of us know each other from Fourth Platoon if not earlier. There's three new faces here. I expect you to make them welcome as well. Everyone has something to contribute, and everyone has a lot to learn. It's about time we got started."

CHAPTER 5

0948 ZULU
88° 55' West, 30° 6' North
Gulf of Mexico
Off the Florida Panhandle

It was training time. For the men of the first Naval Special Materials Detachment, it was always training time. They had been running through their paces for weeks, picking up new skills and polishing them through practice. Only their first week of being a special detachment had been spent back at Little Creek. Since then, they had mainly been on the road training at different facilities. Training, training, and more training. Now, the men were in the warm waters of the Gulf of Mexico, working out of Eglin Air Force Base. With a small cargo ship as their target, they were practicing "underways"—ship takedowns where they had to board a craft while it was moving through open water. And they were still on the uphill side of the learning curve.

The unit had broken into two squads, each working off their own twenty-four-foot RIB. The RIBs had hard fiberglass hulls with inflatable sides, hence their name Rigid Inflatable Boat. As their target cargo ship moved along in the Gulf waters, the two RIBs would pull up alongside the ship and the SEALs would climb aboard. This was the lesson plan, but its execution wasn't meeting Senior Chief Monday's standards. As the two RIBs waited to make another run at the ship, the chief was explaining to his men how their performance was disappointing him.

"Okay," his loud voice boomed out, "that sucked. We're taking way too long to get on board here, people. Kurkowski, if you can't move that fat ass of yours up the ladder, maybe we ought to leave you ashore."

Normally more than ready with a quick retort, Roger Kurkowski was quiet. Even for a jokester in the Teams, when the work had to be done, the playing around stopped. And Roger had been having his trouble getting up the caving ladder, especially with his load of gear.

The unit was practicing one of the hardest jobs they could be asked to do—taking down a ship at sea. The details of how to covertly get on board had been worked out years earlier, so the men of the special materials detachment didn't have to develop the boarding techniques and materials. But they did have to learn them.

The basic technique was simple, as all good combat techniques are. But looks were deceiving. To gain access to the deck of the target ship, the SEALs would have to move up alongside the craft in small boats. A full nine-man unit was in a single boat, which made the situation crowded, but still doable.

Once the coxswain for the small boat pulled up to the target, the hook man in the front of the boat would reach up and set a hook on the gunwale of the ship. A light aluminum painter's pole had been modified for the operation, at the top of which was a two-pronged padded metal hook. On the back of the hook, a bent rod slipped down inside the top of the painter's pole. The bottom of the hook ended with a large ring that had the silver D-ring of a carabiner snaplink through it.

The bent rod on the back of the hook slipped down inside the aluminum painter's pole, and the hook was secured by being tied to the pole with a length of rubber surgical tubing. Shackled to the snaplink on the hook was the end of a steel caving ladder. The ladder was in a coil that unwound to release the ladder's full thirty-two-foot length. Spaced out evenly on the two 3mm steel bales of the ladder were six-inch-wide aluminum bars. The bars acted as steps, and the ladder was relatively light—only three pounds four ounces—and easy to manipulate.

The painter's pole that supported the hook was a telescoping nest of three aluminum tubes that could go from eight feet to twenty-four feet long. To use the system, the hook man would stand in the front of the small boat, holding up the pole with the hook. Another Teammate hangs onto the end of the unrolled caving ladder, keeping it out of the way. Extending the pole as he needed to, the hook man would catch the hook on the edge of the target ship's deck. The hook would pull away from the pole, leaving the caving ladder hanging down. Then the boat would pull up to the ship and the boarding party would climb up the ladder. It sounded easy. And that was about all—it sounded easy.

The hook man had to grab the edge of the target ship's deck, in spite of the heaving and bucking of the small boat he was in and any movement the target ship might be making.

The men got tossed around and banged up learning which of their number would make the best hook man, so they appreciated the padding and boat cushions they had been told to line the front of their small boat with. Once the hook was in place and the pole out of the way, the lead climber took point, going up the ladder to the deck of the ship. His was the most dangerous job. He had to climb up and secure the hook so the rest of his Teammates could get aboard. Then he had to slip up onto the ship, without being noticed by any crew members who might be about.

It was determined during training that Mike Bryant and Larry Stadt were the best hook men and climbers. But everyone had to go up the caving ladders to board the target ship. The ladders only had the aluminum rods as steps, and though the cables the rods were attached to were strong, they were very flexible.

That the cable and rod construction of the caving ladders made them light and portable also had its drawbacks. There was a technique to climbing the ladder that each man had to learn. You couldn't just go up the ladder in a normal, face-on position. Not only was the ladder very narrow, but the flexible construction made it twist and turn as it was climbed. Trying to go up normally could quickly flip a heavily laden SEAL over and slam him against the side of whatever it was they were trying to climb.

The proper technique was to go up along the side of the ladder, with the cable up near a man's chest and between his arms. Hands and feet had to be turned in to use the aluminum-rod steps, the feet on alternate steps, and it took a strong grip to hold onto the relatively thin aluminum rods. But this was the most stable climbing technique to get a SEAL up the ladder and aboard the ship, so it was what the men learned.

Each of the men didn't climb the ladder with the same load of gear strapped to his body, however. Roger Kurkowski and Wayne Alexander were assigned the position of breacher for their squads. It was their job to open doors, hatches, and anything else that might be barring their way. To do this, they had to have certain tools. Explosives were powerful and relatively light, but you didn't run all over a ship blowing the hatches open. Especially not a ship that might be carrying a volatile cargo, such as a chemical or biological warhead.

To open the way, Kurkowski and Alexander were carrying six-pound sledgehammers with the handles cut down a bit, pry bars, and firemen's hooligan tools, which were like crowbars with a wide, split-wedge head at one end and another split-wedge head sticking out ninety degrees from the handle at the other end. They also had Remington 870 twelve-gauge pump action shotguns with eighteen-inch barrels, seven-shot magazine extensions, and pistol grips. Their sidearms were Mark 24 pistols, the SIG P226 9mm semiautomatic that was standard issue in the Teams.

In addition to these tools, the SEAL breachers also had their loads of ammunition—three fifteen-round magazines for their pistols, forty rounds of 00 buckshot ammunition for their shotguns, four flash-crash stun grenades, as well as explosives, detonators, first aid gear, commo gear, gas mask, body armor, web gear, equipment vest, backpack, and more. There were over sixty pieces of gear just for the breacher.

Carrying loads of equipment, weapons, and ammunition around was nothing new for a SEAL. Going up a caving ladder with that big a load strapped to their bodies was a new experience. But SEALs trained to build upper body strength from their earliest days at BUD/S. They needed that strength to carry gear, paddle boats, and now to climb ladders.

Being the shortest guy in the outfit helped Wayne Alexander in the boarding exercises. His fireplug body was almost as wide as it was tall, especially with the huge load of equipment strapped to him. So his center of gravity stayed low and he lumbered up the caving ladder like a black bear going up a tree.

On the other boat, Kurkowski was not having a great time with the training. He was still working out his gear loading, and keeping his balance going up the caving ladder slowed him down considerably. This lack of speed was slowing down the entire squad since they couldn't board the ship any faster than their slowest man could move.

Second squad was looking pretty good on its run. Most of the squad had already gone up the caving ladder. Ed Lopez was acting as the coxswain on the RIB, so he would remain with the boat. Only Kurkowski and shooting partner Sid Mainhart remained to go up the ladder, and Kurkowski had already started his climb.

With Kurkowski bitching the loudest about Sid being "the new guy," Chief Monday thought it fitting that he assign the two men as shooting partners. If Kurkowski felt that Sid wasn't picking up on the training fast enough, he could take the blame as Sid's instructor. The chief felt that since Sid still had a short way to go to complete his probation, it was better that they learn now if he couldn't take the pressure. It wasn't easy on Sid or Kurkowski, but it was efficient.

Now, Sid was waiting at the bottom of the ladder, holding it as Kurkowski pulled himself up and started his climb. Since this was a training exercise, Mike Bryant was watching the security of the hook and caving ladder rather than the perimeter, as he would have on a hot op. The training rule in the Teams was to train as you would fight, so that you could fight as you had trained, but you didn't take unnecessary chances.

The RIB was lifted up on a wave, cutting down on the distance Kurkowski would have to climb, when without warning both Mike Bryant and Ed Lopez heard the engine of the RIB falter. The Volvo Penta Two Iveco diesel engine changed its tone as it coughed, and a shudder ran through the small boat as it lost power.

"Break off!" Bryant shouted. "Break off!"

Before the small boat could pull away from the larger ship, it slid back on the wave it was riding, leaving Kurkowski hanging on the ladder. Lopez was struggling with the RIB, trying to keep it in place until Kurkowski could drop back aboard, but the heavily laden SEAL was tangled in the caving ladder. He couldn't go up and he couldn't climb back down. As he struggled, he lost his grip and fell back from the ladder. But Kurkowski didn't fall free of the caving ladder and land in the RIB. The webbing of his pack frame had snagged on the ladder, wedging itself and the SEAL fast to the cable. And having fallen backward, Kurkowski was hanging upside down on the caving ladder. He couldn't see what had tangled with the ladder, and what he couldn't see, he couldn't free up. The pry bar, hooligan tool, and sledgehammer slipped out of the holsters in his pack.

With the RIB falling away from the ship, Kurkowski was in real danger. If he freed himself, he could drop into the RIB, if it didn't fall away. But if he dropped into the water, he could sink to the bottom with the weight of all his equipment dragging him down. If he inflated the UDT life jacket he wore on top of his chest, it would keep him from drowning. But being on the surface next to the ship was just as bad as drowning, maybe worse. The undertow of the cargo ship would draw him under no matter how hard he swam, sweeping him back to the chopping bronze blades of the slowly rotating ship's screw.

If he remained stuck on the side of the boat rather than dropping, and Lopez didn't break the RIB away from the ship, another wave pushing the RIB against the cargo ship would smash Kurkowski between the smaller boat and the steel hull.

As Lopez nursed and pleaded with the faltering diesel, Mainhart dropped his end of the caving ladder and grabbed up his Teammate. Now, if the RIB lost power completely, both SEALs would be dangling from the ladder, and probably go into the water. Two men were in danger of being lost to the sea or the slicing horror waiting at the back of the ship.

As Kurkowski fell back into Mainhart's arms, the young SEAL was pinned against the side of the RIB and the heavy SEAL. Mainhart couldn't pull his partner away from the ladder, but he could see the nylon webbing straps that were tangled with the cables of the ladder.

Strapped to his left hip, hanging from his belt and behind his flash-crash pouch, was Sid's razor-sharp Mark II K-bar knife, which had served the Teams well since their early days in World War II. Back at BUD/S, the students had been harassed unmercifully if even a tiny spot of rust was found on a knife blade. And Sid knew his knife was clean, sharp—and completely out of reach.

With scarcely a second's thought, he reached down with his right hand and grabbed at his flight suit's front pocket. In the pocket of the suit, in front of his holster, was clipped a custom folding knife— built by Ernie Emerson of California, the Viper MV-1, slim, tough, and with an edge that could cut wire if it had to. With one hand, Sid slipped the knife up and thumbed open the blade.

Its blade locked open, the MV-1 sliced through the tough nylon webbing with a single slash. Kurkowski, freed of his entanglement, dropped heavily into the RIB, bouncing off the inflated rubber side as he fell. As Sid was knocked into the RIB, his right arm was smashed down against the rubber side of the boat, pinned by Kurkowski's sprawling weight. The rubber gave enough to keep Mainhart's arm from breaking, but the blow stunned the SEAL's arm and his custom knife slipped over the side.

From when Mike Bryant had called out for the RIB to break away to the time that Kurkowski and Mainhart were safely inside the boat, no more than six or seven seconds had elapsed. As the RIB's diesel gave a final throb and stopped, the boat had steered away from the cargo ship and safely away from its undertow. Kurkowski rolled over and off of Mainhart. He knew it was a near thing, but had his own way of dealing with the aftermath of danger.

"So, Sid," Kurkowski said from where he lay on the deck, "was it good for you?"

"Uh, I've had better," the young SEAL replied, then realized it was the first time that Kurkowski hadn't called him New Guy, Fresh Meat, or Cherry.

As Mainhart lay on the deck, Kurkowski called over to Lopez, "Hey, Ed, you going to get this thing running or do we have to start paddling?"

From where he was working on the engine controls, Lopez looked up with a wide and relieved smile on his tanned face. "I think it might be better if you started worrying about paying for all that gear that's now at the bottom of the Gulf, Kurkowski."

Laying back with a groan, Kurkowski stuck up a hand and waved it in the air, saying in a high, singsong voice, "Oh, Purser, do let us know when the shuffleboard court is free. This cruise is turning into such a bother."

"Oh, shit," Mainhart said from where he lay on the deck. "I dropped my knife overboard."

"I'll buy you a new one, Teammate," Kurkowski said seriously.

Outside of a careful review of what happened, nothing was made of the incident that almost cost Kurkowski his life. And it could have cost Sid Mainhart a lot more than a good knife. But no one questioned a SEAL going to the aid of a Teammate. They all would have done the same thing.

With new gear gathered up, the training continued. The unit soon got to the point where an entire eight-man squad could catch up to a moving ship and get on board unnoticed in just a few minutes. Once they learned the boarding techniques, the men practiced the clearance of internal and external spaces on a ship.

But before training went on many more days, the men all felt there was a special SEAL tradition that they had to observe.

CHAPTER 6

★ ★ ★ ★

A few days after the incident that almost cost Kurkowski his life, the detachment was standing down from the day's training. It had been another fun-filled day of running boats, climbing ladders, and training, training, training. As the newest man, Mainhart had the privilege of putting away the unit's equipment, stowing and wiping down everything that wasn't a specific man's gear.

Sid had noticed that just about everyone was gone before he had finished up for the day. This was unusual because all the men usually loaned a hand to get the gear stowed. In spite of it being his job, the guys had always helped him before. Only Ed Lopez and Pete Wilkes, who were the coxswains for the units' two RIBs, were still tinkering with their respective boats.

The motel where all of the SEALs were staying had a single large meeting room that they had used as their planning and staging area. The motel was only a few blocks walk down the street from the boat docks, and Sid was looking forward to a solid meal and maybe a beer or two before hitting the rack. But as he got ready to leave, Ed and Pete called him over to give them a hand.

Helping hold tools while the two SEALs finished up with the boat's diesels struck Sid as just another of the make-work bits that were the lot of new guys in military units all over the world. It didn't matter that the SEALs trained for almost a full year just to qualify to conduct a mission. All the little things had to be done as well. So a SEAL could be found cleaning weapons, washing the salt off a boat, or just helping to make sure an engine had its dose of maintenance. The glamorous life of Navy Special Warfare, Sid thought to himself. Funny, the recruiters never talked about this aspect of life in the Teams.

Finally, Lopez and Wilkes were satisfied with whatever they'd been doing, and the engine hatches were lowered and latched into place. Then the three men walked up to the motel together. Sid was keen on heading to his room to get cleaned up before grabbing a bite to eat, but Lopez and Wilkes insisted he come with them to the meeting room. By now, Mainhart didn't even question the directions of the more experienced SEALs, he just did what he was told and tried to learn everything he could along the way.

No one was in sight as they approached the conference room, which was attached to Lieutenant Rockham's room. Sid wasn't expecting anything when they entered the room, but he stopped abruptly when he saw that everyone in the room was standing at attention, each man was wearing the blue and gold T-shirts of the Teams. At each man's left breast shone the gold Trident, the symbol of the Navy Special Warfare operator.

Most of the time, Sid wore plain green fatigues when he was in uniform. But while they were on the road, the unit almost never wore any form of uniform, not even their blue-and-golds. So he was stunned as he stood at the door. On either side of the doorway stood Ed Lopez and Pete Wilkes with wide smiles on their faces. It was obvious now that they had been holding him up while something was being prepared in the room. But what?

Senior Chief Monday's commanding voice boomed out, "Sidney Mainhart, front and center."

Almost as a reflex, Sid drew himself to attention and moved to in front of the group of SEALs facing Chief Monday, who was flanked by Lieutenants Rockham and Daugherty.

"Attention to orders," Rockham called out. "According to longstanding tradition in the Teams, a board was gathered today to decide the situation regarding Second Class Torpedoman's Mate Mainhart's probationary period coming to an end. Having satisfactorily completed his probationary time and demonstrated himself an asset to the Teams, Torpedoman's Mate Sidney Mainhart is hereby awarded the Naval Enlisted Code of 5326 and is authorized to wear the Naval Special Warfare breast insignia."

Lieutenant Rockham stepped forward and reached into his pocket. Pulling out a gold Trident, he pinned it to Mainhart's chest. Then he shook Sid's hand and with a wide grin said, "Congratulations, SEAL."

The Trident pin is almost three inches wide and about one and a half inches tall. The front of the device has an eagle with its wings outstretched behind the anchor symbol of the Navy. In the eagle's right talon is a three-pronged trident, Neptune's spear, held crossways. In the eagle's left talon is a cocked flintlock pistol. The gold-plated metal Trident is one of the largest uniform devices in the Navy, and its weight is noticeable both to the people who see it and the wearer authorized to have it on his chest. At that moment, Sid Mainhart noticed the weight of the Trident he had on, and it felt very good indeed.

Then something very odd happened. As Lieutenant Rockham stepped back, Chief Monday said, "Stand fast!"

Roger Kurkowski stepped away from behind Sid and walked over to the other side of the room. There were a number of the men's suitcases stacked up against the wall, and Kurkowski bent over and opened his up. From inside the case he pulled out his uniform and unpinned the glowing, polished Trident from above its left pocket.

As Sid wondered what was going on, he felt a heavy hand grasp his shoulder. "Don't move," said a quiet voice directly behind him. The hand squeezed once and then withdrew.

It was John Grant, a big Native American who didn't talk much. In fact, in all the weeks they'd been training, Sid couldn't remember Grant saying more than a few dozen words. So whatever it was, he knew it had to be important, which meant he wasn't going to move.

Kurkowski stepped back in from of Mainhart, reached up and pulled off the Trident Rockham had just placed on him. The back of the Trident had three 5/16th-inch-long metal points on it. The points were pressed through the cloth of the uniform, and caps slipped over the ends to hold the device in place. Rockham had held Mainhart's shirt out with his other hand when he stuck the Trident on and never slipped the caps on.

"This is the Trident you were given," Kurkowski said as he slipped the device into Sid's left front pants pocket. "This," Kurkowski said as he held up the Trident he had just taken off his own uniform, "is the one you earned."

And with that, the big man set the Trident in place on Mainhart's chest and slammed it in with the palm of his hand.

The shock of the blow almost knocked Mainhart back. He rocked back for a moment, and again felt that strong hand behind him, this time pushing him back up. Sid had been hit so hard in the chest that he barely felt the three metal prongs sinking into his flesh. Then Kurkowski stepped back and Chief Monday stepped up.

"Never forget that men bled in combat for this symbol," Monday said. Then he too struck the Trident on Sid's chest with the flat of his hand. That one hurt, but Sid only let a slight grunt slip out when the blow landed. Eventually, every SEAL in the room had slapped the Trident to help secure it on its proud new owner.

A sharp, burning pain spread out across the left side of Sid's chest. But that pain seemed almost slight as it was overwhelmed by Sid's flood of feelings. He now belonged to a group of men that few people ever even saw, let alone could call Teammate. And from that day forward he would be able to call these men and the rest of the Teams that—he could call them Teammates for the rest of his life.

As the rest of the unit gathered around him, shaking his hand and congratulating him, Sid felt overwhelmed. Then Kurkowski opened a cooler that was filled to the brim with ice and cold cans of beer.

"First one to the new SEAL," Kurkowski said as he handed Mainhart an open can. "Welcome aboard, brother."

Never had a beer tasted as good to Sid as his first pull from that ice-cold can.

The next day it was back to training. Celebrations aside, they had to push hard to be able to operate by the time Rockham had said they could. So in spite of a few hangovers, several cases of seriously bad breath, and one very sore chest, the men of the Special Materials Detachment once more strapped on their gear and set to work.

Once they arrived at their target—whether they had jumped into a building, swam up to a beach emplacement, or climbed aboard a ship—they had to control the situation. And you only controlled a situation by quickly taking it over. That was the takedown, the actual assault of a target.

The SEALs had to learn how to move as a cohesive unit. What they were doing involved traveling down hallways, corridors, and rooms, clearing out the enemy and asserting their control over an area. It was hard, exacting work. Split-second timing was necessary as well as absolute precision in placing shots. SEALs had been killed conducting this kind of training, so the work was as serious as it could possibly be.

Marksmanship went on for hours at various ranges. The standard submachine gun for the men was the MP5-N. It could be used with a suppressor screwed onto the muzzle, which made the weapon quiet but long and hard to handle in an enclosed area. Or they fired the MP5s with the stock only slightly extended and the guns pushed away from their bodies, tight against braced slings. The 9mm weapons were used as a bullet hose. Spraying bullets with a weapon was something only seen in the movies. Instead, short, two-round controlled bursts were fired, each burst targeted on an area the size of a three-by-five-inch card.

Handguns were not ignored. The SIG P226 semi-automatic pistol was standard issue in the Teams, and in the NSMD as well. Fifteen rounds of 9mm ammunition, the same as fired in their submachine guns, could be pumped out as fast as one could pull the trigger. Again, just like the submachine guns, a quick two rounds to a target, the double tap, made sure the pistol would put an enemy down.

The other standard shoulder arm of the men was the M4 carbine, a slightly shortened version of the M16A2 rifle. The M4 used by the SEALs was capable of full-automatic fire. But it too was used in short, two- or three-round bursts. The 5.56mm projectiles of the M4 carbines were incredibly fast, leaving the barrels at 2,900 feet per second. That made the rounds supersonic. So a sound suppressor on the muzzle of the M4s wouldn't be as quiet as might be needed for some missions.

For almost silent work, the unit's point men and lead climbers, Mike Bryant and Larry Stadt, trained with Ruger Mark II semiautomatic pistols with suppressors built into the barrel. The lightweight Ruger pistols only fired a .22 caliber rimfire round, hardly the most powerful ammunition available. But the weapons were almost silent, and very accurate. With hours of training and practice with their suppressed pistols, both Stadt and Bryant could hit a spot the size of a quarter at up to ten yards. The power of their .22 pistols would be made up for by the precision with which the two men could place their bullets.

Ryan Marks and John Grant were the two snipers in the unit, one per squad. They were the guardians of their teammates. On an operation, the snipers could be required to overlook an entire operational area, and place accurate fire on any threat in that area. To accomplish this, the two men trained with an assortment of rifles, their favorites being the bolt action, customized McMillan/Remington 700 rifles in 7.62mm NATO. In spite of the accuracy of the bolt action rifles, Marks still had a warm spot for the accurized M14 semiautomatic rifle he had carried in the field for years.

For real power, both snipers were proficient with the McMillan M88 bolt action .50 caliber sniper rifles. The huge rifles weighed more than thirty pounds and fired the same round of ammunition as the .50 caliber machine gun—originally designed to destroy tanks during World War I. The huge bullet launched by the .50 rifles—each projectile the size of an average person's little finger—could hit a target more than a mile away. From a standing shot, Marks had nailed a stack of three oil drums at a range of 1,800 meters—over 1.1 miles away.

The men also trained with foreign weapons. The AK-47 and its variants, for instance, were the best weapons for the swimmer-scouts to use coming up on a beach. The Soviet-designed and much copied assault rifle was the only weapon the SEALs had found that could be pulled through the surf zone

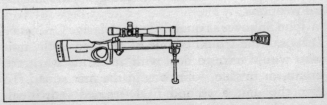

McMILLAN M88

unprotected and still be expected to fire when it was pulled up and the water drained out of the barrel.

Stun grenades, the flash-crash, were carried and worked with. The model the men were using was a conversion of the M116A1 hand grenade simulator. The cardboard-bodied simulator was filled with several ounces of very powerful flash powder. By removing the standard fuse and replacing it with a pull-ring M201-type fuze from a smoke or gas grenade, the flash-crash was created. Pulling the ring and tossing the flash-crash was followed only a second and a half later by a brilliant flash of light and a thunderous concussion, but only cardboard fragmentation. The noise and light were enough to stun anyone exposed too closely to it for several seconds—seconds the SEALs could put to use in taking control of a situation, which was the point of all the weapons training: to take control of a situation and allow their specialists to operate.

Henry Limbaugh and Jack Tinsley were the unit's two corpsmen. Besides learning how to do the boarding and clearing operations, the two corpsmen also underwent specialized training in countering and dealing with biological and chemical weapons.

John Sukov was qualified in Explosive Ordnance Disposal. He would be one of the men in the unit who would have to deal with an exotic warhead, bomb, or missile. John was in the first squad. To give the unit a second EOD-trained individual, Henry Lutz of the second squad was undergoing

EOD training. But Henry would not be able to complete the full course. He was studying under Sukov's tutelage while waiting for a time when he could attend the more formal EOD course.

And all of the men, enlisted and officer, technician, chief, or corpsman, trained in how to conduct a takedown. They knew that even the best training and equipment in the world would do them no good at all if they couldn't quickly and efficiently take control of an area, building, or ship.

So the SEALs studied and practiced.

They had broken down into squads, each squad further divided into two fire teams of two shooter pairs each. The minimum number of men for a room clearance was always two shooters. This number was increased for the larger or more complicated areas such as big rooms or the bridges and engine rooms of ships. The basic formation of the SEAL assault forces was the stack, or "train," in which all the men lined up close to one another so they were able to move as a single unit and communicate by touch.

The front man in the train was normally the point man—Larry Stadt for first squad and Mike Bryant for second squad. Right behind them would be the breachers, Wayne Alexander for first squad and Roger Kurkowski for second. After the first two men came the rest of the squad in a train formation. As the odd-numbered man, the corpsman, either Tinsley or Limbaugh, brought up the rear of the stack and performed rear security.

When the train came up to a door, they would

"stack up" outside the entranceway—closing up their formation tightly. The first two men in the train—the point man and the breacher—would be responsible for opening the door or hatch. The next two men in the stack would go through the open door and clear the room beyond. If necessary, a second pair would follow the first to clear the area.

During all of this action and preparation, the security of the area to the rear would be maintained by the last man in the stack. Once the train was lined up and prepared to clear a room, that last man would squeeze the shoulder of the man in front of him, signaling that he was ready and the area was clear. That squeeze signal would be passed up from the rear to the front of the stack as each man indicated that he was ready. When the squeeze signal reached the front of the stack, the point man would know that everyone was set.

The door would be opened by the breacher, whether by just pushing it open, blowing it with explosives, or knocking the hinges and lock off with shotgun blasts. The point man would maintain forward security for the stack as the next two men in the train, immediately behind the breacher, moved forward and cleared the room.

When a shooter pair entered a room, they immediately moved to opposite sides of the doorway and scanned the room for targets. The number one man in the team, the first man through the door, would move to the left, staying a foot away from the wall and sweeping the room from the left wall to the right. It had been found during testing that flat ricochets off a wall tended to follow along the wall about six to eight inches from the surface, just another detail the SEALs had to learn.

The number two man of the first shooter pair, the second man through the door, would move to the right, again staying away from the wall, and scan the room from right to left. As soon as each man had cleared his field of fire, they would shout out, "Clear!"

As the first pair cleared the room just opened, the rest of the train would prepare to go through the next entranceway down the corridor. As soon as the first door had been breached and the shooter pair entered, the point man and breacher would move down to the next doorway, set up security there, and wait for the rest of the train to catch up. When the first room was cleared and checked, that shooter pair would move out and catch up to the train, taking their positions at the rear of the stack.

This series of movements and actions were complicated and dangerous. The takedown of a target was a fast, lethally choreographed ballet. It would appear to an outside observer as a violent form of line dancing. The men practiced their movements until they were able to do them in their sleep. First run-throughs were done with empty weapons, each movement conducted slowly and deliberately so everyone knew exactly where they were supposed to be and how they were required to move.

These motions were dangerous because each man had not only to be cognizant of his immediate surroundings, but certain about the location of each of his Teammates. Once the men had practiced the procedures on slow walk-throughs, they sped up. And then they did the actions with live weapons in their hands.

Shooting rooms had been set up so the men were able to practice a room clearing with live ammunition. That meant each man had to always know exactly where the muzzle of his weapon was pointing at all times. Safe and effective weapons handling had to become more than second nature to each of the men; it had to be automatic to the point that anything else just felt wrong.

When they had their practice down to the point of conducting live fire exercises, the men were entering and clearing rooms with targets inside them. It might be furniture, desks, chairs, couches, or filing cabinets. And each man would have to clear his side of the room quickly, efficiently, and safely. Targets had to be identified instantly and engaged without question. Hostages or "no-shoot" targets had to be identified just as quickly.

It was in these sudden, fast engagements that all the range time paid off for the SEALs. The threat targets, called "tangos," eventually had three-by-five-inch cards taped to their foreheads. When the SEALs became proficient in their room-clearing techniques, the rounds from their weapons had to hit those cards, and only those cards, in order to count.

Experience had been the instructor for several generations of SEALs and other shooters around the world. Hitting that area of the head—a rectangle roughly outlined by the eyebrows and the tip of the nose—was the only target that would absolutely prevent another action by a tango. A terrorist holding a gun to a hostage's head, or the trigger to a device, would be unable to even close his hand—death would be that sudden.

So the men practiced and practiced, honing their shooting skills and learning the movements of their Teammates. Trains were be rotated, each man taking the position of another man, so they could all learn not only what was expected of them, but the job of every man in the stack. Rooms were entered, bullets fired, and the shouts of "Clear" sounded out around their training areas.

The room clearing and takedown skills were the most necessary and dangerous that the men had to learn. But there were other skills to learn as well. Each man steered the boat, set the caving ladder, or maintained the communications. Just because John Sukov and Henry Lutz were the primary communicators, for first and second squads, respectively, didn't mean that all members of the squad didn't have to be able to work the radios as well.

Free-fall parachute training was as serious as the rest of their work, but most of the SEALs loved the feeling of a free fall. Jumping out of an aircraft at multiple thousands of feet of altitude would strike some people as not the best way to reach old age. It was not a choice for the SEALs. They had to be qualified parachutists just to earn the Trident. And most members of the Teams went on to free-fall jumping and even more complicated versions of a parachute jump.

All of the men had to learn High Altitude, Low Opening—or HALO—jump. The men would exit an aircraft at 30,000 feet or more and free-fall down to 1,500 feet or less. During their fall through the air, the jumpers had to line up with each other and control their fall, tracking across the sky by contorting their bodies. This long free fall was as close to true flying as a human being could come—as long as they didn't forget to open their parachutes before the "flight" came to a sudden halt at ground level.

Mike Bryant loved jumping, and had over a thousand jumps to his credit even before the NSMD was formed. Flying through the air on a drop was great for him, but not for some others in his unit. Roger Kurkowski would jump as much as he had to, but never thought of it as a sport. Dan Able hated jumping, but always did what he had to in order to keep operating with his Teammates.

That was the way of the SEALs. They might love what they did or hate it. But their feelings didn't matter—they had to do everything the job demanded. The Teams were a strictly voluntary organization, and you could volunteer out a lot more easily than you were able to volunteer in.

Completing BUD/S was the only way to join the Teams, but once a Teammate, you could leave just by saying you wanted out. But none of the men in the Teams, and certainly not the Special Materials Detachment, ever considered quitting in order to get out of something they didn't like to do. Besides, where else could you find a job where you got to jump out of planes, blow things up, shoot guns, and generally raise hell on a controlled basis, and get paid for it!

CHAPTER 7

★ ★ ★ ★

Flying along at 26,000 feet would be an exciting time for some people. But after listening to the drone of the four Allison T56-A-T5 turboprop engines of their C-130 cargo plane for the last five hours, it had become more than boring to Greg Rockham and the others. The steady rumbling roar of the turboprops had penetrated every inch of Rockham's body, and he found that the flight had become more tedious than the hours of classroom instruction he and the others had experienced during their training.

Rockham had watched, listened, and learned, as had all of his men. The time spent studying known biological and chemical weapons, protection systems, decontamination procedures, and even laying down disinfectant foam, had seemed long, but it seemed like nothing compared to this plane ride. He was more than ready to leave the aircraft.

There came a time when you had to stop going over and over the plans you had made for yourself and for the men who followed you. You had to just go and do it. It was that time for Rockham and his men.

They were on what would be either their first or last mission, depending on how things went. They'd been training hard for months and in accordance with Admiral Cromarty's preference, were ready to operate six months after they'd begun. Or at least as far as Rockham and the men under him were concerned. The command at JSOC and US-SOCOM, and the Joint Chiefs of Staff, still wanted to see the new Naval Special Materials Detachment carry out a mission.

So the men had been placed under alert and put under lockdown. They hadn't been able to contact their families, go off the base, or do anything other than plan, prepare, and practice for a mission. It was a training mission, but that just meant they wouldn't be using live ammunition, and hopefully the bad guys wouldn't be using real bullets either.

Those in command had put together a joint services operation, with a specific aspect that would use the skills of Rockham and his detachment. According to the scenario, a group of terrorists had a weapon of mass destruction at their base. A unit of Army Rangers would be parachuted in to engage the bulk of the terrorist forces to give Rockham and his men the opportunity to locate and neutralize the WMD.

They would be parachuting into the Ellis Air Force Base complex in Nevada. While the Army Rangers went in on their own operation at the Ellis base facilities, Rockham and his men would be parachuting onto the Indian Springs Air Force Auxiliary Field, across Highway 95 from the town of Indian Springs.

When the men were told about the operation, they were excited, looking forward to jumping, shooting, and scooting again. And when they found out that the target was less than an hour's drive out of Las Vegas, the idea of a very interesting liberty call after the op clearly appealed to a number of them.

The operation would be the most important piece of training the new detachment had yet faced. Their success or failure would determine whether the new unit stayed in existence. This was to be their certification op; they had to succeed. However, no one in the outfit knew the situation except Greg Rockham. He hadn't even told Shaun Daugherty, his second in command. But Shaun was sharp enough to suspect what might be riding on their present flight.

Rockham had pushed the men hard during their forty-eight hours of lockdown prior to going on the op. During their period of isolation, when they were separated from everyone who didn't have a direct need to be with them, the men practiced what they would do on the target site. They knew the basic layout, what to expect in the way of tangos, support, and what they would find on the site.

Intel came in on a regular basis, and they received updates, satellite photos, and so on. But there was only so much they could do to specifically prepare for the op. The rest depended on what they actually found on the ground.

The target itself was a small hangar on the western side of the airfield. The site was isolated so no prying eyes could watch the SEALs go through their paces on the op. A recovery crew at the planned drop zone would pick up the men's parachutes, rather than having the SEALs bury them. Other than that, the mission would remain on a tactical level throughout.

They had their weapons, though Rockham would have preferred M4 carbines. A new ammunition system would allow them to actually shoot the tangos, who were in fact Air Combat Command security people, in relative safety. Their MP5s had been fitted with special barrels so they could function with FX simunition marking cartridges—plastic ammo that carried a load of paint rather than lead.

Special barrel inserts in the MP5s prevented them from chambering or firing a live round of 9mm ammunition. Changing some other parts in the weapons and the MP5s, as well as the unit's SIG P226 handguns, let them both function normally with the FX marking ammo. Mike Bryant and Larry Stadt both had the simunition system fitted to their MP5SD submachine guns.

As the unit's two point men and lead climbers, Bryant and Stadt had the SD, or Schalldampfer,

MP5s models, with almost two-inch-thick, extra long barrels. The thickness and length were due to the integral suppressors built onto the submachine guns. As Rockham looked over, Bryant was double-checking the bright red tape around the last few inches of the muzzle. The brightly colored tape was on the barrels, trigger guards, and pistol grips of all the men's weapons. It was an added safety indicator that their guns had the special conversion kits and couldn't fire live ammunition.

Going in, the men had a lot of ammunition. Everyone had at least seven magazines for their MP5, one in the weapon and another six in two three-cell magazine pouches strapped to their thighs. That gave them over two hundred rounds of FX marking ammunition for the subguns, backed up by another forty-five rounds in the three magazines to their SIG P226 pistols.

Each MP5 had a flashlight attachment on the front grip that allowed the men to illuminate their target with the fingers of their none-firing hand. Over their gray flight suits were sets of body armor, web gear, handcuffs, and plastic tie-ties—tough nylon strips set in two loops that could be pulled tight in an instant and had to be cut in order to open them. The tie-ties were effective, fast, disposable handcuffs.

In the pouches on their gear, the men had four flash-crash grenades and a single canister-type M7A2 CS tear gas grenade. Normally, they would also have a Mark IIIA2 concussion grenade in their munitions issue, but the half-pound TNT charges weren't going along on this training op. Infrared chem lights, red and green chem lights, an Mk 13 flare, an SDU-5/E strobe light fitted with an infrared filter, red-lens pencil light, signal mirror, and pencil flares with their launcher guaranteed that if someone's Motorola MX-300 radio crapped out, they would be able to signal the rest of the team or the extraction bird.

First aid equipment, a black, fireproof/flashproof balaclava hood to cover their heads and most of their face, an M17A1 gas mask, a hood, and impermeable coveralls were in a pack to be worn when they approached their final target, the weapon of mass destruction. AN/PVS-5A night vision goggles, regular goggles for eye protection, a canteen, protec helmet, and even more gear was strapped, fitted, and bagged to each man.

Under all their web gear and armor, the SEALs wore a Special Purpose Insertion/Extraction harness that resembled a regular parachute harness but with carabiner snaplinks at the shoulder. The SPIE rig would allow each man to clip onto—or be secured to, if he was unconscious or wounded—a SPIE rope attached to an emergency extraction helicopter. Though they wouldn't be able to pull out the target weapon with the men, a SPIE extraction could get them all out of a danger area very quickly, dangling underneath a speeding helicopter.

Some of the men had specialty gear. Sukov and Lutz had their EOD toolkits. Tinsley and Limbaugh had detection, testing, and sampling gear, as well as a loadout of chemical weapon antidotes and their corpsmen gear. Kurkowski and Alexander had their breacher gear. And additional equipment was spread out among all of the men. But the heaviest load of all was resting on Greg Rockham's shoulders—he was ultimately responsible for the safety of each of his men, and for the success of their mission.

For the rest of the men, it just looked like any other mission. Everyone had checked their gear multiple times. And they were either resting—it looked like Marks was sleeping—or otherwise occupying themselves. Things had relaxed a lot since their Florida training. The men had come together as a team, they were a cohesive unit.

Friction was little more than what would be expected among any group of extroverts you found in the Teams. Roger Kurkowski, for instance, finally managing to replace Sid Mainhart's lost knife, bitched mightily about what an Emerson MV-1 cost. "If it's such a good damn knife," Kurkowski had groused, "why doesn't he go into production with them?"

Sid didn't have any answer for the big SEAL, but he also knew none was necessary. The two men had become fast friends and Teammates, and the younger man was starting to pick up on some of Kurkowski's habits. Bitching about everything happened to be one of them.

But right now Kurkowski, Mainhart, Wayne Alexander, and Ryan Marks were concentrating hard on a card game they had spread out on cargo containers. Mike Bryant was looking over the shoulders of just about everyone at the game, though Ryan Marks had his hand pulled up so close to his face you would have had to be sitting on his nose to see his cards.

Standing at the rear of the aircraft was Chief Monday. He was the jumpmaster for their HAHO insertion. They would be exiting the plane at 26,000 feet and opening their parachutes almost immediately. On a High Altitude, High Opening jump, the SEALs would be able to glide with their multicell square canopies for miles before setting down on the drop zone. The chief would be giving the signals to get ready for the jump, when they would exit the plane, and all the safety checks in between.

Now, Chief Monday raised his right fist and pointed to his wrist with two fingers of his left hand. It was the signal meaning they had twenty minutes before jump time. The plane was pressurized to an altitude of 10,000 feet. But when they exited the craft, they would be depressurized and breathing bottled oxygen. To get ready, each man put on his pro-tec helmet, buckled the strap under his chin, and put on his oxygen mask.

The MBU3P rubber oxygen masks could be supplied from a walkaround gas bottle like the ones the chief and Rockham had. Or it could be fed gas from the M2900 oxygen console, a large, green tank, about five feet long and a foot in diameter, laying flat along the deck inside a pipe framework almost double the length of the tank. Across the flat board on top of the tank were fourteen gas regulators attached to a high-pressure pipe down the center of the board. Each regulator had its own corrugated rubber hose to connect to the shorter hose dangling from each MBU3P mask. With two consoles secured to the deck, each man had his own oxygen outlet with plenty to spare. Lastly, the masks would be fed oxygen from the two steel bailout bottles each man had on his rig.

Now, each man adjusted his mask and checked it for leaks. Then they hooked up to the M2900 oxygen console. At Chief Monday's signal, Marks had snapped up immediately and he was hooking his mask into place—so much for being asleep. Once the men had their helmets secured and oxygen masks on and operating, they armed the FF-2 auto-actuator on their parachutes.

They were jumping with MT 1XS/SL parachutes. These were rigs that had an upper and lower backpack that held the main canopy and the reserve. The main canopy had 370 square feet of F-111 nylon fabric that would inflate into a rounded rectangular wing when deployed. Just in case it didn't deploy cleanly, the reserve chute had 270 square feet of the same nylon to help keep the jumper from plowing into the ground fast. And if their oxygen failed and a jumper passed out, the FF-2 auto-actuator would deploy their chute automatically once they had passed 1,500 feet. Their drop zone was some 3,133 feet above sea level, so adjustments had to be made to all of the actuators so they would deploy at the proper height. They were a backup system, another safety device.

But no matter what gear the SEALs carried, a parachute insertion was still a dangerous way to get to a target. Four SEALs had been killed off Grenada in 1983 when their water jump went wrong. That was one of the possibilities that made every SEAL commander think twice, and then a third time, about doing an op if it required jumping in. But the parachute insertion was one of the SEALs' skills, and right now Rockham and his men had to demonstrate they could do everything they had to—the hard way if necessary.

So the men sat up in their gear and breathed oxygen as the minutes passed and the plane depressurized. Kurkowski tried to get the card game going again, but it was a bust. With another hand signal, Chief Monday gave everyone the ten-minute warning. With a thumbs-up by each man in turn, Monday confirmed that each one had completed an oxygen check. Then came the six-minute warning.

The red warning lights went on, bathing everything in a bloodred glow. With the warnings on, the rear ramp of the C-130 began to slowly open. The open ramp made the noise level in the cargo cabin so loud that talking was all but impossible. It was why the chief's arm and hand signals were so important.

At the two-minute warning, the signal to stand up was given. As the chief raised his right arm past his head, open palm facing up, the men stood up from their seats. Everyone checked himself and then his partner on either side to be sure no gear was hung up and everyone's equipment was secure.

At the one-minute warning, the chief looked back at his men, extended his arm, bent his arm at the elbow and waved them back to the rear of the aircraft. It was the signal to move to the rear and go on their bailout bottles. Each man went by the numbers, activating their own oxygen bottles and feeling the surge of gas into their masks. Only then did they each unhook their mask hoses from the oxygen console on the deck and wrap the loose hoses around their regulators.

In spite of himself, when Greg Rockham felt the rush of cool gas into his mask, his heart jumped a beat. The oxygen was odorless, but the rubber hoses and mask gave it a taste and smell all its own. It had always reminded him of changing tires back when he was a kid, tasting and smelling the rubber in the air. But with the command to move to the rear, there was no time for memories. Each man staggered under his load of gear and shuffled back to the open ramp.

Within a yard of the edge of the ramp, the slipstream pulled and tugged at every loose bit of cloth and webbing. It was too late to consider anything but the blackness on the outside of the plane. They were doing a night jump, and the lights of Las Vegas could be clearly seen below, well to the rear of them. It had to be the most densely lit city of its kind in the world, Rockham thought. The spread of lights looked like a scattering of dots, golden-white glowing dust, spreading out in the distance. From a center so dense that the lines showed the roadways going through town, to the diminishing lights away from the city, there just wasn't anything like Las Vegas.

Then Chief Monday pulled up a fist with his thumb raised, moving his arm from his waist to his shoulder, commanding them to stand by. There were ten seconds to go. Before many more thoughts went through anyone's head, the overhead light went green and the chief vigorously snapped his hand down and pointed toward the exit, giving the go signal. Everyone stepped to the last edge of the ramp, turned to face the open cargo hold, and jumped backward from the aircraft. Chief Monday was the last person to go out the open door. With the men gone, the plane flew on past, its ramp slowly closing.

The sudden cessation of noise on exiting the aircraft was always startling to Rockham. The men fell through the dark sky, each one twisting his body to achieve a stable free-fall position. As they fell, the men could guide on each other by the light of the SDU-5/E strobe lights taped to the top of their pro-tec helmets. The strobes had a simple red lens over the light, and the flashing light at the top of their heads couldn't be seen by anyone on the ground. Then, when their altimeters indicated the proper height, one by one, each man pulled his ripcord and released his main canopy.

Rockham felt the jerk and drag of his canopy opening up. The square rig opening didn't compare to the gut-wrenching yank upward of the old T-10 round canopies. He looked up reflexively, to check the deployment of his chute, but the black sky showed little more than a blocking out of some stars by a square-cornered black shadow above him. The risers that went up from his shoulders to connect the canopy to his harness were properly taut, the wind didn't seem to be whistling past, and he hadn't hit the ground yet, so he knew that his main canopy must be properly filled out and functioning.

Since Mike Bryant had the experience and skills to lead the unit across the sky, Rockham saw no reason not to use him on point for the insertion. So Bryant was out in front of the roughly V-shaped formation, the point of the V lower than the rear-spreading legs. He was setting the speed and direction for the rest of the SEALs. He turned, and they turned, the men silently flying along under the stars.

As the jumpmaster, Chief Monday had carefully calculated the release point for the jump—when the men would quickly exit the aircraft. He had drawn on his experience, information from their briefings, and up-to-the-minute data from the pilots of the C-130. Monday had shared that information with Bryant so they both could decide on the best compass heading to take on the jump to make the drop zone. Since they'd exited the C-130 while almost fifteen miles from the drop zone, a bad calculation could put them down on the ground miles from their target.

Missing the target would mean a lot more than just a long walk in the desert. They were supposed to be a joint, multiservice mission. The Air Force had already done its part by getting them to the point they were at now, and there were Army Rangers also, and the coordinated timing with them was crucial. The SEALs had to take down their target while the Rangers were engaging the bulk of the enemy forces elsewhere.

No radio communication was allowed except if there were an emergency while they were in the air. Even their relatively low-powered MX-300s could be detected from the ground. And once they were on the ground, it could be too late to cover any missed distance and make up time.

But Rockham had ceded authority on this part of the op to Bryant. He was the man in charge of the drop and was leading it down to the ground. Rockham willingly went along for the ride, because that was the way things were done in the Teams. It didn't matter what a SEAL's rank or position was— if he was the best qualified man to do the job, you put him in charge. The final responsibility for any action or operation was always the officer's, but that responsibility included knowing when to keep your hands off and let the men do their jobs. If a man was in charge of a particular part of an operation, you followed him. It didn't matter if you were an officer and he was an enlisted. Once you had trusted a man to do a job, you let him do it.

Rockham knew that there were a surprising number of officers in other units and services, and even some who'd become executives in the civilian sector, who had forgotten that basic tenet and micromanaged everything. They never learned what it meant to have a group of men whom you could trust to do anything that had to be done. And Rockham trusted his men, and knew they trusted him to back their actions as well.

Right now, following his own guidelines, he steered his chute in a formation, following a faint line of red lights through the dark sky. The ground was anything but dark in places. As the formation tracked across the sky, turning in a series of lazy S-turns, they could all see the headlights of the cars going past on Highway 95 off to their left. It was amusing to wonder just what those people would have thought if they could look up and see the group of parachutes sailing along.

Then again, they might not have thought much at all. This was Nevada, after all. Las Vegas was just off to the east a bit, and there were a lot stranger things to see in that town than a bunch of lumpy skydivers gliding in the air. But Area 51, which was in all of the weird TV shows, was in Nevada someplace as well. Maybe he and his men would be recorded as a UFO if they were seen from the ground. The thought almost made the SEAL officer laugh out loud.

At his position in the front of the formation, Mike Bryant had his own thoughts on the drop. Mostly, he concentrated on reading the compass and altimeter dials that glowed on the chest board he wore. The problems he was constantly solving in his head compared drop rates, the wind pushing them, their forward momentum, and how far they had to go to reach the drop zone.

Bryant was trying hard to maintain a steady forward rate that matched their velocity with their drop rate. The men were moving forward at about forty miles an hour, with the tailwind he'd allowed for, at a seventy-two-degree glide angle, and dropping at a rate of twenty feet per second. The tailwind wasn't too bad, but Bryant had to keep turning the chute from side to side to limit some of their forward motion. The legs between the turns had to be short in order to keep the formation inside the wind cone that would take them down to the target. Without artificially extending the distance the chutes were flying, the formation would overshoot the drop zone. The easiest way to extend the flying distance was to move from side to side while still going forward.

So Bryant had to pay close attention to his compass heading as he steered his canopy. The rest of the men in the formation just had to follow his turns. Pulling down on the right toggle, just in front of the right riser above the shoulder, made the chute turn to the right. Releasing the toggle stopped the turn and the chute just went forward. The left toggle made a left turn, and so the cycle of turns kept repeating.

Rockham heard the sound of the wind blowing past his head, almost unnoticeable with his pro-tec helmet on. What stood out on this jump, as it did on all of his parachute jumps, was the pressure of the leg straps down at his groin and thighs. It told him the straps were there and that they were holding. If they weren't, he would literally fall through his harness and be heading to the ground. The pressure always made him think about the quality of the buckles securing his harness. He hadn't had a bad set break on him—at least not yet.

The turns became flatter and faster as the formation approached the ground. The legs between the turns were shorter as well. The ground was only a darker field in the night; the sliver of moon and starlight gave almost no illumination from their vantage point. But watching the horizon as it came closer to being level with them told the SEALs that they were approaching the ground.

Then Bryant decided it was time to land. They flew past the point he thought was the drop zone, flying about four hundred yards downwind of it. Then the formation turned to the left and went on its base leg for a couple of hundred yards before turning to the left and into the wind for their final approach.

Going into the wind slowed the canopies considerably. Pulling down on both of the toggles at the same time decreased the lift of the chutes while killing a lot of their forward momentum. The ground could be just faintly seen in the limited moonlight, sand, a few rocks, and the occasional chunk of brush and plants.

From a height of about two hundred feet the SEALs pulled their toggles down to shoulder level, the half-brake position. They were flaring their canopies a bit high for a regular jump, but on a night jump it was the safest way. Judging distance to the ground was difficult at night, even for very experienced jumpers. It was better to put on the brakes, flare high and just drift down to the ground.

To prepare for the impact, each man held his feet and knees together, knees slightly bent and toes pointing down. Elbows were locked in to the sides, and leg muscles were held tense. When they hit the ground, they would roll and their bodies would spread out the shock of landing.

Five feet to go, and the ground could just be seen well enough to at least make sure they weren't going to land on any big rocks. Now each SEAL pulled both his toggles down to his crotch. The end cells of the canopies inflated as the leading edge turned down. With full lift and almost no forward speed, the men landed.

In spite of what they did on demonstration jumps, no one even tried to land standing up and staying on their feet. That wasn't something you did on unknown ground when every man needed to stay fully functional for the operation. Broken legs or ankles, or even just a bad sprain, could jeopardize the whole mission and each one of the Teammates who depended on you. So there was no hotdogging. Each SEAL landed in a safe, long sideways roll, a perfect, practiced parachute landing fall.

CHAPTER 8

★ ★ ★ ★

The men were down, they were safe, and no one was hurt. The situation made it officially okay for Rockham to start breathing again. Just because he had a hands-off style of command didn't mean that he wasn't concerned—very concerned—with every aspect of the mission. And a night HAHO insertion onto strange ground was something worth being concerned about.

As the SEALs all gathered up their chutes, the other good aspect of the drop showed up. The unit went "administrative" for a moment as the pickup truck with the parachute recovery crew showed up. They were not only all okay, they were almost dead center of the planned drop zone. Rockham made a mental note that he owed Bryant a beer when the mission was over. The crew from the air base helped gather up the chutes and other drop equipment that the SEALs would have buried in the desert had this been a hot op in a combat zone.

The drop zone was almost due north of the airfield itself. They were a klick and a half, 1,500 meters, from the target hangar on the west side of the field. The distance wasn't quite a mile, and they were on schedule. They coordinated on Rockham, and he directed Bryant to take point and lead the squads out.

They weren't expecting much in the way of action from the base itself. The normal operating hours for the field only ran from 0730 to 1630 hours on weekdays. It was closed on weekends and holidays. So the base being closed so early on a Saturday morning wouldn't strike anyone as being out of the ordinary. At least the base's schedule wouldn't strike any of the locals as odd.

During the briefing and workup on the operation, the men had been told what to expect and why. When Kurkowski heard that the Air Force only ran the field during normal working hours, he barked, "Less than a dozen flights a day, and they're off at four-thirty every day, and they get weekends off? All of this not an hour outside of Las Vegas. Fuck this! I've got to transfer to the Air Force."

But despite his complaints regarding the strenuous schedule followed at Indian Springs, Kurkowski had settled down and worked just as hard as every other member of the unit during the preparation and workup for the op. They had found an aircraft hangar at Oceanic Naval Air Station near Virginia Beach that was close in size and layout to the building they were about to hit. They didn't have a floor plan of the structure, and so practiced assaulting the hangar a number of different ways.

Since their briefing on the op had said the weapon of mass destruction was "suspected" to be a large chemical device, Rockham and the others agreed on a general course of action. Second squad under Shaun Daugherty and Chief Monday would take the large hangar area itself as their target, clearing and securing it. Since it had been specified that the weapon was "large," the easiest access to handling equipment, forklifts, and vehicles would be in the large hangar bay through either of the two twenty-eight-foot-tall sliding doors.

If second squad located the device, they would secure it while first squad conducted their part of the operation. Though a commander is never comfortable with splitting his team, splitting the unit into its two nine-man squads would be the fastest way to cover the large building. So while second squad concentrated on the device, Rockham would lead first squad in clearing out the office area on the west side of the hangar.

Their intel had reported that a possible ten to fifteen tangos would remain inside the building while the rest of the terrorists engaged the Rangers. The Rangers were actually miles away, at a remote location on the Nellis Air Force bombing and gunnery range. There, the Army forces could conduct a live-fire exercise while also working against the Air Combat Security Command forces.

The SEALs would be using their special simunition-adapted weapons and firing on Air

Combat Security Command tangos who would be similarly equipped. The SEALs were all wearing their body armor, pro-tec helmets—now with the strobe lights turned off—and heavy goggles. The bright splashes of paint from the FX marking ammunition would be safe, and guarantee to show if a hit was made.

Now they moved out in a combat formation behind Bryant and Stadt, who were switching off the point position between themselves. Every day of training—which meant every day of the week for months—the men of the unit had been conducting physical training. Their workouts hadn't been just calisthenics. To build up the muscles needed for climbing and moving, they'd worked for hours on weight machines. When they weren't lifting weights, they were running or swimming. Now, having to cross almost a mile of desert with all their equipment on them, their physical training was paying off.

Kurkowski moved along with his breacher's loadout settled in, worn like a heavy coat. Wayne Alexander had just as heavy a load, but he appeared to have been born part mule. He never seemed to slow down, no matter how much weight he was carrying. He never seemed to speed up either, but he could hump the biggest load in the unit and just keep going.

Everyone was strong, fit, and able to move silently. The only sign of their passing were eighteen black shadows moving across the Nevada desert. To avoid being silhouetted against the skyline, the men all kept low and didn't cross any of the paved airstrips between themselves and their target.

Every other man in the unit was wearing a set of AN/PVS-5A night vision goggles. The goggles gathered all the available light and multiplied it thousands of times. To the men wearing them, the desert took on an unreal air. Through the NVGs they were able to see every brush, shrub, rock, and gully clearly, in sparkling green relief. They weren't actually looking through the tubes of the goggles at the surrounding countryside. Instead, the goggles electronically magnified the available light and made a picture appear on a green screen in front of each eye.

But the use of NVGs robbed the men of normal night vision, which was why only half of them wore the goggles, though everyone had a pair. The men's eyes had become adjusted to the darkness and could make out objects and their surroundings at a distance from where they were moving, and the NVGs had a limited range and ran on batteries. Thus, the unit was ready for all aspects of night fighting.

They came to at a small gully only a few hundred meters from the target hangar. They were approaching from the north and no movement could be seen anywhere around the building. The two squads would now separate. From this point on, one group or the other would get to the device and secure it. Once the area was secure, their extraction bird would be called in. Without a word having been spoken since exiting the aircraft, the men went on with their part of the mission. The next time they saw each other, they would either be successful or not.

The rectangular steel building was the only structure for hundreds of meters in any direction. To the south of it lay the main runway; to the north, a concrete apron ran out into the desert and ended. A single lightbulb burned above the south-facing hangar door; no other lights could be seen anywhere, either inside or outside the building. The structure was 125 feet wide and a hundred feet deep, according to their briefing information. The main hangar bay would be a hundred feet square. The additional twenty-five feet of building width made up the office area. The west side of the building had several doors and posts indicating parking slots along the wall. That would be the office area of the hangar and first squad's responsibility.

The east side of the building was a large, flat expanse of corrugated metal. Long vertical stringers stiffened the walls and gave them some texture. But the large expanse was only broken by a row of windows across the top, just underneath the overhang of the roof, and a single doorway in the middle of the wall. There was a rectangular extrusion out from the wall at the northeast corner of the building. By the look of the posts, junction boxes, and conduits around it, it was likely to be the main electrical junction for the structure. A large vent pipe ran up the inside corner of the wall where it turned out from the building. That corner was going to be Mike Bryant's stairway into the structure.

Early in the planning for the operation, it had been decided that the large hangar doors couldn't be opened without drawing the attention of everyone nearby. The building was known to be an all-steel structure, so a wall could be easily cut through with a linear-shaped charge. With such a charge, the power of a very small amount of explosive was focused into a cutting jet. A door-size opening could be instantly cut through a steel wall, eliminating the need to use any of the normal doorways. Such doors would be guarded by the tangos, one way or another.

But the target for the operation was a possible chemical weapon. The possibility of damage to such a device eliminated any thought of using explosive breaching. So Bryant and his shooting partner, Henry Lutz, were going to penetrate the building another way.

Bryant was going to climb up to the roof edge and enter through one of the windows. If he saw that the area was clear, he would climb down to the floor and open the outside door for his squad. Henry Lutz was going to back him up both on the ground and in the building. If the target weapon was spotted, Henry was the most qualified man in the squad to deal with it.

With the rest of the squad covering them from the edge of the concrete apron, the two SEALs dashed for the wall of the structure. No fire came at them from the night as they made it to the corner where the pipe stood.

The eaves of the roof were twenty feet above the ground, the windows extending down another three feet. Bryant went up the pipe with his feet braced against the wall as easily as if he were walking up a flight of stairs. After first peering across the roof and sweeping his field of vision with his MP5SD, he swung up and onto the roof proper.

Now being covered by Bryant, Lutz also went up the pipe, not quite as quickly as Bryant, but fast enough to get to the edge of the roof in a few moments. Sliding out onto the roof of the building extension, Lutz covered the area of the outside wall and was able to see through the dirty windows into the darkened hangar.

Reaching down with his Leatherman—a pocketknife that unfolded into a pair of pliers and held a number of useful tools—Bryant opened the window quickly and efficiently. A few squirts of oil from a bottle in his pocket made sure that the hinges of the window would not squeak when moved. Silently easing the window open, Bryant waited and watched for any reaction within.

After a full minute had passed, he reached down to a pouch strapped onto his leg and pulled out one end of a rolled length of tubular nylon tape. The tape was nearly as strong as a 13mm climbing rope and took up much less space than an equal length of regular line. Tying the end to the steel pipe he'd used to climb up to the roof, Bryant looped the tape through the snaplink he'd attached at the left shoulder of his SPIE harness.

Under their vests, each man wore the SPIE harness, which could be attached to a rope rig hanging underneath a helicopter for a very quick extraction. Bryant was now going to use the harness as an attachment point for the snaplink he was using as a makeshift descender. By pulling on the lower end of the nylon tape with his left hand, he could lower himself as quickly, or slowly, as he wished with just the pressure of his left hand. As he lowered himself, the nylon tape would unwind from the roll in the leg pouch, and his right hand would be free to handle his weapon.

With his preparations complete, Bryant keyed the mike button on his MX-300R radio and said quietly, "Six . . . six . . . six."

The number, repeated three times, meant that he was in place and ready to enter. Within a minute everyone on the net heard "Four . . . four . . . four" through their earpieces. First squad was ready and in place for the takedown on the hangar.

Now, with Bryant and Lutz covering, the rest of second squad moved across the concrete apron and set up in a train just outside the door in the middle of the wall. Silently and carefully, Bryant slipped over the open windowsill and into the hangar's dark interior.

Wearing his NVGs, he could see a portion of the inside of the hangar. Even with the light-magnifying power of the NVGs, there was only a small amount of the limited moonlight and starlight, which had penetrated through the windows into the main hangar bay. Some dim light could be seen on the far wall, the glows coming from what might have been office windows covered with blackout material. But in the hangar proper, there was little more to see than the outlines of stacks of boxes, drums, and other unidentifiable materials.

As he slipped halfway down to the floor, a soft

sound caused Bryant to squeeze his left hand, halting his descent. With his right hand around the pistol grip of his MP5SD suppressed submachine gun, he scanned the area to see what might have made the noise. With the gun pushed out hard against the shoulder strap that went across his back, Bryant tracked the muzzle along his line of sight.

Another soft sound drew his attention, along with the muzzle of his weapon. Halfway across the bay he saw a figure move. The boxes had masked the man from Bryant's view until he stood up from where he'd been sitting. The man stretched and began to walk toward the side door, on the other side of which Bryant's Teammates had set up to enter the building.

As the man walked, he flashed the thin red beam of a masked flashlight in front of him. The red light would be hard to detect to the naked eye at any distance, but it would enable the man to see while still protecting his night vision. The beam shone brilliantly through Bryant's NVGs, allowing him to carefully direct his weapon to follow the man across the room. As the figure stepped around a large, covered mound on the floor, he moved to within thirty feet of where Bryant hung.

Though the SEAL was motionless and silent, something caused the man on the ground to stop and look around. On the front of his helmet was a clear, lexan face shield. It wrapped halfway around the helmet and completely protected the man's face. In his right hand was an MP5 submachine gun supported by its shoulder strap.

His curiosity piqued, the man looked up and

started to raise the beam of his red flashlight. As the beam went up the wall, the man saw a huge black shadow resolve itself into what flashed through his mind as a gigantic spider hanging from its web. The startling thought froze him in place for a second. There was a soft snapping sound, and a pink flower of paint further surprised the man as it bloomed across his face shield.

Quickly dropping the rest of the way to the floor, Bryant kept the muzzle of his weapon trained on the "dead" tango. Snapping free of his descent line and its carrying bag, Bryant keyed his radio mike and said softly but clearly, "Execute . . . execute . . . execute."

If he had been able to reach the doorway, the triple-repeated signal would have been the spoken number "Two." Then first squad would have triggered the takedown with the execute order. But Bryant had no way of being sure that the tango he'd dropped wouldn't make any noise. The rules of engagement they were operating under for the exercise said that he wouldn't. If any man—SEAL or "enemy"—received a solid hit from the simunition rounds, he was supposed to be dead and not do anything more that could help his side. But the SEAL couldn't take the chance that this "dead" tango wouldn't cheat, and leave his Teammates to pay the bill.

Within a second of the order going out on the net, there was a heavy bang and the door a few dozen feet from Bryant burst out toward the desert. Kurkowski had placed the duckbill of his hooligan tool between

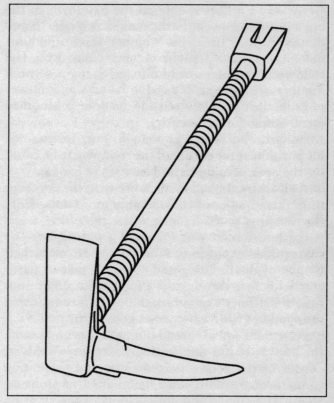

HOOLIGAN TOOL

the doorjamb and edge of the steel door. The SEAL's immense arm strength had ripped the lock free of the metal doorjamb, and Sid Mainhart, in the point man position, had pulled the door open.

The number one and two men in the train, John

Grant and Ed Lopez, entered the bay through the open door and swept to their right and left. Immediately behind them the number three and four men, Lieutenant Daugherty and Chief Monday, followed. The men spread out and each one, by the numbers, called out, "Clear!"

From their positions outside the door, where they were holding rear security, in came Kurkowski, Mainhart, and Henry Limbaugh. Lutz maintained his position at the corner of the roof, where he could see the open area north and east of the hangar.

As Kurkowski had made noise with the hooligan tool, there had been considerably more noise from the east area of the hangar, where the offices were. A crashing sound was followed a second later by two muffled explosions. First squad had made their breach of the building and sent in a pair of flash-crashes before entering. The furious sound of multiple short bursts of submachine-gun fire followed the sound of the flash-crashes going off.

As second squad spread out to secure and search the hangar bay, a double door near the southwest corner of the room banged open and three men came through. With sudden and efficient violence, Shaun Daugherty and John Grant opened fire on the three men. Multiple bursts targeted the men before they had a chance to react to the shots coming out of the darkness toward them. They may not have seen who was firing, but the sting and spread of the soft plastic paint-filled FX bullets as they impacted on their clothes and face shields left little doubt that they were out of the game.

"Clear," Grant shouted, quickly followed by the same shout from Daugherty.

When Bryant's signal went out over the net, first squad was already in place and ready to initiate the takedown. The signal "Two" repeated three times from Bryant would have meant that second squad had made a surreptitious entry into the hangar bay. But the "Execute" signal meant that something had gone wrong and it was time for the main event to start.

There was no hesitation on the part of any member of first squad or their officer, Lieutenant Rockham. The initial quiet entry plan was out the window, so the takedown was started in full.

The double doors at the northeast corner of the building had swung inward with a blow from Alexander's sledgehammer nailing the doors right on the lock. The in-swinging doors were immediately followed by a pair of flash-crashes thrown by Rockham and Mike Ferber.

When the thunderous bang and brilliant light of the flash-crashes rang out, the number three and four men in the train, Ryan Marks and Dan Able, went through the door, spreading out and moving down against the opposite walls. Three tangos were in the room, all of them disoriented by the noise and light of the flash-crashes. The smoke from the exploded grenades parted in lines connecting the muzzles of Marks's and Able's weapons to the staggering tango targets.

As Marks and Able were clearing the room, John Sukov and Peter Wilkes, the number five and six men in the train, entered and spread out along their respective walls. The two SEALs added their fire to that of their Teammates already clearing the room. With the impact of at least six bullets to each man, the tangos knew this was the end of their involvement in the exercise.

With the sound of "Clear" ringing out, Rockham and Ferber came into the room. Without slowing down, they went to the hallway mouth that centered in the south wall and took position to the left of the opening. Wayne Alexander and Larry Stadt came into the room and moved behind Rockham and Ferber. At no time did any of the men expose themselves to anyone who might have been down the hallway, except when Marks and Wilkes had stepped across and cleared the east side of the room.

Jack Tinsley came into the room and covered the three downed tangos while keeping rear security on the outer door. Now the train had reformed to move down the hallway, which was the same size as a corridor found in most houses. This meant that the train could only move in a single file. A double column would have been used in a wider corridor to double the amount of forward firepower that could be brought to bear.

When the train was reformed, the squad moved out down the hallway. Marks and Wilkes stood at their position on the east side of the hallway entrance. To rejoin the train, they would be the first entry team on the door just inside the hallway. Tinsley was maintaining his watch at the rear and would be establishing the tango detainment area once the takedown and clearing were completed.

There were eight doorways facing the thirty-foot-long corridor. At its far end was an opening into another room. There was no movement in the distance and nothing could be heard by the SEALs as they set up. Moving quickly, Larry Stadt moved out on point, followed immediately by Wayne Alexander, both men starting out at Rockham's hand signal.

The first doorway in the hall was on the west side and just past the beginning of the hall. When the ready squeeze signal was passed up from the rear, Stadt moved down the hallway just past the door, keeping his weapon trained to the south. Alexander swung around with his sledgehammer and struck the first door square on the end of the lock. The heavy blow blasted the door open, and it crashed inward against something.

As the door was knocked open, Ryan Marks stepped into the door and pushed hard against it, Wilkes immediately behind him. Marks shouted "Clear" but didn't go through to the janitor's closet they'd just breached. Instead, he and Wilkes stepped back and followed Alexander as they all set up on the first door on the east side of the hallway.

This door didn't have a lock, only a push plate. The sign MEN told the SEALs what was on the other side, as far as a room went. But a tango could take cover in a head as well as any other kind of room, so they had to clear it as well.

Procedure was followed, but only with Marks and Wilkes in the train behind Alexander. Stadt maintained security down the hallway, observed by

Rockham, who was kneeling on the floor, and Ferber behind him. Alexander banged open the door once they set up an abbreviated train on the east side of the hall and Marks squeezed his shoulder. A flash-crash went through the open door. Right behind the explosion was Wilkes, followed by Marks. They found nothing other than two commodes, a urinal, and a lot of smoke.

With the beginning of the hallway cleared, the train moved down faster, forming up behind the point man and the breacher. As each room was passed, it would be crashed, then entered and cleared. As the train passed the cleared room, the men would come out and rejoin the end of the train line.

The third doorway on the west side of the hallway opened up onto the flight planning office. When Alexander breached the door, Rockham and Ferber went in to clear the room behind the crashes tossed in by Sukov. As the two SEALs went through the door, a fusillade of gunshots rang out.

Two tangos were in what was apparently the flight planning room for the hangar. The flash-crash explosion had disoriented them, but one man was able to swing around and pull the trigger back on his MP5, though he was firing wildly, rather than at the SEALs.

Rockham and Ferber had entered the room and immediately spread out, as dictated by their training. The tango continued to fire wildly even after Rockham had stitched him square in the chest. Ferber had nailed the other tango in the room with a quick burst, and that man remained on the floor. But Rockham's tango refused to go down. As the SEAL officer stepped up to the man and knocked his submachine gun up into the air, where the bullets splattered across the ceiling, Ferber stepped up behind the man and knocked him down.

A short, hard struggle between Ferber and the tango ended with the man on the floor finding himself wearing several sets of tie-ties, on his wrists and ankles. In all of the other rooms the SEALs cleared, only four more tangos were found and eliminated. None of the SEALs took a hit from any of the very limited return fire the tangos put out.

When it was determined that the hangar had been cleared of tangos, the remaining enemy "dead" were gathered in the front office under the careful eyes of Sid Mainhart and Roger Kurkowski. The one uncooperative tango who had been secured by Ferber was picked up bodily by Marks and Able and simply dumped in with the others. If the man didn't want to play by the rules, the SEALs decided, he could suffer as they played by his rules.

The large hangar bay was searched, as were the office rooms. Anything of intelligence value—which meant every piece of paper, photograph, map, or other items—was gathered up by the SEALs and stuffed into bags brought along for the purpose. The "dead" tangos were searched, and the contents of their pockets included in the bags. For further information, the tangos were photographed as they lay on the ground.

Under the tarp Bryant had seen covering a large

mound in the hangar bay, the SEALs made their final discovery. Sitting in a large metal rack was a long, conical warhead. It was gray in color, about two feet in diameter, and six feet long. John Sukov was brought in to examine the device along with Henry Limbaugh and Jack Tinsley.

Sukov looked at the warhead as it sat in its rack and said, "Son of a bitch. This thing's made from the warhead to a Scud missile. The fuze is missing from the nose, but there's three caps on what look like burster wells. There's one well under the nose here where the fuze is missing, and two I can see at the back. Whatever this is, it isn't a normal HE warhead."

"Is it safe to move?" Rockham asked.

"There're no antihandling devices that I can see. The burster wells are empty, and I've checked for any exterior charges or fuzes. There's a filler agent that gives it weight, but no explosives that I can find."

"Tinsley, Limbaugh," Rockham said to the two corpsmen. "Your opinions?"

"It matches the descriptions we have of a Soviet chemical warhead with some variations," Tinsley said.

"I agree," Sukov said. "This thing is a chemical warhead for a Scud B missile. It could be filled with GB or VX nerve gas."

"Okay," Rockham said. "If it's safe to move, we take it with us."

"It weighs about eight hundred pounds," Shaun Daugherty said as he heard the orders.

"Call in the extraction birds," Rockham said,

"and get Marks, Alexander, Kurkowski, and Able in here."

Looking up at Mike Bryant and Larry Stadt, Rockham said, "Break out that nylon tape of yours and put three double loops of it under this thing."

The SEALs did as their officer ordered. As the extraction helicopters came in to pick the men up, they had an additional load for one of the birds. Staggering out of the south hangar doors, the six strongest SEALs emerged carrying out the warhead. With the nylon tube doubled for extra strength, the men had the extra length of the nylon pulled across their shoulders. Their lieutenant wanted it on board the bird, and that was what they were going to do.

The entire takedown of the building had taken less than ten minutes once they were on site. With the eastern sky just starting to glow with the rosy light of dawn, the helicopters, SEALs, and their prize lifted off.

"So, after our debrief we get to pull some liberty in Vegas on a Saturday night," Kurkowski said hopefully over the noise of the helicopter blades.

"I'm not sure that if I let you do that, they won't strap a live version of that warhead to my ass, Kurkowski," Rockham said with a grin.

CHAPTER 9

★ ★ ★ ★

Not every SEAL who left the Teams did so on a fully voluntary basis. There were a number who retired and left the Navy, and there were some who paid the price of the high-speed day-to-day training it took to remain and be an active SEAL. Sometimes wounds and injuries sustained in combat caused a man to leave the Teams and the Navy on a medical retirement. Sometimes those same medical retirements were due to simple, stupid accidents.

When Ken Fleming, a member of SEAL Team Two's Fourth Platoon back during Operation Endurance, broke his knee, it was due to a bad landing on a practice parachute jump. The result was the end of a SEAL career.

But the men who make the Teams are resourceful, and Fleming, taking his medical retirement pay and his own savings and combining them with the skill and enjoyment of cooking, opened the Iceberg Bar & Grill. A burgeoning catering service added to the success of the new eating establishment, and Fleming looked like he was well on his way to beating the old restaurateur's rule: "To make a small fortune in the restaurant business, start with a large one."

But the men of Fourth Platoon had not forgotten their Teammate. Certainly not when that Teammate had a place with a liquor license. The entire Special Materials Detachment was gathered at the Iceberg waiting for their boss, Lieutenant Rockham, to show up with his report on what was going on up in D.C. The Iceberg had become a second home to the men of the SMD, and they were made welcome by their former Teammate. There was a lot of good-natured joking and ribbing, and the men were sorry not to have Fleming with them in the new unit, but glad that he was becoming a success.

Fleming had made sure his old Teammates had a private place to stay after duty hours and talk freely among themselves. The Iceberg had a back room, ostensibly for large parties and receptions. But to the public, the private dining room always seemed to be taken during the evening hours. It had become the place where the SEALs could relax, have a few beers, and develop the unit cohesion that made the Teams work so smoothly.

The wait staff at the Iceberg knew the SEALs well. Many of the waitresses had experienced the

exuberance of the men of the Teams at other estab-
lishments throughout the Norfolk and Virginia
Beach area. Even though things never got out of
hand at the Iceberg, only the head waitress normally served the guys in the back room. And she
was just about the only woman there who was willing to go in the room when the SEALs were in the
house.

There was an old rubber swim fin—the type
known as a "Duck Foot"—that the men inside the
room would hang on the doorknob when they
wanted privacy. Then not even the head waitress
would enter. During those times, Ken Fleming would
either serve his old Teammates or they would come
out and serve themselves.

When Rockham returned from his Pentagon
meeting late in the afternoon, he found that Chief
Monday had released the men on liberty, which
meant they were all expected to be at the Iceberg. A
few quick phone calls got the few men who were at
home with their families into town and to the Iceberg, and by the time the lieutenant had arrived, all
of the men of his unit were waiting quietly in the
back for him and his news. The old swim fin was
hanging from the doorknob.

"Okay," Rockham said, "that's it, guys, we've
been officially certified to operate. We're good to go
for any mission that comes up for us."

A loud round of cheers followed Rockham's announcement. The men had all been working long,
hard hours to get to this point, and it felt good to finally be there. As Kurkowski put it, they'd crammed

twenty-six hours of training into each twenty-four-hour day. Though they were professional warriors, recognition still felt good which was the reason behind Rockham's next announcement.

"And Admiral Cromarty sends his personal 'Bravo Zulu' for a job well done," he said proudly. The expression "Bravo Zulu" was a traditional way of expressing congratulations officially in the Navy. Those words from the admiral sounded pretty good to the SEALs who had worked so hard to earn them.

When the cheering died down, Rockham continued, "And the admiral sends along the best regard of the support staff for our last little exercise. It seems the Air Force had a little trouble managing to extract some warhead they found the Navy had inserted into one of their birds."

That announcement drew a particularly loud round of laughter from the men.

"The Air Force never could pull one out of their ass," Kurkowski said.

"Serves them right," Wayne Alexander said solemnly. "They consider just riding a bike to be a PT test."

The physically active men of the Teams held the general level of physical fitness in the Air Force in less than high regard. The bulk of the jokes and jabs were merely part of the usual interservice rivalry. Each man in the room had respect for what the other services could do. But they also had little respect for what the other services could not do. And the Air Force wasn't considered to have much of a physical training program. Of course, according to the SEALs, even the Olympics only had an adequate training level.

"Dr. Sharon Taylor—you do remember her, don't you?" Rockham said with a wide grin.

A thunderous chorus of whistles and catcalls followed the mention of the beautiful CIA biowar expert.

When the noise had died down, Rockham continued, "Well, she sends her best too."

"You did mention to her that Ferber's still waiting for some of that best, didn't you?" Kurkowski said.

Mike Ferber, the detachment's leading petty officer and the object of Kurkowski's jab, had struck up a light relationship with Sharon Taylor when the unit had been aboard the *Archerfish*. Nothing had come of the situation, since Ferber wasn't one of the womanizing SEAL types. And they had been in the middle of a mission well inside Soviet territorial waters at the time.

The joke and the laughter of the men had the effect Kurkowski had been working for—it caused the rugged SEAL petty officer to blush, which brought the house down. Even the usually stoic John Grant was roaring with laughter at Ferber's embarrassment. It was rare for a SEAL to show embarrassment, and to most of the men in the room, Mike Ferber was the only SEAL they knew who even could blush.

"Okay, settle down," Rockham said as the laughter died away. "I have some serious information for you."

All attention in the room was centered on the SEAL officer. The men liked their play and a good time, but they could settle in to work in an instant when it was required.

"Just because we're certified to operate doesn't mean we don't have to keep up the long hours of training," Rockham said. "In fact, it means even more work for us.

"Now, we're going to have an alert system put in place for us. One squad will be on first alert status, while the second squad will be on second alert. First alert status means a one hour response time for that squad. If the alert goes out for an op, that squad has to be on base within an hour, and ready to deploy within six hours."

The men groaned over that news. Being on that short an alert time meant they could go home, and that was about it. The short deployment time was something new. They would have to keep their bags packed at all times to be able to make that schedule.

"Settle down," Chief Monday's voice rang out. "You don't have to like it, just do it."

"I can't say I'm all that thrilled about the time crunch either," Rockham said. "And it's not going to be all that great for the other squad. There's only the eighteen of us all in the whole Navy right now who are qualified to conduct operations against weapons of mass destruction. Until the higher-ups decide more people should be assigned, we're it.

"Those on second alert status will have the luxurious time of four hours in which to report. That time period does not mean you get to sleep in. It's intended to allow you to leave the Little Creek/Virginia Beach area in order to conduct training."

"But not very damned far away," Mike Bryant said from the back of the room.

"Nope, not very," Rockham agreed. "I think that particular time period was intended to allow your command staff the luxury of going up to D.C. for meetings and still have enough time to get back down here for an alert without collecting too many speeding tickets along the way.

"And the second alert squad also has six hours to get ready to deploy. So the squad on first alert status has seven hours total from when the alert goes out to being in a wheels-up status. Second alert status means you have a total of ten hours to do the same thing. Of course, if the balloon goes up, I expect everyone to be here ASAP, and we all leave together if at all possible. We are our own support, for the most part.

"Command may have been stingy with the time they've given us to train up. And our alert times are pretty damned short as well. Where they haven't been cheap is spending money. You may have noticed that we have a load of gear—more than enough to equip a detachment twice our size."

A low grumble of assent went through the men. In the last months, loads of equipment and materials had been arriving at their detachment headquarters at Little Creek. The gear had been piling up, becoming a problem in the cramped quarters they were allotted on the base. It was one of the reasons why the men moved out to the Iceberg whenever possible.

"Well, now you know what all that gear is for," Rockham continued. "That's the only way we're going to make that deployment time. Gear boxes will be prepackaged and ready at all times. In the armory at Team Two will be a complete set of weapons for each man—tested, zeroed, cleaned, and ready to go. The same thing for the magazines. A full ordnance loadout will be packaged at all times. Weapon's magazines, explosives, munitions, the whole nine yards.

"And that gear and those supplies will not remain static. We will be rotating weapons, ammunition, commo, everything. When a squad changes alert status, they change over their gear. Jack, Henry?" Rockham addressed the two corpsmen. "That means the same thing for all our consumables, be it in Medical, Sub Ops, Air Ops, or our specialized chemical protection and detection gear. Everything not only has to be ready to go at a moment's notice, it has to be fresh enough to have at least a ninety-day operational life.

"They have given us six hours to be good to go for up to a ninety-day deployment without resupply. I don't intend for us to need that whole six hours. Somewhere in this navy, somebody was surprised by the sudden drop in their allotted funds. I don't know if it's from a tin can out in the Indian Ocean somewhere, or some admiral's wife isn't going to be able to redecorate their quarters this year—or for the next several years, come to think of it. The Navy sank a bucketful of money into this outfit as soon as they could see we were going to be worth spending it on. They are going to get their money's worth.

"And there is a reason for all of this taxpayer's money being spent," Rockham continued in a serious tone. "Part of the briefing I just received up in D.C. included the listing of some very bad people in the world out there. These fuckers think playing with bugs and gas is a good thing. Some of them have already used such weapons, even against their own people.

"They don't think anyone's going to be able to catch them pissing in the sandbox. And if they do get caught, they don't care, they'll just deny it and let the diplomats wrangle things out for years. We're going to prevent that from ever happening. And if it does happen, those immediately responsible get to meet up with us, probably in a dark place."

For a moment all that could be heard in the room were the faint rattle of pots and the clink of glasses through the far wall, abutting the kitchen.

Then Rockham grabbed a beer from the table and took a drink. "By the way, since I'm still going to be shuttling back and forth between here and D.C. for a while, second squad is going to be the first of us to enjoy first alert status. Come on up here and get your prize, Shaun."

Reaching into his pocket, Rockham pulled out a small pager, identical to the one clipped to his belt. As Daugherty walked up to where Rockham sat on the edge of the table, the men clapped and whistled. The situation was serious, and everyone in the room knew it, but they still acted as if their junior officer had won some kind of prize.

Reaching over, Rockham clipped the pager to Daugherty's belt. "That's it, guys," he said. "Everyone gets one of these issued to them, and you keep it on your person at all times. I don't care if you're eating, sleeping, or banging away at your latest pickup—you keep this thing within earshot."

"Do you have two of them for Kurkowski?" Mike Bryant said. "That guy can sleep through a collision alarm, and he snores enough to drown out jet wash."

"He sleeps through an alert," Chief Monday said after the laughter died down, "and I'll personally hook his up to a squib and tape it to his ass."

The idea of the big SEAL having an electrically detonated firecracker taped to his posterior struck his Teammates as particularly fitting.

CHAPTER 10

★ ★ ★ ★

1322 ZULU
Grid Zone NI 37-12, Coordinates NM436748
South of the Wadi Haurān
Al Anbar Governorate
Western Iraq

The big missile tore down from the sky and struck the desert with a dull explosion. Instead of the heavy rolling thunder a weapon of that size should have made, the explosion of the warhead was relatively slight, muffled and filled with black smoke. The pink cloud that would have formed from the leftover oxidizer in the ruptured tanks was slight. This missile hadn't been fully fueled for its flight.

Within a few minutes a small tan-colored UAZ-469 truck arrived on the scene, three men riding in the open cab. It pulled near the impact sight of the missile, and the men got out to look. They stood with their hands in the pockets of their blue uniform coveralls and watched the smoke rise from the wreckage.

The impact sight held little interest for the men, and they quickly went around to the back of the vehicle and began opening boxes filled with equipment. A number of Soviet KPO-1 sampling kits were placed out on the side of the truck bed, their tops opened to show the lines of bottles and containers inside the pouches.

Slipping dark green Romanian M-74 gas masks over their faces, the men pulled on rubber gloves. Then, taking up odd-looking four-foot-long poles with sharpened ends and T-shaped handles, they slipped the carrying straps of several KPO-1 sampling kits over their shoulders and moved onto the impact site. Each man drove a stake into the ground near the center of the site, hooked a ring over it, and unrolled a coil of line attached to the ring, stretching it out away from the missile. The line had more rings spaced at regular intervals along its length.

Once the lines were spread out from the impact site like the radiating spokes of a wheel, the men began taking samples at the point of each ring along the line. The odd poles were useful now, as the men stuck them into the ground for an inch or so, then lifted up the small core sample, dropping it into one of the containers in the KPO-1 kit.

The men were methodical in their sampling, eventually moving the lines farther away and in other directions from the impact site. Within a half an hour they had samples from all around the site. As another, much larger ZIL-131 stake bed truck drove up, the three blue-suited men completed their

sampling task. They pulled off their gas masks as
regular green-uniformed soldiers began getting out
of the back of the ZIL, carrying tools no more sophisticated than shovels.

0915 ZULU
32° 46' North, 44° 17' East
Al Hakum Special Weapons Facility
Iraq

In the center of the open field stood a pair of
two-foot-tall posts, a nose-down aircraft bomb
with the fin section removed secured on top of each
one. Even without the fins, the light gray bomb cas-
ings stood over four feet tall and a foot in diameter.
A thin cluster of cables ran into the distance from
underneath the tip of the weapons.

Radiating out from around the bombs were
some animal cages, most of the various critters inside the cages protesting the cool morning air of the
desert. Other lines radiating from the posts were
merely open dishes appearing to hold a layer of
jelly and nothing more.

With sudden violence, the bombs exploded,
though with relatively little force for a weapon of
their size. The contents of the bombs were sprayed
out in a round pattern, overlapping each other in
places and terrifying the occupants of the cages. As
the mist from the bombs settled out, it lay across
the cages and the open glass dishes, coating them
with a thin, adhering dust.

From a bunker a short distance away, men now approached the bomb site. They wore complete biological protection suits. Rubberized cloth, including sealed boots and gloves, covered every inch of their bodies. Over their heads were hoods with clear plastic face shields. Their humped backs held air packs that allowed the men to breathe without taking in any of the surrounding air.

With exaggerated care they began picking up the cages and covering the dishes with lids.

1235 ZULU
33° 20' North, 44° 10' East
Aby Ghurayb Research Institute
Five miles west of Baghdad
Iraq

The two-story building was nondescript. It was just another plain concrete and glass structure like so many others throughout Iraq. Inside, there were eight fully equipped laboratories and a number of conference rooms and smaller offices. Several technicians and scientists were having a meeting in one of the conference rooms.

Badra Hushmand was an attractive woman by either Western or Eastern standards. Her penchant for dressing in flashy, Western-style clothes was unusual in Iraq. Her brother Saeed was the director of the institute but preferred to conduct actual experiments and research instead of conducting meetings and planning sessions. This fit Badra's preferences well. She was the more ambitious and aggressive of the pair, and liked to "crack the whip" and display her power over her workers.

"I want to know what happened to the warhead!" she said loudly across the table. "What went wrong? It flew correctly and struck the target area. But the contamination of the site was minimal. It was supposed to work—it should have!"

At the silence around the conference table, the irate woman's dark eyes flashed in a face framed with long black hair. But the tight-set lips and glare removed any beauty from Badra Hushmand's expression. No one in the room wanted to admit to being the cause of the failure and bring down the wrath of a very upset associate institute director.

But remaining silent just caused the woman's ire to increase. She lashed out at everyone in the room.

"The bombs worked," she said loudly. "The burst pattern wasn't optimal, but it was satisfactory. The dual testing showed that both the anthrax simulant and the botulinum toxin fillings work. They even complement each other in their effects. The anthrax takes some time to affect a target, while the botulinum toxin starts working within hours. But the powers in Baghdad want a missile warhead, not a simple iron bomb that any fool can drop."

Finally, one of the senior technicians decided the best way to get the situation over with was to speak his mind. He had serious suspicions that he knew what the problem was. And Badra wasn't going to like what he said.

Abu Waheed was the oldest son of Tariq Waheed. He had served in the army as an ordnance technician and knew weapons, especially explosive weapons and their characteristics, very well. He was from Tikrit, but had few political ambitions, either in the army or at the research institute. He knew that Badra would be more careful about attacking him when he spoke up, but not much.

"The problem isn't in the weapon," Abu said, "it's a combination of the style of agent used and the delivery system. We can't solve the problem with our present method of filling the warhead."

Turning to the technician, Badra aimed her dark eyes at him as if they were the muzzles of two guns. "And just what do you think the problem is?"

"The agent isn't spreading from the missiles because we're loading a wet slurry," Abu said, ignoring the look Badra was giving him.

The wet slurry was a thick coffee-colored liquid, the result of the growing process for anthrax and the anthrax simulant *Bacillus subtilis*, which was used to conduct some of the developmental testing. The growth medium that the anthrax and simulant thrived in was gathered and concentrated after the bacteria had reached their peak density. Various chemical, mechanical, and other techniques were used to force the bacteria to form spores. Then the media was reduced to a thick slurry, heavy with the bacteria.

The wet slurry could be handled like any other dangerous material. And it could be loaded into munitions, shells, bombs, and missile warheads with normal loading equipment suitable for some chemical agents. This made the slurry a favored way of weaponizing the biological agents. And Badra's brother Saeed had developed the technique for growing the bacteria and concentrating the slurry.

"The problem centers on the fact that the bombs remain in a relatively protected environment during testing," Abu explained. "The missile warheads do not. The Scud—and especially the new long-range design—are ballistic missiles. They fly high in the atmosphere to reach their target. It's very cold that high up. The wet slurries are simply freezing in the warheads. And they don't have the time to thaw before impact.

"The reports and analysis of the warhead tests prove this out," Abu continued as he warmed to his subject. "The agent was in the area, but it wasn't evenly disbursed. There were literally chunks of agent spread out over the desert. But most of the pieces had thawed before they were reached. It was only a few bits that were still frozen, where they were protected by the shade of the wreckage recovered later by one of the workers who was picking up the missile remains. The sample testing crew never even saw the chunks."

Badra's expression had changed from anger to thoughtfulness. She was a scientist in her own right, holding a master's degree in microbiology, as well as speaking Arabic, English, and German. She and her brother had studied in Germany for years before coming back to Iraq to run Project 324, the development and production of biological weapons. She was smart enough to quickly see that Abu was right.

"All right," she said evenly, "I can see your logic, though I'll want to see your report in writing. I spent years developing this program. It was only within the last year that we've been given the funding and priority to really get some research done. I won't see our efforts go to waste. Those alchemists and their stinks are being hailed as the heroes of our war with Iran. I know our project can do even more for Iraq, and Saddam. So what is the answer to the problem?"

"Well," Abu said, "we know that there isn't a problem in creating a large enough quantity of the basic agent. Our fermenters can grow the cultures, and the shock techniques the Soviets gave us causes the anthrax to form spores very well. The slurry works as a bomb filler, but is too wet to work in the warheads. The answer then is simple—we take out the water.

"With freeze-drying techniques, we can still use the slurry results from our growth processes. But we have to dry the slurry out and then mill the results into a powder form. There will be some technical problems with the milling down, but we can work that out. Even with the bombs having worked in tests, we'll find their efficiency going up an order of magnitude if we used a freeze-dried powder form.

"Liquid slurry is the easiest material to handle, but it's probably the worst form of biological agent to try and spread as an explosive-formed aerosol. If we grind down the powder to one to five micron-sized particles, it will be the most efficient way to spread the weapon as a breathable aerosol."

"And what do we need to start this process?" Badra asked.

"There are some freeze-drying machines available from a Danish manufacturer that are purpose-designed for what we want to do," Abu replied. "They are used to produce materials for the creation of biological pesticides based on bacteria. Even the grinding machines we need are on the international market."

"You make a list of what you want, and I'll see you get it," Badra said with a bright smile.

Some of the men around the table felt that the woman was even more dangerous when she was smiling.

CHAPTER 11

★ ★ ★ ★

1020 ZULU
Room 3D467
The Pentagon
Arlington, Virginia

The relative importance of an individual's job in the Pentagon could sometimes be deduced just by going through the doors to get to the proper office. Greg Rockham had by now made a number of trips to the command center of the U.S. military during the creation of his new SEAL unit, so he could find his way around the Pentagon fairly well. And he'd learned something about the status of a person's door in the huge building.

The office he was reporting to now was an inner room of a suite. The outer door had a five-pin cipher lock on it, but the door was open during business hours, and so the SEAL lieutenant walked in. When he'd identified himself to the yeoman in the outer office, he was told to proceed into the inner office. By the weight of it, the inner door was of painted steel and carried a Sargent dial-type combination lock. Whatever went on inside this office was meant to be secure. And in the Pentagon, security meant importance.

Rockham was now fairly certain that the yeoman in the outer office had very quick access to a firearm if he wanted one. And what went on inside this office was important, though Rockham had yet to learn his part in that importance.

As he entered the office, his attention first went to the officer behind the large wooden desk that took up the far wall of the room. Then he took in the pleasant length of nylon-encased legs crossed at the ankle, which led up to the woman sitting in one of the two armchairs in front of the desk. It was hard not to give a lot of attention to the attractive blonde in the smartly tailored suit to whom the legs belonged. And it was a familiar face framed by that blond hair.

The Pentagon was a military location, though, and military protocols overrode social ones. From the silver eagles on the collar and the name tag on the uniform of the officer behind the desk, Rockham knew he was facing Captain Moisen of the Navy. The captain stood up behind his desk and reached out a hand as Rockham approached.

"Lieutenant Rockham," the captain said, "I'm Nick Moisen, Naval Intelligence. I'm very glad we can finally meet in person. I believe you know Dr. Sharon Taylor?"

As he shook hands with Moisen, Greg replied, "Yes, sir, Dr. Taylor and I have met before." Turning to the smiling woman in the chair, he said, "How are you, Dr. Taylor?"

"Very well, Greg," Sharon said, giving the SEAL officer a dazzling smile.

"Please take a seat, Lieutenant," Moisen said. "I'm very familiar with where and when you met Dr. Taylor. And in just what you and your SEALs accomplished during Operation Endurance. The results of that mission are one of the reasons you were chosen to head this new unit."

"Yes sir," Rockham said noncommittally as he sat down. Security habits built up over the years were hard-learned. He wasn't going to say much to anyone, not even in the hallowed halls of the Pentagon.

"You were asked here today, Lieutenant," Moisen said, "to try and give you a little more background on just what we're trying to accomplish with your unit. That, and I wanted to meet you face-to-face. You see, I'm going to be one of the two primary liaisons for your unit's missions. The other is going to be Dr. Taylor here."

"My understanding was that we would be receiving our orders from SOCOM through JSOC," Rockham said.

"And you still will," Sharon Taylor said, leaning forward in her chair. "But you'll also be receiving directions, intelligence, and support through both Captain Moisen's offices and those of the CIA."

"The last set of directions I received from the CIA almost cost me two men," Rockham said in a grim tone.

"And the fact that you took a difficult situation and made it work for you is one of the reasons you're here today, Lieutenant," Moisen said. "Don't get the idea that you're going to turn into some kind of covert cowboys for the Agency. That isn't the reason we spent so much time and money putting your unit together."

"Then just what is the reason, sir?" Rockham asked.

Leaning back in his chair, Moisen continued, "Exactly as you were told by Admiral Cromarty last year. You and your SEALs are going to be a quick reaction force against weapons of mass destruction in a maritime environment. But we aren't just going to be waiting around for someone to make a threat with a weapon, or worse still, manage to get one in place to use, before acting."

Sharon Taylor spoke up. "When a viable threat comes up, your team may be sent in to deal with it. But you also may be sent in to make sure a threat really exists—or even to establish that the means to make a WMD threat exist."

"If you find a threat," Moisen said simply, "you will be expected to deal with it. As the commander on the scene, you'll receive the complete backing of this office, the Navy, and the U.S. government."

"That's quite a bit of responsibility for a simple Navy lieutenant and a bunch of SEALs, sir," Rockham said. "Even for as good a group of men as I have working with me."

"You have more than proven that the actions you took during Operation Endurance weren't a

fluke," Moisen said. "Dr. Taylor here speaks very
highly of you and your men. Your actions impressed her a great deal—and I know her to be
someone not easily impressed. But even if she didn't
speak so well of you, the afteraction report of your
operation in Nevada says enough by itself."

There were several manila folders on Moisen's
desk, red TOP SECRET warning placards attached to
their covers. Picking up one of them and flipping
through several pages, he looked up at Rockham
and raised an eyebrow quizzically.

"It seems you and your men have a penchant for
collecting the odd bit of ordnance while on an operation," he said. "You physically took an eight-
hundred-pound warhead from a building secured
by twelve terrorists. Then you hand-carried the device to your extraction helicopter and manhandled
it aboard. Why?"

"It seemed like the proper thing to do at the
time," Rockham said. "Besides, it had been an easy
op and my men needed the workout."

"I understand the helicopter crew didn't think so
later," Moisen said. "They had to call for handling
equipment to get the warhead off the bird."

"They could have used some more time in the
gym, yes sir," Rockham said.

"Any other reason you took that warhead, Lieutenant?" Moisen asked pointedly. He gave the appearance of a senior officer who was not going to
accept another flippant answer.

"Yes sir," Rockham said. "Past experience told
me that just bringing home a sample of a weapon

isn't as good as bringing out the entire device. And destroying one of those damned things isn't as simple as disarming a bomb. You take a fuze out, and someone can still cause a lot of damage and contaminate a large area just by shooting some holes in the casing. The easiest way to prevent that is to just make sure the device doesn't stay there. My men could do the job, so we did it as completely as we knew how."

"A better answer," Moisen said as he leaned back in his chair again. "And one I expected from you. Do you know how many rogue countries or organizations there are that could create such a weapon as you found out in Nevada?"

"Not really, sir," Rockham said truthfully. "But there can't be that many of them or someone would have used such a thing by now."

"We're not sure that someone hasn't used such a weapon yet, Lieutenant," Moisen said. "But to answer what I asked, there are seven states that we believe have viable programs to produce weapons of mass destruction. Putting nuclear programs to the side for the moment and just concerning ourselves with chemical and biological weapons, the Soviet Union, China, North Korea, Iran, Syria, Libya, and Iraq have been going forward with programs to develop these weapons."

"As you well know," Dr. Taylor said, "the Soviet Union has the most advanced biological weapons program on the planet. And the same could be said about their chemical weapons as well. But the country is in turmoil internally. Their economy is in a shambles and the Iron Curtain appears to be rusting apart. The collapse of the Berlin Wall last November and the possible reunification of Germany is speeding up what looks like the collapse of the Soviet empire. Unless they start World War Three while lashing about in the death throes of communism—and Gorbachev does not act like the suicidal type—the Soviet Union is not presently considered a primary threat."

"What could be a secondary threat from the Soviet Union, even in the shape it's in now," said Moisen, "would be the unauthorized release, sale, or outright theft of a WMD by a rogue military group, criminals, or terrorists. The diplomatic machinery between their government and ours has already been moving to limit that possibility."

"If it hasn't already happened," said Rockham.

"Yes," Moisen said, "those Russian troops you ran into. I know your afteraction report states that you thought they were Spetsnaz."

"I still do," Rockham said.

"Your experience still holds some weight with a number of people, Lieutenant, myself included. But everything we've been able to learn about that operation says it was a local KGB border guard officer who was planning the theft for some time. If those were Spetsnaz you ran into up in the Arctic, they've fallen off the radar, ours and the Soviets'. It may be that the Soviets have taken care of them as an internal matter. None of our sources can find out anything that doesn't point to a rogue KGB man's op. We may never know. But there are some very real threats out there.

"Muammar Gadhafy in Libya has been trying to purchase chemical expertise from just about anyone who would sell it to him. But since he's anti-Marxist as well as anti-West, the Chinese and Soviets haven't cozied up to him as much as they could. But his oil money has bought materials and technical assistance from out of Europe."

"One of the big problems with both chemical and biological weapons production," Dr. Taylor said, "is the fact that much of the technology has multiple uses. The same plant that produces pesticides, and even a lot of the precursor chemicals, can also be used to produce chemical weapons such as nerve gas, without a lot of major changes. Biological weapons too. A fermenter can be used to produce alcohol or any number of useful, safe products. It can also be used to turn out anthrax and other bioweapons."

"In the Mideast, Iran and Syria both have chemical weapons programs going on," Moisen said. "Hell, even out in the Pacific, we know that North Korea has an ongoing program to produce weapons of mass destruction. They want to push hard for their own nuke, but they've accepted bios and chemicals as a near substitute since shortly after the Korean War ended.

"But all of these countries haven't used chemical or biological weapons that we've been able to confirm. The only one that has was Iraq during their war with Iran. Saddam Hussein has an ongoing chemical weapons program that has not only stockpiled chemical agents, he used them against the Iranians and even his own people. When the Kurdish tribesmen in northern Iraq looked like they were going to side with Iran, Hussein didn't hesitate to use mustard gas, cyanide, and even nerve gas against them.

"And Saddam isn't going to just remain satisfied with having chemical weapons. What he really wants is a nuke, what he calls an 'Arab bomb,' to counteract the nuclear arsenal in Israeli hands. It looked like all of his other WMD programs had taken a backseat to the nuclear one, but the success of his chemical weapons in Iran has changed that.

"Iraq has had a biological weapons program going on for years. But it looked like at least the bioweapons program had lost priority and funding to their nuclear and chemical options. That may have something to do with a personal fear Saddam has of disease and germs. Whatever the reason for not pushing bioweapons in the past, that situation has changed. Our intelligence reports have Iraq field testing bioloaded artillery rockets and aircraft bombs several times in the last year. With Saddam's functional missile program, it's just going to be a matter of time until he has biowarheads for his Scuds—and it may not be all that long a time.

"Saddam Hussein styles himself to be the savior of Iraq—and he intends to be the same for the whole of the Arab world. He absolutely hates Israel, even more so since they bombed his Osirak reactor at al-Tuwaitha back in July 1982. That single act set his nuclear program back years, if not decades. And as I said, it looks like he intends countering Israel's nuclear threat with a chemical and biological one of his own.

"And just how does this affect my men and me?" Rockham asked.

Moisen leaned back in his chair and smiled thinly. "Lieutenant, you and your SEALs are trained from the very first to operate in a normally lethal and certainly hostile environment—underwater. There isn't any question that you can handle yourselves in any environment on the planet. And you think on your feet, take the initiative, and get the job done.

"Our military and the present administration will not just react to a WMD incident, or the possibility of one. If we have the information that can lead us to a solid target, we will act on that information. And that action could mean that we send you and your men in to gather proof, samples, or to destroy a facility.

"Since we are effectively a peacetime military now, there isn't a lot of opportunity for a hot op. You and your men have proven that they can stand on the sharp end and do what has to be done. And you're going to be given the opportunity to do that again."

CHAPTER 12

★ ★ ★ ★

The end of the Iran-Iraq War was a victory for Iraq, but one that came with heavy costs. Eight years of combat had left Iraq deeply in debt to much of the rest of the world. Arab countries had poured loans into Iraq's coffers, and then allowed Saddam and his people to do the fighting. The threat of Iran exporting its Fundamentalist revolution to the rest of the Persian Gulf states and Muslim world had been blunted.

With Iran held in check, Saddam Hussein wanted the billions of dollars in war loans to Iraq forgiven by his Arab neighbors. Besides the elimination of his country's debt, he also wanted several countries to give him an additional $10 billion each to help rebuild Iraq's damaged economy. But forgiveness of the outstanding loans was not going to come from the other Persian Gulf states, nor was any further money. So Saddam and Iraq were left bloodied by the war losses, in debt almost to the point of bankruptcy—and in control of the fourth largest standing army in the world.

In 1990, Iraq had nearly one million troops under arms, and almost half again that in the reserves. Many of these troops were blooded combat veterans. Backing the men on the ground were 5,500 tanks, 3,500 pieces of artillery—over half of them larger than 100mm in caliber—and more than 650 combat aircraft. This volume of forces and weapons made Iraq the most powerful military force in the Persian Gulf, second only to Israel in modern military fighting power in the whole of the Mideast.

The Iraqi economy hadn't been rebuilt after the Iran-Iraq War. Instead, Saddam continued to pour wealth into building up his armed forces and weapons programs. He wanted to unite the Arab world under his leadership. Behind the vanguard of his army, Saddam Hussein wanted to personally lead the destruction of Israel, which he deeply hated. He believed that he would become the patriarch of the Arab world were he to be proclaimed as the man who ended the Israeli "problem." But he needed money to complete his ambitious plans, money that could only come from the oil wells of Iraq.

Iraq has the second largest proven oil reserves in the world, behind only Saudi Arabia. To gain the maximum benefit from Iraqi oil production, Saddam had to have the rest of the oil-producing countries—especially the Gulf states—cut back their production. A drop in oil production would cause a rise in the price paid per barrel, and an influx of hard currency was what Iraq needed desperately.

During a July 10 meeting of the Gulf states' oil ministers in Jedda, Saudi Arabia, Iraq, and its previous enemy, Iran, accused Kuwait and other Arab Gulf states—notably the United Arab Emirates—of overproducing oil and exceeding the agreed-upon quotas. The quotas were intended to maintain the level of oil prices in the world, while overproduction, even by only a few countries, would cause them to drop.

Kuwait and the UAE had been producing more oil than they were supposed to have. Extremely xenophobic, Saddam Hussein would often see conspiracies, especially foreign conspiracies, being plotted against him in all quarters. The oil production by Kuwait and other countries seemed to prove as much.

The Iraqi military began moving units toward the Kuwaiti border. To try and placate Saddam, both Kuwait and the UAE offered to limit oil production. Kuwait also offered a money payment to Iraq of $500 million paid over a three-year period. The sum was so small in comparison to Iraq's needs that it was considered insulting in Baghdad. And Saddam's decision about what to do with Kuwait had been made weeks before.

By July 21, 1990, intelligence sources reported the movement of 30,000 Iraqi troops to the Kuwaiti border. By the beginning of August 1990 a massive buildup of Iraqi forces along that border was complete. Eight Republican Guard divisions, the elite of Saddam's army, had by then moved to the border. Some considered it his version of the Nazi Waffen SS. They were among the most trusted forces under Saddam's direct command, lavishly equipped with the best materials he could purchase.

The Republican divisions included two armored, one mechanized, four infantry, and one special forces unit. This was in addition to the regular Iraqi army units that had been sent to the border area. Saddam now had 140,000 troops and 1,500 tanks and infantry vehicles poised near Kuwait. In contrast, the total forces Kuwait could bring to face the Iraqis included 16,000 troops, 245 tanks, seventy pieces of artillery, and twenty-three combat aircraft.

Because of his deep distrust of the regular military units, Saddam had not allowed them to load up their vehicles and tanks with the normal load of ammunition. Most of the regular army T-54, T-55, and T-62 tanks had only one or two rounds of cannon ammunition for their main gun. The aircraft waiting on the fields had been stripped of their external armament, missiles, and bombs, for their flyover of Baghdad in mid-July for the celebration of the date of the Ba'athist party taking control of the Iraqi government.

Saddam was not going to attend a military parade and let armed aircraft and tanks pass by close to him. But his Republican Guard units were a different story. The T-72 tanks of the Republican Guard armored divisions had full racks of ammunition. And they had their marching orders in hand—orders that had been hand-delivered by messenger, or over military phone lines, so as not to be intercepted by governments dependent on electronic technology for their intelligence gathering.

On Wednesday, August 1, the ambassador from Iraq met with a number of U.S. State Department officials only a short distance from the White House. The Iraqi ambassador did not refute completely the intelligence reports on Iraqi troop and vehicle movements, but he stated they were unimportant activities. The ambassador went on to say that the rhetoric of the Americans was raising fears in the Persian Gulf more than any minor military exercises by the Iraqis.

Two hours after that meeting, U.S. officials from the State Department, the CIA, the Joint Chiefs of Staff, and the White House met in a secure conference room at the State Department. The deputy director of the CIA brought the latest intelligence reports available from all sources. In the deputy director's opinion, the Iraqi ambassador had been laying out a smoke screen. He believed the Iraqis would invade Kuwait within the next twenty-four hours. That prediction was made at approximately five P.M. EST in Washington, D.C. In Kuwait it was midnight, and Thursday August 2 was just beginning.

2300 ZULU
30° 5' North, 47° 42' East
Customs post
Highway 12
Northernmost point on the Kuwait-Iraq border

It was two A.M. on a Thursday morning, not considered a particularly busy time for even an in-

ternational border crossing point. The customs
agents and guards at their posts could see a long
way across the flat sands of the Shamiyah Desert, illuminated by the modern sodium lamps high up on
metal poles. There had been little traffic all day on
the eight-lane divided highway that ran north and
south through Kuwait and into Iraq, especially
coming down from Iraq.

But this Thursday morning was soon filled with
the sound of diesel engines roaring all about the
small clutch of customs buildings. The grinding of
metal against metal filled the air, a sound made by
the continuous tracks used on heavy armored
tanks.

Iraq's best military divisions were rolling into
Kuwait in huge numbers. Over 100,000 Iraqi
troops and hundreds of tanks crossed the border in
those early morning hours. The entire population
of Kuwait was less than the number of men filling
the ranks of Saddam's army. Between the border
and the capital at Kuwait City there was about 110
kilometers of modern superhighway, and little else.
The Iraqi military units sped along the highway as
other units crossed the desert sands around them.

Kuwait fell quickly. Seven hours after the first
tank had crossed the border, there was no one in
authority from the royal family left in the country.
Resistance hadn't been organized, or orders even
given to the military, while the government escaped
into exile. Inside of two days the Iraqi forces had
complete control of the country. Behind the ad-
vancing Iraqi troops was the Mukhabarat, the Iraqi

secret police. They quickly began gathering up individuals who would be able to resist the new order being imposed on Kuwait.

Army reinforcements came down from Iraq in air-conditioned buses. Four Iraqi divisions of infantry troops moved into southern Kuwait to the border with Saudi Arabia. There, they began building defensive positions. The first of thousands of mines were buried in the sand. On the shores of Kuwait, tanks and artillery were dug in and fortifications put up to block any invasion from the sea.

An Iraqi news agency broadcast to the Iraqi people and the world that the government of Kuwait had been overthrown by revolutionaries. These same revolutionaries, the reports claimed, had then asked Iraq for help in defending their country from the greedy hands of the royal family and their ministers. In the provisional government of Kuwait, an acting prime minister took over. He turned out to be a Mukhabarat officer and a relative of Saddam Hussein. On August 8, Saddam Hussein announced the end of Kuwait as a country and its annexation as the nineteenth province of Iraq. Then even the sham of the provisional "revolutionary" government was dropped and not heard of again.

CHAPTER 13
★ ★ ★ ★

The U.S. response to the invasion of Kuwait was immediate. The threat was not only the occupation of Kuwait, but the very real possibility that Saddam might continue south with his forces, invading and occupying Saudi Arabia. The occupation of Kuwait was not a situation that could be allowed to stand. Further actions by the Iraqis in the Persian Gulf would not only have to be prevented, the Iraqis would have to be pushed back into their own country.

Meetings took place at the White House from the morning of August 2 and into the afternoon. The rest of the world also demonstrated its immediate concern about the situation in the Persian Gulf. By that evening, the UN in New York had adopted Resolution 660, condemning Iraq's invasion of Kuwait and demanding the immediate withdrawal of all Iraqi forces from the devastated country.

But the U.S. was moving forward with much stronger measures than the resolution issued by the

UN. Iraq simply ignored what the UN was saying and went on with its reinforcement of the forces in Kuwait. Within only four days of the invasion, U.S. Secretary of Defense Dick Cheney and General Norman Schwarzkopf were meeting with King Fahd of Saudi Arabia, who welcomed U.S. forces onto Saudi soil. This was no small feat since the country held two of the most sacred sites in the Muslim religion, Mecca and Medina. Foreign troops—especially infidel, nonbeliever troops—could spell disaster for the Saudi government if the rest of the Muslim world protested the act. But the possibility of Saddam Hussein invading Saudi Arabia was considered a greater threat.

At 2150 on August 6 the President of the United States signed the deployment order sending U.S. troops on their way to the Persian Gulf. The immediate execution of OPLAN 1002–90 had been ordered. The actual deployment of combat forces to the operational theater started taking place the next day. After some discussion between Generals Powell and Schwarzkopf and the White House, a communiqué was issued to the military and the public at large. The mission—the defense of Saudi Arabia and the buildup of U.S. forces in the Persian Gulf—was now officially known as Operation Desert Shield.

A few days earlier the UN had adopted the second of its resolutions regarding the Persian Gulf and the invasion of Kuwait. Resolution 661 imposed trade sanctions on all cargoes originating in or heading to Iraq or Kuwait. The only items allowed by the sanctions were medical supplies and, under humanitarian circumstances, food. The immediate effect of the embargo was to stop the sale of Iraqi oil on the world market. It was also intended to choke off supplies, spare parts, and equipment to Saddam's army and degrade that army's performance.

But there were no teeth in the UN resolution. Orders from President Bush to begin enforcement of the embargo went out on August 16, but only a few ships were stopped and turned back before the Iraqis forced the U.S. Navy's hand. The use of force to stop civilian cargo ships wasn't fully authorized, and the fragile coalition of nations against Iraq was just being built up. Some warning shots were fired, and that was about all. The U.S. couldn't afford to precipitate open hostilities with Iraq, not until enough forces were on the ground in Saudi Arabia to stop a possible invasion.

The coalition of forces against Saddam Hussein and the Iraqi invasion was building up, even during the first weeks after the invasion. The first of the Arab countries to offer troops and support to the U.S.-led effort was Egypt. Its president, Hosni Mubarak, despised what Hussein had done, and he also could see advantages for his country in supporting the coalition forces. In the end he not only allowed the U.S. to set up several forward operating bases in Egypt, along the Red Sea, but committed 40,000 troops to the action in Kuwait, which would not be without danger to both President Mubarak and his country.

1545 ZULU
Special Materials Detachment Headquarters
Naval Amphibious Base
Little Creek, Virginia

Since the first day of the invasion of Kuwait, the U.S. armed services had been on a heightened state of alert. At the Navy facilities around Norfolk, the level of activity had reached an almost frenzied level in just a few days as major naval assets prepared to put to sea. At Little Creek the SEAL Teams were also on a high alert status, even though there was little difference in the day-to-day running of the Teams that could be seen by an outside observer.

The tighter security around the amphibious base itself, however, was obvious. As at all U.S. military installations, the threat of possible terrorist attacks caused the bases to go to THREATCON WHITE, a category at which gates were closed to the general public and a complete ID check was required. This was an imposition to a number of dependents who habitually shopped at the bases, but the demands of security overrode the inconvenience.

Most of the Special Materials Detachment were on base continuing with their jobs while under alert status. Both first and second squads were present. Even though first squad was under first alert status, given the present situation, second squad wasn't

THE MIDEAST

going to conduct any training away from Little Creek. The farthest any of the men were going was either home or to the Iceberg.

At his desk, Chief Monday received a phone call, and after speaking for a few minutes, he hung up and turned to the men in the room with him. "Get everyone in here," he said. "That was Rockham over at Group Two. We're on alert for an op as of right now."

"About half of the guys are over at Team Two working out on their weight pile," Henry Lutz said. "Ferber and Sukov are with Mr. Daugherty, checking out the ordnance loadouts in the magazine area."

"And Mainhart's in the head," Roger Kurkowski said, entering the room. "Why the list of everybody?"

"We're on alert," Lutz said as Monday picked the phone up and started to punch buttons.

Before Kurkowski could say anything more, the beeper on his belt went off. The shrill *beep* . . . *beep* . . . *beep* sounded in the room as the beepers on everyone's belt went off.

"Well," Lutz said, "that should bring them running."

"Five bucks says Mainhart is still running when he comes through the door."

"No bet," Lutz replied. "I think I just heard the door to the head slam."

The object of the two SEALs comments came rushing through the door a moment later. The youngest member of the unit charged into the room and almost skidded to a stop.

"Isn't that cute," Kurkowski said. "He comes when you call. Now zip up your fly, sailor."

Mainhart grabbed at his crotch and looked down while Lutz and Kurkowski broke out in laughter. Even Chief Monday cracked a smile as he went back to pulling papers out of his desk.

"Enough fucking around," the chief said before Mainhart had spoken a word. "Take your checklists and start going through them. Rockham's going to be here in minutes with some guy from Intel to start our briefing. We are under isolation as of now."

Being put under isolation meant that the men of the detachment were restricted to the building except for meals and required movements. Married personnel couldn't call home, and no one could leave the base. Whatever was going down, the chances were that this would be a real operation and not a drill.

The joking stopped as the work began. The rest of the unit began entering, several of the men still wearing sweat-soaked workout clothes. Each man started in on whatever his predeployment assignment would be. They had drilled a number of times over the last few months in just what to do when an alert rang out. The level of excitement was higher in the room because this time the men knew it wasn't a drill.

But the veteran SEALs also knew not to get excited about a possible operation. Only when the wheels of their aircraft had left the runway and they were on their way would some of them start looking forward to a mission—some would even wait past that point. It didn't pay to get excited and then disappointed. The highs and lows could drain a man. Then when the situation was real, their reactions might be off.

The men were professionals, and they went about their business in a professional manner. They would be told what they needed to know as soon as it was practical, so questions were at a minimum. Anticipating anything just used up energy.

Within ten minutes of the alert signal going out, the entire unit was gathered in their headquarters. Lieutenant Rockham had come in from the command headquarters at Navy Special Warfare Group Two alone to give the men a heads-up on what was going on.

"Okay, listen up," he said as the men gathered in the now crowded room. "I just got off the horn to D.C. We have a hot op going down in the Middle East. For right now, all I have is that we should plan for a possible boat takedown at sea. Some Intel types are flying down from D.C. to give us a full briefing. They should be here within a couple of hours. Until then I want everything ready for a full deployment. We're going to hit the deck running, gentlemen. Department heads, report to me as soon as you have a heads-up on your status."

There was no confusion, and no questions following Rockham's statement. They knew that if he had more information to give them, he would have. So each man went back about his business. They'd been preparing for just such an announcement since news of the Iraqi invasion of Kuwait the week before. The men who were in charge of individual departments—such as Ordnance for weapons, ammunition, and explosives; Sub Ops for diving gear; Air Ops for parachuting and airdropping their gear—knew what they had, how it was packed, and where it was laid up. They reported in to Rockham within minutes of each other.

It had been 1045 local time when the alert went out for the detachment. At twenty minutes past noon a Navy captain arrived at the unit's headquarters, having flown down from the Pentagon by helicopter. Accompanying him was an officious-looking man in a gray business suit. Early August in southern Virginia is not a good time to be wearing a business suit, and the short-statured man looked anything but comfortable.

"Ten-hut," shouted Chief Monday as the captain entered the room.

"At ease, gentlemen," Captain Moisen said as the SEALs snapped up to stand at attention.

The men relaxed as Moisen moved to where Rockham had gotten up from his desk.

"Good afternoon, Captain," Rockham said as he saluted. "Welcome aboard."

"Glad to finally meet your men," Moisen said as he returned Rockham's salute. "And I think they're going to be glad to meet me in another minute.

"Gentlemen," Moisen said, turning to the SEALs in the room, "I'm Captain Moisen and I'm glad to finally get a chance to meet all of you. I've read nothing but good reports on your progress in training, and I'm glad to tell you that you may have a chance to put that training to use a lot sooner than anyone expected.

"This gentleman," Moisen said, turning to the man who had come in with him, "is Mr. Turner, an intelligence analyst for the deputy director of Operations at Langley."

Kurkowski bit his lip before saying anything about a "desk spook" as Chief Monday looked straight at him. The captain didn't notice the exchange as he went on.

"Mr. Turner," Moisen said, "is going to brief you on the situation as it is developing. Mr. Turner . . ." He turned and motioned to the man.

"Thank you, Captain," Turner said in a soft voice. "Could someone please hang this up for me where everyone can see it?"

Taking the tube from the man's outstretched hand, Mike Bryant and John Sukov unrolled the map. They stuck it up on the plywood wall, covering several notices and bulletins as they secured it in place with pushpins. The map depicted a large section of the Middle East, centering on the Red Sea, cutting diagonally across the middle of the sheet. Africa was to the west, Saudi Arabia to the east, and the Suez Canal and then the Mediterranean at the upper left.

"This is the Red Sea with the Suez Canal to the northwest at the top and the Horn of Africa at the lower left." Turner had pulled a telescoping pointer from his pocket and was indicating the areas as he mentioned them.

"Most of the attention of the world is on what's

going on in Iraq and Kuwait up here at the upper right. But we have reports of an action taking place in the Red Sea that requires your particular expertise.

"We have reports from very reliable sources that Saddam Hussein has struck a deal with General al Bashir, the ruling military dictator of Sudan, to accept missiles being smuggled from Iraq to his country. We have reason to believe that at least one of these missiles may be mounted with a chemical or AOB warhead and—"

"An AOB warhead," Kurkowski said from the back of the room. "Just what is that?"

"That is an 'agent of biological origin,'" the CIA man replied.

"Thank you," Kurkowski said, unimpressed with Turner's attempt to use shop talk during a briefing.

As a chuckle went around the room, Chief Monday growled softly, "Belay that," and looked up at the CIA man. "Sir," he said, inviting him to continue.

Mollified, Turner went on. "It looks like Hussein is trying to cause as much trouble as he can for Egypt. President Mubarak has joined with the coalition forces. His was the first country outside of Saudi Arabia to do so. And he has pledged men, equipment, and staging areas on Egyptian soil to help drive Iraq out of Kuwait. This is no small thing, as Egypt still wields a lot of influence in the Mideast Arab community.

"Egypt will not only give material and personnel

support to the coalition, President Mubarak has given priority to Navy ships and supply transports moving through the Suez Canal. This helps us get the assets of the Sixth Fleet from the Mediterranean to the Red Sea and within a good striking distance of Iraq. The nuclear carrier *Eisenhower* and its task group have already traversed the Suez Canal and are in the Red Sea right now.

"To counter this action by Egypt, Saddam is arming Sudan with a weapon capable of reaching the Aswan Dam. Chemical or biological warheads could strike major population areas in the Nile Valley of Egypt. If Egypt gets hit while the rest of the world is watching Kuwait, the Sudanese will take up a chunk of her territory. That will cause us to split our forces and defend Egypt as well as take back Kuwait."

"So how does this affect my men and I?" Rockham asked.

Captain Moisen spoke up. "It looks like Saddam is going to be smuggling at least one or more of his modified Scud B missiles on board an old cargo ship that makes a regular run along the coast of the Red Sea. The missile is expected to go on board the ship at Al Aqabah at the head of the Gulf of Aqaba in Jordan. It may already be aboard."

"Jordan is right in Israel's backyard," Daugherty said, "and they also have port facilities on the gulf. Why don't they just stop the ship and take the missile?"

"Normally, they probably would," Moisen said.

"Or at the very least, the ship would meet with an accident. But our government has asked the Israelis to keep their hands off this one."

"Why?" Rockham asked.

"Because Saddam was very careful in choosing this particular ship," Moisen said.

"The *Pilgrim's Hope* is an old U.S.-built Victory ship from World War Two," Turner said. "She sails under the Yemen flag and travels up and down the coast of Saudi Arabia, Egypt, Sudan, and Ethiopia before crossing over to Yemen to do the whole trip again. She carries cargo and passengers, and it's the passengers who are the problem.

"One of the ports of call for the *Pilgrim's Hope* is Jiddah in Saudi Arabia. There, she drops off Muslim pilgrims on their way to Mecca. And she picks up pilgrims on their way back to their countries.

"It's those pilgrims who concern us," Moisen said. "Not only are they possible hostages, but they are also devout Muslims. If anything was to happen to a group of Muslim pilgrims, it could shatter the coalition of Arab states that are just starting to come together. If it was Israelis who caused any harm to come to a bunch of devout Muslims, that could just about touch off a holy war in the Mideast. And Saddam is right there to make sure it would happen."

"The *Pilgrim's Hope* is going to be tailed on her entire trip through the Red Sea by the USS *Oklahoma City*. She's a Los Angeles–class nuclear attack sub assigned to the *Eisenhower*'s task group. We have constant updates from her on the position of the *Pilgrim's Hope*. The only time she won't be on the cargo ship's tail is when she surfaces to pick up you and your detachment.

"The port we expect the *Pilgrim's Hope* to offload the Scud at," Turner said, "is on the northern coast of Sudan. It's a little fishing village called Muhammad Qol in Dungunab Bay. There is an old fort and a mosque at Qol, and the *Pilgrim's Hope* has it as a regular port of call when she's on her rounds. The pilgrims on board usually offload and pray at the mosque. It's a perfect location for a covert delivery of a missile.

"There's a single pier at the village that can accept the cargo ship," Turner continued. "Our reports say the *Pilgrim's Hope* is capable of using her own handling equipment to offload the missile, which is concealed in a standard cargo container. From there it would be a simple matter to truck the missile up into the mountains surrounding the Nubian Desert and hide it until it would be used against Egypt.

"We have made arrangements that the pier will be occupied when the *Pilgrim's Hope* arrives. It is our best chance to get to the missile while minimizing the chances of any hostages being aboard. Even

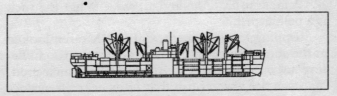

VICTORY SHIP

if the ship couldn't offload the missile, any pilgrims aboard would use the local fishermen's boat to move ashore for prayers."

"The Red Sea is long and thin," Moisen said, taking over, "but her waters run very deep. Just to seaward of Dungunab Bay, the water drops to several thousand feet very quickly. But the reefs around the bay make any approach by surface ships almost impossible. There's just one channel that a shallow draft ship can pass. The submarine can get you within striking distance of the target, but your SEALs are going to have to move to the *Pilgrim's Hope* underwater on their own power.

"There's only one good protected anchorage at the mouth of Dungunab Bay, several miles southeast from Muhammad Qol. That's on the lee side of this sandstone island, Mukawwar Island. It's protected to the north by the Angarosh Reef. That's where we plan on your team crossing into the bay. It's a flat-topped cake reef, with sheer dropoff on three sides. There's a lot of fish activity in the area, both reef species and pelagic fish from the deep water. It's one of the reasons the fishing village has been there for the last several hundred years, if not longer."

"Pelagic fish?" Alexander said. "What the fuck is a pelagic fish?"

Stopping for a moment, Captain Moisen looked at the short, heavy-built SEAL across the room. Before anyone could say anything, Moisen answered.

"It's a deep-water fish that feeds near the surface and usually travels in schools. Tuna, herring, and mackerel are all pelagic fish; so are some sharks. Ever seen barracuda?"

"No, sir," Alexander said, "at least none that I know of."

"You will, the reef's full of them," Moisen said. "And they travel in packs."

Alexander sat back with a thoughtful expression on his face. Though no SEAL was ever attacked by a barracuda, there was a reason they had the nickname "Wolves of the Sea."

"All of that is the good news," Moisen said with a tight smile. "Now the bad news. The *Pilgrim's Hope* moves along at the astounding pace of seven to eight knots. Her top speed used to be eleven knots, but there's more than a few thousand hours on those engines and she probably hasn't been able to hit that speed for decades.

"She has to travel just under six hundred nautical miles from Al Aqabah to reach Muhammad Qol. She usually averages four stops along the way to drop off or pick up pilgrims. These stops are at Hurghadax, Port Safaga, Marsa Alam, and Ras Banas in Egypt before she reaches Sudan. But with her special cargo on board, those stops may be passed up on this trip. That means if she leaves on the next ebb tide, as we expect her to, we have a certain maximum of seventy-four hours as of noon today to be on site and ready to go.

"Your specific mission will be to board and take control of the *Pilgrim's Hope* with minimal risk to any civilians on board. Once the ship is in your control, you will locate and render harmless any missiles or weapons of mass destruction aboard. The mission will take place in the national waters of Sudan, so if you find any WMD that you cannot physically remove or destroy, you will take the ship out to where the weapons can be taken under U.S. Navy control."

CHAPTER 14

★ ★ ★ ★

After all the training they had done, for a takedown such as this one, there wasn't any way the unit would turn down a hot operation, not if there looked to be any kind of reasonable chance to pull it off. Briefing packages were left for all of the men, with additional materials for Lieutenants Rockham and Daugherty.

The unit's gear was ready to go, and they could hit the plane at any time. It would take them the better part of twenty hours of flight time to get from Norfolk to Saudi Arabia and then from there onto the aircraft carrier *Eisenhower*. From the carrier, it would be a short hop to rendezvous with the submarine *Oklahoma City*. That gave them a cushion of about twenty-four hours before they had to lift off, and they could put that time to good use.

The intelligence package said that the *Pilgrim's Hope* was an old Victory-type cargo ship that had been built by the thousands in the U.S. during World War II. That meant the ship was at least forty-five years old and that its layout could have been altered in any number of ways over the years.

But some things that were visible in the surveillance pictures they had of the ship had not changed.

There were five holds in the ship, numbered one to five from the bow back. The three holds in the front half of the ship were separated from the two at the rear by the machinery spaces and the superstructure of the ship above them. The target they were looking for was reportedly inside a standard cargo container, to hide what it was. The massive MAZ-543 Transporter/Erector/Launcher vehicle, probably wasn't traveling with the missile.

The MAZ-543 was a huge trucklike transporter for Scuds that could move the missiles while they lay flat in a cradle, raise them into firing position, and launch them from any site the vehicle could reach. The MAZ-543 made the Scuds a mobile system, but there would be no way to hide the huge eight-wheeled vehicle inside any kind of container since the MAZ-543 was larger than the average fire engine, and stood out from the landscape even more so. That meant the missile would

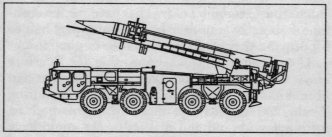

MAZ-543

probably be on the simple wheeled transport trailer that was little more than a framework with wheels.

The size and weight of the missile meant that it could fit into just about any of the cargo holds on the ship. Until they had more up-to-the-minute surveillance photos, they couldn't know for certain that the cargo wasn't being secured on deck. But that wasn't the way Rockham would have played it, and Daugherty, Monday, and Ferber agreed. The most likely location for their target would be in the number two hold.

All of the holds had lifting booms over them, but only the number two and three holds had the heavy fifty-ton-capacity lifting boom up forward, which could service either hold. A Scud B missile, and especially the enlarged Iraqi al-Hussein version, would weigh over 13,000 pounds when it was fueled. The empty weight of the missile was much less, in the neighborhood of 5,000 pounds. That meant that the ship's own booms and handling gear could move a container holding the missile on its trailer.

The number three hold was right in front of the superstructure. It would undoubtedly be under constant guard from anyone on the bridge. Rockham knew that if he'd wanted to move a missile covertly and securely, that's where he would put it. The SEALs' search of the ship would begin on the number three hold and move on from there to the number two hold. The number three hold was the most secure, but the number two was the

longest on the ship. Anything the size of an extra-
long cargo container would have to be in one of
those two locations.

But to search the ship meant they had to have it
under their control. Intel had estimated a crew of
fifteen to twenty men serving on the ship. And there
could be any number of Iraqi soldiers and technicians to protect and operate the missile. On top of
that, the SEALs could have to deal with any number of pilgrims who could be aboard.

In this situation, the six "S" rules of prisoner
handling—speed, secure, search, silence, separate,
and safeguard—would have to be followed closely.
Once they had the ship secured, moving the prisoners to the fantail looked to be the best way to
guard them with a minimum of SEALs. That
would leave the other men to deal with searching
the rest of the ship.

But to secure the ship, they first had to board her.
Practice and rehearsal of an operation was one of
the things that helped give the SEALs their edge in
an operation like this. And they had a great opportunity for practice less than twenty miles from Little Creek. At the Fort Eustis Military Reservation
on the James River, the U.S. Maritime Administration of the Department of Transportation had a
large number of ships tied up to reinforce the mer-
chant fleet in time of war. Among them were Victory ships like the one the SEALs would be
boarding in the Red Sea.

Normally, there was a time-consuming set procedure required when using another government

agency's assets, and the one thing the men of the Special Materials Detachment didn't have was time. Every moment mattered. So while phone calls were going around government offices, and admirals were telling bureaucrats just what would be done, the SEALs continued to plan and prepare.

By three o'clock that afternoon, Ferber and Daugherty had driven over to Fort Eustis and were checking out the ships available. By four o'clock the rest of the SEALs were there also checking out the ships, which were little more than relics of World War II.

Though the internal spaces were in pretty good shape, the outside of the ships were mostly a mass of rust, peeling paint, and seagull droppings. Kurkowski mentioned that tetanus shots might be the order of the day and that he needed one just for standing on the deck. Jokes aside, the decision was made to wear work gloves while conducting boarding training, to try and hold the number of cuts and abrasions to a minimum.

The ships were gathered in groups, called nests, where they were anchored alternating bow to stern. Only the outermost ships in the nest had the sides of their hulls exposed, which were the ones the SEALs would practice boarding. The old cargo ships were completely empty and rode high in the water. The big eighteen-foot-diameter bronze screw at the rear of each ship was half exposed. All of this meant that the SEALs would have to climb a little higher on their caving ladders to get aboard.

With the fast walk-through completed, the

SEALs did what SEALs do the most—they got wet. Through the waning hours of the afternoon and into the evening, the men of the SMD practiced placing the climbing hooks at the end of their caving ladders onto the deck of their target ship. Once the hooks were set, the point man would go up the flexible ladder to gain the main deck of the ship.

Though they had practiced swimmer boarding techniques during their qualification training, this practice had more of an edge to it. In only a few days they would be doing this for real, and so when this work started, the joking stopped. If a man spoke up, it was to either point out a problem or suggest a possible solution. But though problems came up, they went on with the exercise. Training hard, training to win, was the only way they knew to get the job done. The old SEAL axiom, "The more you sweat in training, the less you bleed in war," was something they all believed in.

Boarding plans were examined, discussed, tested, and changed as they worked with the ship. There were two mast and boom assemblies forward of the superstructure. The masts were between the number two and three holds and the one and two holds. The support materials for the masts and booms— the cables, winches, lines, and extra booms lying across the deck—made movement difficult.

In the center of the ship rose the superstructure, the midship house. Made up of three decks, it rose above the main deck and held most of the ship's functioning areas. The top deck was the smallest deck, and it held the bridge—the command area of the ship. On the second deck, the cabin deck, most of the ship's crew and officers bunked. The third deck, just above the main deck of the ship, was the boat deck. It was longer and wider than either the cabin or bridge decks. All the decks were even at the bow, with only the bridge deck jutting forward slightly to give it the most unobstructed view.

On the port and starboard sides of the boat deck were the davits holding the ship's four lifeboats. On the ship where the SEALs practiced, the lifeboat cradles were empty, the huge inverted L-shaped hooks leaning back against their curved rails. On the active ship the SEALs would be assaulting, the cradles would each be filled with a twenty-five-man lifeboat. That would seriously hamper the SEALs' movements as they took the ship down.

Each deck of the midships house was smaller than the one below it. The cabin deck had a passageway on either side, and a small open deck at its stern. The bridge deck was smaller still than the cabin deck. It also had a passageway on either side, as well as a larger rear deck toward the stern. At the stern area and along each side passageway, ladders, which in fact were stairways, connected the decks together on the outside.

The boat deck contained the galley, mess, ship's storage, and other common areas. Below the superstructure was the huge, multideck engine and boiler rooms. The volume of the boiler and engine rooms was larger than the whole of the midships house. On the inside of the midships house and engine rooms, internal ladders and passageways allowed access to the decks without exposure to the outside elements. Off the engine and boiler room spaces there were also access hatchways that led to both the fore and aft cargo holds.

The primary targets to be secured during a takedown of the ship were the bridge and the engine room. The chart room would be behind the bridge. Most important, the radio room would be located on the deck below the bridge on a Victory ship. These were the areas the SEALs would have to capture and control as quickly and efficiently as possible. It didn't matter how quickly they made the takedown if they missed someone as they passed— someone who could raise the alarm before the SEALs had control.

So the takedown would have to move quickly while still maintaining as much control as possible. At no point could they let the security of the assault force be sacrificed for speed. Estimates had the SEALs being outnumbered two to one by the crew and any Iraqi forces on board. Then there could be the added complication of any possible pilgrims. The only way to conduct the assault quickly and efficiently was through as much practice as they could squeeze in before they had to lift off the next day.

The plan of assault for the unit had already been changed several times during the practice runs. The machinery and material scattered across the deck in front of the midships house prevented the SEALs from climbing aboard anywhere in the bow area. The lifeboat davits and other clutter would complicate any covert boarding at the midships area. Coming in over the stern looked to be the best bet, especially since the ship they'd assault would be at anchor and the heavy propeller stilled. But during their practice assaults, another problem came up.

At the stern of the Victory ships there was a raised, circular deck, open on the top and heavily reinforced underneath. That deck, which they knew would be on the target ship, was originally intended for a five-inch gun, a heavy cannon for the cargo ship to defend itself with. There were several gun decks around the ship at the bow and sides, but these were smaller decks intended for 20mm guns, with a 40mm gun at the bow. It was the size of the rear gun deck that would constitute a bad choke point for the SEALs coming in over the stern.

Using two ladders would put both squads on the deck twice as fast, but coordinating the movement between the squads was very difficult. Radio traffic had to be kept to a minimum for security's sake, and eliminated entirely if possible. And that couldn't be done and coordinate the two squads during a climb. So the squads would go up a single caving ladder, with the second pole man and his ladder held in reserve.

But when the SEALs came in over the stern, the crowded area under the gun platform blocked them in badly, and nothing they tried could eliminate the choke point as a problem. So the decision was made to come in on the side of the ship, behind the midships house, in the area of the number four hold.

With their general plan worked out, the SEALs

practiced their assault tactics and techniques several times while it was still daylight, then broke for chow and a checkout of all their gear. Each of the department heads made sure everything was ready for the deployment the next day. Then each man went over his gear again for the evening practice.

The assault rehearsals that evening would be different than those they'd done during the day. Three squads from SEAL Team Two, twenty-four SEALs, would act the part of the ship's crew and officers. They would be armed the same as the men of the SMD, with MP5-N submachine guns that had been converted to fire the simunition paint-marking rounds.

The hours of practice and rehearsal were long and hard. But the men knew the value of what they were doing. The lack of sleep now could mean a lack of casualties later. Besides, they could always sleep on the long plane flight to the Mideast. So with a quick meal under their belts, it was back to the dark waters of the James River and an old World War II cargo ship. Since they were in isolation for the operation, the men could not communicate with their homes or outside the base. But those who had families had been through this situation before. It was one of the things that put a strain on relationships for those in the Teams; just another price for being a SEAL.

As the sky started to turn pink the next morning, a very tired group of SEALs left Fort Eustis and returned to Little Creek. It would still be a while before any of them could get some rest. The gear they had been using had to be cleaned and put away. Then the last minute checks of anything that had to be changed for their deployment had to be done.

The men of the SMD knew which way to turn, where to go, and what to do in taking down a Victory-class ship. There would be differences between the ship they'd practiced on and their actual target. No ship could be used for decades without some changes taking place in the machinery and other spaces. But the locations of the hatches, ladders, and main compartments was something that wouldn't change. And each of the SEALs knew where everything could be expected to be aboard a Victory ship.

Their lessons were hard-learned. The paint splotches on their uniforms, accompanied by the occasional bruises, cuts, and abrasions, showed that they had gone up the steep side of the learning curve for that particular kind of ship takedown. A point of pride for the SEALs of the SMD was that their fellow SEALs, their Teammates from SEAL Team Two, displayed a much larger number of paint splotches on their uniforms, with each man showing at least several obvious signs of the SMD's marksmanship skills.

CHAPTER 15

★★★★

The men were ready and the gear was packed. The bulk of their equipment and supplies were stowed in operational and personnel bags, and these bags were in turn secured in a four-by-four-foot cardboard "triwall" box. The box was sealed and covered with a protective plastic bag before it was banded down onto a metal forklift pallet. All of their equipment loaded up several pallets, including one for their diving gear, another for their boats and motors, and still more for their personal gear and weapons.

Forklifts lifted their equipment pallets onto a truck for the trip to the air base. Then the rest of the unit piled on board a Navy bus. The Air Force people at the base would load the pallets aboard the plane—while also under the careful supervision of several SEALs.

The Air Force loadmaster would undoubtedly have been alarmed had he known how some of the SEALs' gear was packed. Everything they were taking with them, from their personal bags to their Zodiac F470 boats and thirty-five horsepower outboard motors, was packed in a man-portable container. In the case of the Zodiacs, "man-portable" was a relative term. The boats in their transport bags weighed over 265 pounds each.

But nothing—no bag, container, motor, or boat—could be thirty inches in diameter, width, or thickness. Most of the bags were intentionally under twenty-six inches at their thickest point. The biggest single items were the Zodiac boats, each one packaged in a cylindrical bag, 29.5 inches in diameter and fifty-nine inches long.

The reason for this was that the hatches on the submarine they would be boarding were only twenty-six or thirty inches in diameter. Everything the SEALs would be bringing with them had to fit through one of those hatch sizes. There would be no external lockers or storage on the outside of the sub's hull.

What would have most bothered the loadmaster was the fact that each man had his full basic load of small arms ammunition in his gear bag. The ammunition was loaded into the magazines that filled the pouches of each man's personal web gear. As far as the SEALs were concerned, the grenades, explosives, pyrotechnics, and flash-crashes were all properly stowed for air transport, and the weapons weren't loaded. The situation was completely safe—and what the Air Force didn't know wouldn't hurt them. The SEALs were operating under combat rules, even if the Air Force hadn't been told. The SEALs didn't feel they would have a lot of time before they reached the target, certainly not extra time to break ammunition out of sealed crates, then steel cans, and finally cardboard boxes, just to load it into magazines.

The twenty-four-mile trip to Langley Air Force Base near Hampton, north of Little Creek and Norfolk, took the SEALs across the mouth of the James River and was over fairly quickly. The Air Force technical sergeant who met them at the gate seemed delighted at all of the activity around them. Moving gear, troops, and planes around meant that the Air Force was getting things done. The man's incessant talk and constant grin became irritating to the SEALS as he rode in the bus and directed them to where they had to board their plane. The traffic patterns were so heavy that they had to stop and wait a number of times when other materials blocked their way.

Some of the tired SEALs wanted to simply kill the guy as a professional favor to the Air Force, then go on and just commandeer the next aircraft they came to. But Kurkowski reminded them that killing a crazy person was considered bad luck—and they might want to keep all of their good luck for later.

By 1130 hours the SEALs were finally aboard their C-141B Starlifter, which belonged to the

437th Military Airlift Wing out of Charleston, South Carolina. The Starlifter had been in use with the military since 1964 and was still a major mover of personnel and cargo. With the situation in Kuwait and the Persian Gulf just starting to build up, the Starlifter had been converted to move both personnel and cargo.

To convert the Starlifter, a large module was slipped into the cargo compartment and secured to the deck. The module mounted 166 older-style airline seats in multiple tiers—not the most comfortable seats in the world, but the tired SEALs thought they were just fine.

Additional modifications to the interior included a module that contained toilet facilities and a galley. The module just slid in on built-in floor rollers and secured. The remainder of the space in the cabin was taken up by high-priority cargo and equipment bound for Riyadh and the developing U.S. military command center there. Among the cargo containers were the packages that belonged to the SEALs.

The Starlifter might have been an old design, but the B model had been given more than a few upgrades in the late 1970s. Besides being stretched in length more than twenty-three feet to increase cargo capacity, the C-141B was given an in-flight refueling capacity. That meant the aircraft was going to be able to make the entire trip to Riyadh nonstop. Somewhere along the way, the big cargo plane would meet up with a flying tanker. The thirsty Starlifter would be able to suck out over

23,000 gallons of fuel in twenty-six minutes, if it needed that much.

But before they could consider an in-flight refueling, the Starlifter had to lift off and be on its way. The passenger module was close to being filled. Most of the people sitting in the seats were high-ranking officers. Rockham and Daugherty were the only two lieutenants in sight, among colonels in the Air Force and Army, several generals, and even a couple of admirals and Navy captains.

Space on flights heading directly to Saudi Arabia was hard to come by. General Schwarzkopf, in overall command of the Desert Shield effort, had given priority to putting armor—M1A1 main battle tanks and Bradley fighting vehicles—on every piece of heavy lift aircraft in the Air Force's inventory. Schwarzkopf did not hold a high opinion of Special Operations forces at that time, so the SEALs had to make do with what they could get. The flight they were on would be the fastest way to get to Saudi Arabia. The fact that it was going to Riyadh, the location of the new U.S. Central Command center, explained the large number of officers on board the Starlifter.

But the SEALs' mission was important. Its high priority meant that a block of seats had been held by the plane's crew for the SEALs, to allow them to sit together and discuss whatever they had to in what privacy was available. But they had arrived at the plane late, and it had been sitting and waiting for them. During that time, a short, balding, rotund

Air Force major had made himself at home in the
SEALs' section of seats. He'd opened up his brief-
case and had papers spread out over several seats.

When he was asked by the crewman of the Starlifter to move, the officer simply ignored the man.
When Rockham asked the man to make room for
his men, the major looked up once and then went
back to his paper shuffling. "Enlisted men can find
seats where they are available, Lieutenant," the of-
ficious little officer said. "I'm busy here with important work."

It looked to Rockham as if the man was intentionally trying to be a pain in the ass, or maybe he
was one of those pencil-pushing officers who was
just a martinet because he never actually did anything, just managed paper. The materials he'd
spread out all over looked to be logistical work, important enough, but not something Rockham was
going to accept as a reason he couldn't sit with all
of his men.

Before the SEAL officer could say another word,
a rear admiral walked over from where he'd been
sitting, leaned over and spoke in the major's ear.
The top of the major's head turned even redder
than it had been, and he quickly gathered up his papers and stuffed them into his case. Without looking in Rockham's eye, the major got up and moved
to another seat some distance away.

Before Rockham could say a word, the admiral
said with a smile, "Class twenty-six, Coronado.
Dropped on a medical. I never did earn one of

those," and he indicated the Special Warfare insignia, the Trident, on Rockham's uniform. "Good luck," he said, and walked back to his seat.

There wasn't much to say after that. The SEALs got into their seats and buckled in. In a few minutes the Starlifer began to move. Its next planned stop would be in Saudi Arabia, some 6,866 miles and thirteen hours away.

More than half a day of traveling aboard a military aircraft could wear on anyone. Most of the SEALs took the situation in stride. Several of them stretched out in their seats and promptly went to sleep. Just because they had proved at BUD/S that any of them could go without sleep for extended periods didn't mean that the average SEAL wouldn't grab some shut-eye whenever he could.

When Wayne Alexander started snoring, that did cause some consternation among the passengers. The horrible buzzing roar was thought by some to be a sign that an engine was getting ready to tear loose from its mounting. A hard poke by Chief Monday caused Alexander to grunt, move about, and stop snoring—for the moment. But the short SEAL soon ended up with his head back and that stentorian noise coming out of his face.

Twelve hours and forty-five minutes in the air. A long time by anyone's standards. Rockham, Daugherty, Ferber, and Monday spent a lot of the time going over manifests, diagrams, maps, and other intelligence reports to see if there was anything they had missed in their plans for the op. The high points of the trip centered around a few surprises dragged out of a container brought on board by Chief Monday.

Even though the unit had been under isolation, information always seemed to slide through the cracks and into the unofficial SEAL support net. Families were always taken care of. If a husband was away on deployment, a wife could rest assured that if an appliance broke, the car needed work, or any household needs came up, someone from the Teams would come by and take care of the situation. And the support network didn't just extend out to the families, as Chief Monday was about to reveal.

When the time came to break out the meals, Chief Monday told the Air Force crew members to keep their box lunches, that the SEALs had brought their own chow. While the rest of the men looked on, Monday opened up a large box secured with some of their gear and began pulling out white Styrofoam boxes. The smells that came out of the boxes told the SEALs that their Teammate at the Iceberg hadn't forgotten them. That morning, a large box had shown up over at SEAL Team Two, with the understanding that it would be delivered to the SMD when they returned from training.

The aroma of hot soup, thick roast beef sandwiches, and fried chicken overrode the smells in the cargo hold of the aircraft and packed humanity. None of even the higher ranking officers around the SEALs thought to ask to share in their bounty. Somehow, getting between these men and their food didn't seem a good idea, though when Kurkowski started carving up one of the several large apple pies with his new Emerson folding knife, the temptation to ask for a spare slice was hard to resist.

The Starlifter caught up with the night and moved on through the darkness. Somewhere in the skies near Spain they rendezvoused with a KC-135R Stratotanker aircraft and refueled. The next major part of the journey took them across nearly the length of the Mediterranean, until they turned south along Egypt, the Red Sea, and crossed into Saudi Arabia. The last several hours of their flight took place during the dawning hours of Friday, August 17. The morning light showed little but their flight over sands and barren gravel plains, only very occasionally broken by the dark ribbon of a road.

The Starlifter touched down at the King Faisal Air Academy air base at Riyadh and taxied across the large airport facility. In spite of its size, the airfield was busy, nearly as crowded as Langley had been the day before. It was 0820 hours local time, and military aircraft of all colors were moving about, being unloaded, fueled, and made ready for further flight. A large number of smaller planes carrying the markings of the Royal Saudi Air Defense Force were parked. There were also several rows of C-130H, KC-130H, and other transport craft with the same markings.

As the Starlifter pulled up to the unloading area for their aircraft, a much smaller plane was visible nearby. It was a two-engined turboprop-driven craft with a light blue and gray color scheme, and it carried the markings of the U.S. Navy.

Even that early in the morning, the cool of the desert night had given way to the hot August sun. The side doors of the C-141B opened into the glare of the sun, and the heat struck the men as they filed out like a physical blow.

"Yeah, but it's a dry heat," Kurkowski said.

"So's an oven," Ryan Marks snapped back. The black man's bald head already had beads of sweat starting to form on the shiny skin.

Vehicles were pulling up to pick up the various VIP passengers. Chief Monday went over to speak to the ground crew, which was preparing to unload some cargo through the opening clamshell doors at the rear of the aircraft. Trotting over to Lieutenant Rockham was a hot-looking U.S. Navy officer wearing a flight suit.

"Lieutenant Rockham?" the flier said.

"That's me," Rockham answered. "What can I do for you?"

"I'm Lieutenant Candless," the Navy man said. "I've been sent from the *Eisenhower* to pick up you and your men and get you out to her ASAP. I've been waiting here a couple of hours, and we're set to go as soon as your men and their equipment are on board."

"That your bird over there?" Rockham asked, pointing to the C-2A Greyhound with the U.S. Navy markings that he'd noticed earlier. The plane had the letters COD, for Carrier Onboard Delivery, printed on her engine nacelles in big black letters.

"That's her," Candless said. "Let's see about getting your gear aboard."

"I think my chief is already handling that," Rockham said.

At the rear of the Starlifter, the SEALs three cargo pallets were being pulled off and stacked to the side of the aircraft. The ground crew running the forklifts continued to unload the Starlifter, but after being told about their situation in a quick few words from Chief Monday while John Grant and Dan Able stood to either side of him, the forklift operators turned to the SEALs' pallets and moved them to the C-2A Greyhound as expeditiously as possible. The fact that John Grant was ready to take the forklift from one of the men and run it himself was not lost on the ground crew.

"You bitched about the heat," Rockham said to the SEALs. "Now we're going to get out of it for a while. Everybody on board the plane."

Within twenty minutes of the Starlifter opening her doors, the Greyhound, with the SEALs and all of their gear aboard, was wheels-up and on her way. This second leg of the trip was going to cover some 675 miles, most of the distance over the sandy wastes of Saudi Arabia. According to the navigator of the Greyhound, they would be over the deck of the *Eisenhower* in two hours and fifteen minutes.

For the best part of two hours, the SEALs could sit and listen to the drone of the turboprops. The only option was looking out one of the few portholes at the almost unchanging desert passing beneath them. For the last twenty minutes of their flight, and the last hundred miles, the Greyhound passed over the deep blue waters of the Red Sea.

Then they were inside the area covered by the screening ships of the *Eisenhower*'s battle group.

The huge nuclear-powered *Eisenhower*, CVN 69, was a Nimitz-class ship and over a thousand feet in length. Every SEAL was at heart a Navy man, and it was stirring to that heart to look down on one of the largest warships in the world. From the keel to the top of the mast, it was 244 feet, equal to the height of a twenty-four-story building. And the mast and superstructure were dwarfed by the size of the flight deck. Just barely short of 1,100 feet long, and nearly a quarter of that—254 feet— wide, the 4.5 acres of flight deck was one of the busiest, and most dangerous, places to work on earth.

Over 6,000 sailors crewed the massive ship, and supported the eighty-five to ninety aircraft in the *Eisenhower*'s flight wing. Only a nuclear-powered ballistic missile submarine carried more firepower than a Nimitz-class carrier. The *Eisenhower* and her support ships had crossed the Suez Canal in almost record time to get on-station in the Red Sea. And the *Eisenhower* was only the second nuclear-powered carrier to even pass through the Suez Canal.

The presence of the mighty ship was enough to at least give Saddam Hussein pause to think about a further invasion. The twenty F14 Tomcat and twenty F/A-18 Hornet fighters aboard could back up the EA-6B Prowlers and A-6E Intruders as they made a hash of Iraqi ground positions and air cover. Saddam might not think that the U.S. would use the might of her Navy against him, but if he was wrong, the mistake would be a costly one from this single ship alone. And now the SEALs were being added to the mix.

CHAPTER 16

★ ★ ★ ★

0755 ZULU
24° 8' North, 36° 12' East
Flight Deck approach
CVN 69 *Eisenhower*
Red Sea

In spite of the size of the aircraft carrier, it looked like there wasn't enough room for the C-2A Greyhound to land. Particular care had to be taken by the pilot in the landing approach due to the over eighty-foot wingspan of the boxy cargo plane. Some of the SEALs were concerned—most of them had never witnessed a carrier landing, let alone been involved in one—but the Greyhound set down easily, her tail hook grabbing the arresting wire and the plane quickly coming to a stop.

"Welcome aboard the *Ike*, gentlemen," Lieutenant Candless said over the aircraft's PA system. After the craft had taxied to a waiting area, the four men of the Greyhound's crew unsnapped their safety harnesses and told the SEALs they could do the same.

SUDAN MAP

"Okay, everybody out and stay by the plane until we get further direction," Chief Monday said, "and somebody wake up Alexander."

On the busy flight deck, there weren't any aircraft taking off or landing, but the place was still a hive of activity. Jets were being moved, loaded, fueled, and otherwise prepared for flight. The four huge elevators along the side of the *Eisenhower*—three on the starboard (right) side and one on the port—were lifting and lowering aircraft into the cavernous deck spaces below.

An odd but welcome sight to several of the SEALs was the olive-drab helicopter parked forward on the port side. The twin-rotor Chinook was the standard medium-lift helicopter in the U.S. Army, and one of the more popular birds of its type in the world. The CH-47D could lift its own weight in cargo and travel over a hundred miles with it, and the SEALs could conduct some interesting missions with the Chinook.

"Lieutenant Rockham?" a young ensign shouted over the noise of the deck activity. He had walked up to the Greyhound as the SEALs were getting out of the cargo plane.

"That's me," Rockham shouted back.

"I'm Ensign Coppersmith," the young officer shouted. "Could you and your men please come with me?"

"Chief, detail a man to watch the gear, and the rest of you come with me," Rockham said. "Lead on, Mr. Coppersmith."

"Alexander, you're well rested," Chief Monday said. "Watch the gear."

Then the rest of the SEALs followed their own officer and the ensign through the hatchway in the side of the "island"—the superstructure rising up on the starboard side of the flight deck.

Going through the hatchway, it became obvious why the ensign had been sent to act as their guide. The inside of the carrier was a maze of passageways, compartments, and decks. Without quite knowing exactly where they were, the SEALs soon arrived at a room lined with well-upholstered seats facing a raised platform, with map and chalkboards on the bulkhead behind it.

"This is the pilot's briefing room," Ensign Coppersmith said in a normal tone of voice. "If you could make yourselves comfortable, the XO and intel officer will be down to brief you shortly. There's coffee in the urn there." Coppersmith pointed to a low table at the back of the compartment.

The SEALs settled in to follow the age-old military tradition of "Hurry up and wait." This time, they didn't have very long to wait.

Within five minutes a tall, black officer came in, accompanied by a short, intense-looking older officer. Looking about the compartment, the black officer noticed Rockham's rank insignia on his uniform collar.

"Lieutenant Rockham," he said as he walked over and put out his hand. "I'm Commander Washington, executive officer of the *Ike*." Turning to introduce the officer with him, Washington said, "And this is Lieutenant Commander Maxwell, the head of our Intelligence department."

"Glad to meet you," Rockham said as he shook each man's hand in turn. "This is Lieutenant Daugherty, my second in command."

Daugherty shook the two officers hands in turn.

"Okay," Washington said. "We haven't much time, and we need to bring you up to date on what's been going on since you've been in the air."

Maxwell went up to the podium and unrolled a large chart of the Red Sea. "Gentlemen," he began as he turned back to face the SEALs, "I have not been given the full details of your mission, but our job here on the *Ike* is to get you on board the *Oklahoma City* as soon as possible and give you all the material support we can.

"We are here," he said, and pointed to a spot in the northern Red Sea off the coast of Egypt. "And we are going to transport you by helicopter to here." He pointed to a spot in the empty ocean.

"This is just a bit over a hundred miles from the *Eisenhower* as we steam to the southeast. But it is still well inside the range of the CH-47 ready for you up on the flight deck. At this rendezvous point, the *Oklahoma City* will surface to pick you up. Once on board the submarine, you'll be given the most recent target intelligence that they have generated.

"The submarine will surface after she has received a radio signal from the helicopter. Our technicians have double-checked the communications gear on board the helicopter and have made certain that it is compatible with that on the submarine.

"The equipment you asked for is ready and waiting out on the hangar deck. Two of the *Ike*'s rescue swimmers will be going with you on the insertion, using our own boats. That way we'll be able to ensure that you arrive on the sub with full fuel tanks. When you've finished inspecting the equipment on the hangar deck, you can have it raised in place to the flight deck by using the elevator. XO?"

Commander Washington stepped up onto the podium and addressed the men. "Chow has been laid on for you in the mess hall. You can eat immediately if you wish. The helicopter will take about forty minutes of flying time to get you to the rendezvous point. The *Oklahoma City* is expecting to pick you up at 1300 hours. You shouldn't miss her, she's the only Los Angeles attack sub in these waters—to the best of our knowledge."

The SEALs chuckled at the thought of getting on the wrong sub in the middle of the Red Sea.

"That should give you about ninety minutes from now to get ready," Commander Washington continued. "Ensign Coppersmith will act as your liaison with the *Ike* and assist you in any way he can. Are there any questions?"

Chief Monday was the only one of the men to raise his hand.

"Yes, Senior Chief?" Washington said.

"We need to fill up our outboard's fuel bladders

before we lift off," Monday said. "We didn't travel with them full."

"Not a problem, Senior Chief," Commander Washington replied. "A gasoline supply commensurate with your needs has been laid on. And there are spare fuel containers to take with you for topping off. Anything else?"

"No, thank you, sir," Monday said.

"Having spent the better part of a full day in the air," Rockham said, "we should paddle our way to the sub—we could use the exercise. Commander Washington, we appreciate everything you've done."

"You and your men are welcome, Mr. Rockham," Washington replied. "After all, we're all on the same team. If there's nothing else, I'll let you get on with your preparations. Your pilots will meet you to load the bird. I have been told that they are very experienced in the kind of insertion you intend. Good luck, gentlemen."

It was a very busy hour and a half for the SEALs to get their gear ready. The triwall containers that had transported their gear were unwrapped. The various-size bags and containers were laid out and either set aside or packed into the two Zodiac boats that were waiting for them on the hangar deck. The two rescue swimmers, Ed Griffith and Mark Turner, were able to help the SEALs prep the two boats. Splitting up into squads, the SEALs grabbed a hot meal and still got all of the gear ready well inside their time limit.

Traveling up to the flight deck was an experience. They carried their boats out a mammoth set of doors to the outside of the hull. There, the huge elevator platform—big enough to move a jet fighter easily—lifted them up to the flight deck. It was something to ride up to that deck in an elevator larger than a two-car garage.

The CH-47D had been chosen as the best bird to conduct a "swamp duck" insertion, which meant that the helicopter would actually land on the water, weather permitting, and flood the inside of the cargo compartment. The two Zodiacs inside could then just float out of the helicopter, propelled by some of the SEALs with paddles. Once clear of the helicopter, the outboard motors would be started and the boats moved out to the submarine.

It had been decided to use the swamp duck for several reasons. If the weather hadn't permitted that kind of operation, the SEALs would have conducted a "soft duck" and just pushed the Zodiacs out the rear of the helicopter. Then the men would have jumped into the water and continued with the mission. But that technique would have meant abandoning the two insertion Zodiacs. With the rescue swimmers from the *Ike* on board, the two inflated Zodiacs could be turned around and driven right back up the flooded ramp of the CH-47D.

The time factor involved made the SEALs use extra boats to get on board the submarine. To have taken their packed boats and inflated them for the insertion would have meant deflating them before they could be moved into the submarine. The fif-

teen to twenty minutes it would have taken to de-
flate, roll up, and pack the boats on the curved deck
of the submarine was considered too long a time
for the nuke boat to be on the surface. Every moment she was exposed increased the chance of
somebody seeing her.

So the SEALs would be taking their own boats
into the sub. And the *Ike* wasn't going to have to
lose two Zodiacs, since the SEALs would have cut
the flotation cells and sunk the boats rather than
try and pack them into the sub. Another advantage
to using the *Ike*'s Zodiacs and outboards was that
the SEALs would have only cold motors to man-
handle into the sub.

Fit, fed, packed, and good to go, the SEALs
boarded the Chinook a little ahead of schedule.
The helicopter lifted off from the *Eisenhower* and
headed south.

Deep blue water, miles and miles of it, passed below the helicopter. The Red Sea was over a mile deep
at this point, a long gash in the sea floor below them
giving the water its depth. But for all the beauty of
the water, the SEALs and crew of the helicopter were
looking for something else—the long, black torpedo
shape of one of the man-made killers of the sea.

Captain Palmer, U.S. Army, was on the radio
calling out the identification code phrase to the
waiting submarine.

"Lieutenant Rockham," Palmer shouted into the
microphone attached to his headset, "I've made
contact, she's close by. You should see her surfacing
off to our left!"

"Roger that, Captain, thanks," Rockham acknowledged.

All of the SEALs were looking out of the port side of the Chinook. The sharp eyes of Ryan Marks, the detachment's sniper, were the first to spot the small mark on the blue ocean.

"There's something at about two o'clock," Marks said, "maybe a quarter mile away. There's a white line in the water."

The SEAL had spotted the small white tail kicked up by the antenna array of the *Oklahoma City*. As the SEALs watched fascinated, the black shadow of the nuclear submarine could be seen coming up from the depths. Given its size, it seemed to move in slow motion, first the sail of the submarine breaking the surface, then the long, black hull, white foam rolling away from her in the disturbed water.

"Okay, make ready," Chief Monday shouted.

The SEALs all took their positions as the helicopter started to lose altitude. The crew chief of the bird opened the rear cargo ramp and looked out. The noise level in the helicopter rose as the open end of the bird let the sound of the rotors roar in. The SEALs and the two rescue swimmers from the *Ike* were standing at the ready to release the securing straps on their boats.

The Chinook was lowered until the rear ramp touched the water. Then it continued down according to the instructions the pilot was receiving from the crew chief. The water lapped up the ramp and started to enter the cargo hold. The two sixty-foot-

diameter rotors at either end of the helicopter kept
the bird steady, and the pilot continued to lower it
into the water. At a signal from the crew chief, the
SEALs completed their release of the boats and
pushed them down the ramps.

The two rescue swimmers were acting as the
coxswains of both Zodiacs as the boats entered the
water. They unlocked the outboards and let them
tilt back into the water. Both motors started on the
first pull, quickly settling down into a dull roar.

As the boats went back off the ramp, the SEALs
jumped into the water on either side. It was a long-
perfected skill the SEALs used to climb into the two
Zodiacs. From their very earliest days at BUD/S,
SEALs learned how to get into a rubber boat without flipping it over. Now, with the men settled in on
the sides of the boats, the two rescue swimmers
steered for the surfaced nuclear submarine only a
few hundred yards away.

1000 ZULU
22° 50' North, 37° 14' East
SSN *Oklahoma City*
Red Sea

With the center of each boat filled with gear
bags, the SEALs straddled the buoyancy tubes. Lying flat along the twenty-inch-diameter black tubes,
the SEALs rode along with one leg inside the boat
and the other outside the hull, the knee bent back
to keep the foot from dragging in the water. Sheaths
in the hull held six black, soundproof paddles. But

the efficiently running outboard motors prevented any need to break out the paddles.

In spite of the calm seas, the submarine had been positioned to run with the seas on her port quarter. Moving forward at barely three knots, hardly a brisk walk, there was no wash over the rounded deck of the sub at all and she left almost no visible wake. At Rockham's and Daugherty's directions, the two coxswains steered the boats over to the sub's starboard side.

Crewmen wearing red safety vests were on the deck of the submarine to assist the SEALs in getting on board. Besides the vests, the crewmen had lines running from their waists to a track cut in the deck of the sub. The lines were free to run along the track, and would help keep a crewman from going overboard or from being sucked into the prop if he did go into the water.

The SEALs did not have such safety equipment, other than the inflatable life vests they all wore. They scrambled aboard the submarine, then Rockham and Daugherty, each in the bow of their respective boats, threw a line attached to the boats to one of the deckhands on the sub. The deckhands in turn made the lines fast by securing them to a deck cleat. The coxswains throttled back the outboard motors but kept them idling in case they had to break away suddenly. Now the unloading of the Zodiacs could begin.

In spite of the large piles of bags and various containers in the boats, the unloading went quickly. A short, heavyset man with master chief anchors on his collar directed the SEALs to move their gear down to the weapons loading hatch forward of the sub's sail. Each kit bag, rucksack, and container had at least one hoisting line attached to it. The heavier items, such as the packed Zodiacs and outboard motors, had more than a single hoisting line. The Zodiacs were so heavy and difficult to handle on the curved hull of the sub, they had four hoisting lines each attached to them.

Recognizing the man giving the directions as the chief of the boat, a COB, Chief Monday clambered up onto the hull after passing up the heaving lines attached to the fuel bladders for the SEALs' outboards.

The round hull of the submarine had an odd feel underfoot, like the give of a thick, hard carpet. In fact, it was covered with special anechoic rubber blocks. The blocks were glued to the H-80 steel of the submarine's hull to help cut down on sound echoes off the metal, and helped add a sonar "stealth" capability to the sub, and were smooth to aid the flow of water over their skin. The upper part of the hull was coated with an antislip compound to increase the grip of footwear against the rubber surface.

Going up to the COB, Chief Monday introduced himself and asked for help getting the fuel bladders into the external line locker. The COB, Master Chief Chase Bonner, having anticipated the request, had the special X-shaped wrench to unlock and open the line hatch.

The external line locker was inletted into the deck, with only the outline of the hatch and the socket for the wrench head to identify it. After COB opened the hatch, Chief Monday could see that there was plenty of room for the SEALs four fuel bladders but not enough room for either of the Zodiacs.

The line locker was not accessible from inside the submarine. But it was a convenient and safe place to store the hazardous materials represented by the gasoline in the full fuel bladders. And it would have saved the trouble of dragging the Zodiacs into and out of the sub's hatches when it came time to use them.

While the COB and Chief Monday were securing the fuel bladders, the rest of the SEALs moved rapidly ahead with unloading and moving their gear into the submarine. High up on the sail was the open bridge. The submarine's captain and his executive officer, accompanied by the officer of the deck, were standing in the small open area of the bridge watching the activity on the deck below them. Standing up on the sail behind the bridge were two of the sub's crewmen, each man scanning the horizon with binoculars as he stood lookout watch.

The SEALs didn't have much time to notice who was on deck. They were busy pulling their gear bags up and lowering them down the open weapons loading hatch. The large open hatch made the submarine vulnerable. She wouldn't dive with men on the deck, and she couldn't dive with the hatch open. Being on the surface while at sea is never a favorite situation for a submariner. The big nuke boats were at home under the waves, cutting through the deeps under a thick blanket of water.

To speed things up, Wayne Alexander and Ryan Marks were already down inside the submarine, moving bags and stacking them to the side as they came down the hatch. Within about five minutes from the time they pulled up to the sub, the SEALs had all of their gear off the deck and inside the hatch. The men followed their gear on board, leaving the clearing of the deck and sealing the hatch up to the sub's crewmen. The last man down the weapons loading hatch, the COB, pulled the heavy outer hatch shut against its counterbalance system.

As the *Oklahoma City* was sealing up, the circling CH-47 helicopter descended back down to the surface of the water. Again, following the directions of the crew chief, the pilot set the bird down lower and lower, so that her rear ramp and cargo bay slowly flooded as the helicopter went down by the stern. With a shallow depth of water in the bird, the Zodiacs came into the bird at speed, the rescue swimmers pulling up the outboard motors as the rubber boats hit the ramps.

With both of the Zodiacs recovered, the CH-47 lifted off, trailing water as she headed back to the *Eisenhower*. Even without any radio traffic, the carrier would have had a good idea of what had been going on in the Red Sea over a hundred miles from the ship. The *Ike*'s SPS-49 long-range air-search had a range of over 275 miles and was able to watch the helicopter dip and rise twice as she conducted her mission.

The SPS-48 height finder radar on the *Eisenhower* had a lesser range of only 244 miles. That still was considerably more than the distance from the *Ike* to the *Oklahoma City*. The commander of the nuclear attack sub would have been less than happy about just how well his tall sail showed up on the *Eisenhower's* radar. But he was about to eliminate any radar signature his boat would make. Only he and a few others remained outside of the submarine, and he was going to change that situation immediately.

CHAPTER 17

★ ★ ★ ★

On the small bridge on top of the sail of the *Oklahoma City*, Commander Robert Wilson, captain of the submarine, could see that the helicopter had taken off with her rubber boats safely aboard. As the last of the crewmen on the deck entered the submarine and secured the weapons loading hatch behind them, it was time to go back to the environment the submarine operated best in.

"Officer of the Deck," Wilson said in his usually gruff voice, "are the passengers and cargo below?"

"Yes, sir," said Lieutenant Jeff Ritter from his station just behind the captain.

"XO, take her down," Captain Wilson ordered.

"Take her down," repeated Bill Wotton, standing to Wilson's right. "Aye, sir."

Picking up the handset from the small console in front of him, Wotton called down to the control room, "Control, Bridge. Sounding?"

"Bridge, Control," came back over the phone. "Sounding, one three double zero fathoms."

"Lookouts, clear the bridge," Wotton ordered.

"Clear the bridge, aye, sir," the two sailors answered as they climbed down from their position on the upper part of the sail.

"Officer of the Deck, prepare to dive," Wotton said.

As the XO's words were echoed through the submarine, the big ship went from being simply busy to a flurry of activity. Men moved across compartments, through passageways, and up or down ladders, to prepare for the dive. In spite of the apparent rush to get to diving stations, the SEALs standing in the passageway just a short distance behind the enlisted mess could see that there was no confusion in any sailors' movements. This was a carefully choreographed and long practiced series of actions.

On the deck above the SEALs, Captain Wilson came down the ladder from the bridge, through the sail, and into the control room/attack center. The chief of the boat, having entered the control room from the weapons loading hatch up forward of the sail, was already waiting when the captain came down from the bridge.

"Captain is down," Wilson said quietly.

"The captain is down," the COB repeated in a much louder tone.

"XO down," Wotton said as his feet hit the deck of the control room.

"XO is down," the COB repeated.

Up on the bridge, Lieutenant Ritter, as the officer of the deck, took one last look around to make certain that everyone was clear and all was as it should be. Then he too went down the bridge hatch and into the control room.

When Captain Wilson saw Ritter, he said in a strong voice, "Submerge the ship."

"Diving officer," Wotton said, "dive the ship. Make your depth one five zero feet."

"Make my depth one five zero feet, aye, sir," the COB repeated. "Chief of the watch, on the 1-MC, dive, dive."

As the announcement of the dive went out over the public address system, valves were opened and air gushed out of the buoyancy tanks on either side of the hull. The water rushed in, and the air blew out of vents along the upper surface of the hull, carrying a heavy load of mist into the air. As if it was a living thing, the huge black shape of the nuclear submarine appeared to be blowing multiple spouts, as a whale would prior to slipping beneath the waves.

Turning to the planesman sitting at his station in front of a yoke-type wheel, the COB ordered, "Make your depth one five zero feet, five degree down bubble."

As orders echoed through the ship and each man did as he'd been drilled, the young planesman pushed his wheel forward against its control column. The bow planes tilted to meet the wheel's command, and the black shape slipped beneath the waves.

"Come about and make your course one seven zero, flank speed," Wilson ordered.

"Course one seven zero, flank speed," the COB repeated.

The helmsman at his station to the right of the planesman repeated the orders and turned his control wheel until the ship's course indicator lined up with the proper heading. Turning the knob of the engine order telegraph through the forward speed commands of one-third, two-thirds, full, and flank, told the engine room to increase the power to the propeller shaft to its highest normal degree.

A slight vibration went through the craft as it picked up speed and started to head almost due south. Aside from that small shudder, gone almost before it could be noticed, the ride was so smooth that there was no real feeling of movement. But the big submarine was starting to go through the water at near her top speed of thirty-two knots, or about thirty-seven miles an hour.

A quiet settled over the ship as the submarine moved through the environment it most belonged in. Men continued with their duties in a very quiet manner. Hatches weren't shut hard, tools were not knocked about, even voices were spoken at a lower tone. The world of the submarine was one of quiet. In an attack submarine such as the *Oklahoma City*, the first one to hear an enemy had the advantage—the acoustic advantage, as submariners said. And the *Oklahoma City* never intended to give that advantage away.

"XO, please see to our guests," said Wilson. "Give my compliments to their commander and have him and his XO meet me in the wardroom in fifteen minutes, please."

"Aye, sir," Wotton said. Then he turned to the stern of the ship and the ladder that led to the lower decks.

The control room was the heart of the submarine. In its immediate vicinity was all the information the captain would need to make his decisions, which determined the success or failure of a mission, or even the life and death of his submarine. Forward of the control room was the sonar room, the ears of the submarine. Detecting sound was the most important sense for a submarine in the underwater world. Visibility was minimal at the best of times. Light only penetrated for the first hundred feet or so of the ocean, then all became twilight, and finally darkness.

It was through this darkness that the *Oklahoma City* sped. In her sonar room, four seats were bolted to the deck, each in front of a AN/BSY-1 sonar console. Using the "busy-one" electronics in the sonar room, the huge spherical and hull array of the BQQ-5A(V)1 sonar sensors in the nose of the submarine could be "read" by the sonar men.

An acoustic spectrum analyzer in the corner of the sonar room helped tell them just what they were listening to. But the final analysis on a target had to be done by the human operators sitting at their consoles. The library of sounds in the analyzer not only listed a vast number of past identifications, it also held a record of everything the sonar men had detected on their present cruise.

Any contact made could be listened to over a sonar man's headsets. But the electronic trace of the contact was usually analyses from the glowing lines projected on a CRT screen. A glowing white line across a frequency band would show that a contact was made, and help identify just what it was the men had found.

As the submarine began her chase to the south, the sonar men started listening for a specific surface contact. That contact was the cargo ship *Pilgrim's Hope*. Identified as target contact Sierra One-one-five, the sonar men did not know the name of the ship they had followed for days. But they did know every squeak, groan, rumble, and thump her engines and machinery made.

As the submarine continued with its mission, the SEALs prepared for their part. The men had already begun setting up housekeeping in the torpedo room, down in what felt like the bowels of the sub. Several members of the sub's crew had assisted the SEALs in moving their gear bags and containers down to the third deck of the submarine. The SEALs had accepted the help, given that they had to carry each item down two sets of ladders, the equivalent of two flights of stairs in the civilian world.

The torpedo room was one of the largest single compartments aboard. As in every other compartment on the submarines, almost all of the available space was taken up by machinery and the electronics to support that machinery. The space in the torpedo room was necessary for the three huge racks of ordnance taking up the two sides and center of the compartment.

The two racks on either side of the compartment had spaces for six torpedoes, or harpoon missiles encapsulated for launching from a torpedo tube. The side racks held their weapons in two layers of three. The outboard top two torpedoes in each of the side racks were missing. In their place were the white bunk pads with lengthwise blue stripes that the SEALs were used to seeing throughout the Navy.

The crew had arranged their ordnance load to accommodate their passengers and at least give the SEALs a minimum of comfort. This was not a small thing on board a Los Angeles–class boat. The design of the submarine had been made to fit a number of parameters, and to reach their goals the designers had to trim back in other areas to make room. A result of this was that there were never enough bunks for the enlisted crew aboard a Los Angeles–class sub. The junior enlisted men shared a two-bunk assignment to three men. The procedure was known as "hot bunking," as the sleeping space was never empty long enough to cool off from its previous occupant.

Their bunking arrangements aside, the SEALs could see that the large center ordnance rack had no empty spaces. The long, green-painted shapes of the Mark 48 ADCAP (Advanced Capacity) torpedoes were in two layers of six. The twenty-one-inch-diameter torpedoes were nineteen feet long and tipped with a flat-nosed plastic cap. Each of the Mark 48 torpedoes could drive its 645-pound PBXN high explosive warhead out to a target over twenty-eight miles away. And the torpedo could get to that target at a speed of over sixty miles an hour.

But the Mark 48 torpedoes were only in the two side racks and the bottom layer of the central rack. The six weapons on the top layer of the central rack weren't torpedoes, they were encapsulated A/R/UGM-84D Harpoon missiles, which was actually a turbojet-driven, rocket-launched cruise missile.

The encapsulated Harpoon could be launched from the Mark 67 533mm (twenty-one-inch) torpedo tubes of the *Oklahoma City* and other submarines. It would travel to the surface, where the capsule would separate explosively and the rocket ignite to launch the Harpoon into the air. The guidance system of the Harpoon would direct it to a target over fifty-seven miles away at a speed of Mach 0.85, over six hundred miles an hour. The almost 450-pound high explosive warhead of the Harpoon could do serious damage to the largest naval craft in the world.

In the front of the compartment was the bewildering array of electronic, hydraulic, and compressed air systems needed to operate the two torpedo tubes on either side of the bulkhead. The breaches of the four tubes—numbers two and four on the port side, one and three on the starboard side—each bore an ominous red-lettered placard that read: WARNING—WARSHOT LOADED.

Between the two sets of torpedo tube breaches was the launch control console. On the bulkhead behind the console, a huge rack of electronics supported the torpedo tubes and the vertical launch system.

Unlike other attack submarines, the newer ships of the Los Angeles class were fitted with the VLS. On the upper bow of the submarine were twelve hatches inletted into the deck. Underneath each one of those hatches was a UGM-109C Tomahawk Land Attack or Anti-Ship Missile (TLAM or TASM). The Tomahawk could be launched while the submarine was submerged, and carry its thousand-pound high explosive, or even nuclear, warhead to a target over eight-hundred miles away. And the guidance system of the Tomahawk would let it hit a target the size of a garage door at its maximum range.

The *Oklahoma City* was heavily armed with some of the most deadly naval ordnance ever fielded by the U.S. Navy. And setting up their gear and checking their bags while surrounded by all that destructive power were the eighteen SEALs of the Special Materials Detachment. The amount of high explosive surrounding them didn't bother the SEALs in the least. They had worked with explosives, and a number had already faced far worse weapons made up from the tiny world of bacteriological diseases.

For Sid Mainhart, operating from the *Oklahoma City* was like coming home, a home he had outgrown and left over a year earlier. The young torpe-

doman's mate had spent a lot of time standing
watches in the torpedo room of the Sturgeon-class
boat, the *Archerfish*. Now on ground familiar to
him, he could offer some information and skills to
his Teammates that they might not be as familiar
with as he was. All in all, the youngest member of
the SMD was very happy with the situation.

The two SEAL officers were a little less happy
with the situation, but only because of their concern for the mission. Rockham and Daugherty had
made sure that their men were settling in and that
there were no problems that couldn't be immediately resolved. Then Commander Wotton had
come into the torpedo room to make sure that
everything was all right with the SEALs and to ask
Rockham and Daugherty to come with him to the
officers' wardroom to meet with the captain.

The officers' wardroom was on the second deck
of the submarine, aft of the enlisted berthing. The
well-appointed room acted as a dining area for the
officers of the *Oklahoma City*, as well as a study
area, office space for paperwork, and even an en-
tertainment center. The rich brown wood paneling
gave the wardroom a warmer feeling than the average submarine compartment. Padded chairs surrounded a long table now covered with a cloth, but
which could also be converted into an efficient hos-
pital operating and treatment table if necessary. In
the various cabinets around the sides of the wardroom were both medical supplies and materials to
turn the room into the sub's sick bay.

At the moment, the wardroom only held the XO

and the two SEAL officers. None of the men felt that they needed the compartment converted into the sick bay, at least not for the moment. They were sitting at the table quietly waiting for the captain, a cup of good Navy coffee in front of each man. When Captain Wilson came in, they all snapped to attention, relaxing only a little and sitting back down at his quick "As you were," command.

Walking over to the coffee urn and drawing himself a cup, Captain Wilson turned and stepped to the table.

"Finding everything to your satisfaction, Mr. Rockham?" he asked as he sat down at the head of the table.

"Yes, sir," Rockham answered. "No problems that I can see so far."

"Excellent," Wilson said. "Any difficulties, and you bring them to the XO's or my attention immediately. The timetable for this little parade is a tight one."

Wilson leaned back in his seat. "Mr. Rockham," he began, "right now I have my ship moving at flank speed to intercept the *Pilgrim's Hope* according to her last observed position and plotted course. Flank speed isn't something we like to run at in an attack boat. It makes us noisy, and that makes us easier to find. But we have to catch up with that miserable rusting hulk of a freighter to get you and your men aboard.

"The accommodations aboard the *Oklahoma* don't allow for much extra room. The Los Angeles class of attack submarine was not designed to support your kind of operation as easily as other boats might be able to. But you and your men may be aboard for as little as a day. I understand that the XO has seen to it that there are at least a few comforts for you and your men down in the torpedo room?"

"Yes, sir," Rockham answered. "There's enough in the way of rack space and pads for my men to be able to get some rest before the operation. We've operated on a sub before and are used to having to make do with tight spaces. Your crew have been more than generous in helping us move our gear and settle in. But as you said, we may not be here very long."

"I've used my prerogative to let my crew know what we're trying to do," Wilson said, "or at least enough of the mission so they can conduct their part of it more readily. Part of that reason is the new orders I have regarding your target. Those orders are that if you find a weapon of mass destruction on that ship and are not able to destroy it, I will. I have the choice of using a Harpoon or Tomahawk missile that I can drop down on top of that ship and send it to the bottom in large pieces.

"Given that my Tomahawks cost a million dollars each, and that ship might have a scrap value of a couple of thousand, I have decided to use our Harpoon antiship missiles on her. Admittedly, that will be like hitting flies with a sledgehammer. The hundred kilos of high explosive in the Harpoon warhead will pretty much split that ship in two. But the waters are too shallow for us to line up any kind of a torpedo shot across the reefs.

"So it's either going to be up to you and your SEALs, or me and my missiles, Mr. Rockham. I would much rather it be your SEALs, since they can do a hands-on job of destroying anything worthwhile that they find. But if you and your men are unable to destroy the target—I will."

"We don't see any problem with the destruction of the target right now," Rockham said. "The big problem for us will be to gain control of the ship and make sure that any nonhostiles aren't put into harm's way. It was the possibility of hostages or just innocents aboard that boat that kept the Navy from sending her to the bottom already. But what is our timetable now?"

"We have about three hours before we should close with the target," Wotton said. "Even then, she should still be about four hours steaming time to go to get to her anchorage. Our most recent reports still have the pier at Muhammad Qol being put out of operation in time to block our target's unloading. So for right now all we can do is head to the target with all speed."

"You and your men should get what rest they can," Captain Wilson said. "The mess has been informed to have a hot meal ready for them, and you and your XO can use the wardroom here for any planning you wish. XO, see to it that they have everything that they need," Wilson said as he got up from the table.

The other three officers in the room immediately snapped to attention as the captain rose from his seat. "Aye, sir," Wotton said as the captain left the wardroom.

"Was it just me," Daugherty said after the door to the wardroom had closed, "or was he pissed at us about bothering his routine?"

"Routine is what we live on, Mr. Daugherty," Wotton said. "Besides, we're on the last few weeks of a long cruise. We would be heading back to the States right now if everything hadn't hit the fan out here. The only real worry the captain has about that is that our supplies are starting to run low. And now we have to do a sneak and peek into shallow waters. That isn't the favorite place for an attack sub."

"So we've learned," Rockham said. "But we'll be able to leave your boat in deeper water while we go in with our Zodiacs."

"Speaking of your boats," Wotton said, "do we have to surface for you to launch them?"

"No," Rockham said. "We can do a lockout while the sub is still submerged. But since we can only have a few men at a time go through the escape trunk, getting all of our men and gear out will take some time. Even with our using both trunks, it will be a long job to get the men and gear out."

"Okay," Wotton said, "the captain and I discussed this. If there isn't any sign of radar activity in the area, we can surface far enough offshore that no one on shore should be able to see anything. The island will block the ship's radar. We confirmed that the *Pilgrim's Hope* has operational radar while we were trailing her. It was the big reason that we went so far out to sea to pick you up from the *Ike*. While we were tracking the target visually, the radar antenna on top of the periscope head picked up radar emissions from her. So we wanted to be well out of their radar range before we surfaced to get you and your men on board."

"If we can surface for the insertion," Daugherty said, "it will speed up our getting off the boat. We should be able to launch our boats within five minutes of surfacing. Locking out through the escape trunk, even if we use them both, will stretch that time out to more like a half hour or greater. It won't just be trying to lift the gear up and out of the escape trunks. We'll only be able to send out three men at a time."

"We can conduct an underwater lockout," Rockham said. "It's something we've trained for. But a surface launch is a lot faster and a lot fewer things can go wrong. Our Zodiacs and their motors give us enough range that we can deploy from the sub while she's over the horizon from the target."

"That would make the round trip something over forty nautical miles," Wotton said. "That won't throw off your timetable and still let you have a margin for error?"

"It would just mean that we leave the submarine at about the same time we would have to if we did a lockout closer in to shore," Rockham said. "Only the extra time would be used up by our just getting off this boat and under way. As far as the safety margin goes, that shouldn't be a problem. We brought more than enough fuel with us for the outboards. Besides, I'd rather have to paddle the boats partway back to the sub than breathe down our rigs and use up our oxygen just getting under way."

"Okay," Wotton said. "I'll take your recommendations to the captain. Here's the most recent photos and data we have on the target." Wotton handed a manila folder to each of the SEAL officers. "The photos were taken through our Type 18 search periscope at thirty-two power. They should have enough detail to be of use to you."

"Thank you, Mr. Wotton," Rockham said.

"The name's Bill," Wotton said with a smile. "You can remain here in the wardroom and discuss the intel in private for the next hour or so. I suggest you take advantage of it. Privacy isn't something we have a lot of aboard the *Oklahoma*."

The XO left the two SEALs to discuss their plans in the wardroom. He returned to the control room to get an update on the sub's position. The sonar men on watch had nothing to report—not that they expected to locate the target they had been shadowing for days. That target, Sierra 115, was not expected to show up on their sonar displays for some hours yet.

Very faintly, from far off in the distance, came the trace of a "thump" in the water on the sonar screens. The faint trace was on the screen for only an instant and then it was gone, not even showing up long enough to be considered a contact. The sonar men had missed a very significant part of the mission, even though they had known nothing about it.

CHAPTER 18

★ ★ ★ ★

1237 ZULU
Customs Pier
Muhammad Qol
South of Dungunab Bay
Sudan

Abrahim Shafaq was a fisherman, as his father had been, and his father before him. It was an honest way to earn a living. It fed people, kept his family together, and allowed the people farther inland to have a chance at the bounty of the sea. Being a fisherman was a good way to spend a life, or at least it had been.

The year before, Sudan had been shaken by another political upheaval. At the end of June 1989 the military had replaced the government with one led by their own officers, with General Omar al Bashir at its head.

The change in government wasn't anything new. The overthrow of one regime was done by the next, which would later be overthrown when its time came. That seemed to be the way of things in Sudan for decades. But the drought that had plagued the southern parts of the country in 1987 and 1988 caused starvation for thousands. Massive floods in 1988 left more than two million people homeless, and made the shortage of food even more acutely felt.

These were details that Abrahim Shafaq didn't bother himself with. What he knew was that a new government meant new problems for him and his family. With his boat having its own engine, which allowed him to fish farther out to sea in a single day, he was one of the wealthier, more prosperous fishermen in his small village. And that meant he was a target.

Abrahim had been a good Muslim all of his life, as had his fathers before him. But this new wave of Islamic Fundamentalism sweeping through his country went against what he had been taught was the true meaning of the Koran. There had been peace between the Christians and Muslims in his country years before, but that peace was nothing but a distant memory now.

The rebels in the south were fighting harder than ever against the government troops. If things got much worse, his two older sons could easily be called up to fight a thousand miles from their home. The army coup last year had done nothing to improve the situation. It might be only a matter of time until his fishing boat was too valuable for the government to allow him to keep.

It was time for the Shafaq clan to move from Sudan to a more stable environment. To the north and west was Egypt, and farther to the west there was Morocco and Tunisia, which held promise for someone who knew how to wrest a living from the sea. But to move away from Sudan would take money, a good deal of it. Much more money than even a prosperous fisherman could expect to save in a lifetime. At least, such was the case until recently.

Abrahim did not know which government was supporting his old friend who had come to see him a few weeks earlier. It could be the Egyptians, or possibly the Americans or the English. It might have been the rebels, or even the Israelis. What his friend offered him was not only escape from the dangers rising around him, but the means and a reason for doing so.

The motive was simple. His friend's friends, whoever they were, wanted the customs pier, the only real docking facility in the area, to be unusable for several days. They were very specific about when they wanted the pier blocked, and they had a suggestion as to how it could be done.

The "suggestion" was sitting down below, next to the fuel supply to his engine. Abrahim thought it was too bad that the day's catch was also going to go to waste. The fish would have done well in the local market. But what the fish would have brought was nothing compared to the money that he had already hidden away, money paid to him by his friend. And there would be considerably more paid out after the pier was blocked.

It was coming up to noon, and the morning's fishermen were pulling up to the pier to unload before noon prayers. Abrahim was among them, his bigger boat moving up to a spot where it blocked the deep side of the pier. Pulling on the string leading back to the box near his engine caused the sequence of events inside to start. Abrahim did not know just what would happen, only that his boat was not going to last out the day. And his engine was now not going to start.

The shouted commands of the people up on the pier did nothing to help what looked like a stalled engine. Abrahim climbed up onto the pier with his sons and said he was going to go get the mechanic to repair the engine. He hadn't traveled more than a few blocks with his sons when the call went out for noon prayers. After the prescribed time of prayer, while bowing toward Mecca across the Red Sea, Abrahim again continued on his way with his sons. Since it was the beginning of the holy day, it would not be easy to convince the mechanic to come down to the pier. But the government people there had been insistent that he move his boat before that evening.

The sudden whooshing explosion from the direction of the pier told Abrahim that perhaps getting the mechanic for his boat wasn't as important as it had once been. Back at the pier, it looked as if the fuel supply of his boat had caught fire and exploded. Both the pier and the boat were engulfed by flames.

The fire on the pier was controlled and soon put

out. The boat was gutted and sank at its mooring. It would be at least until the next day before the crews would be back at their posts to work the one operating loading boom on the pier. Then the gutted hulk of Abrahim's fishing boat could be moved out of the way and the pier would be once again usable.

1508 ZULU
21° 38' North, 37° 12' East
Red Sea

At his watch station in the sonar room, Sonar Technician Third Class Scott Reynolds saw a white line appear on his sonar display. At the same time, he heard a familiar set of sounds come in over his headphones. Calling his supervisor over, he reported the contact. Chief William Parker noted what Reynolds showed him on his screen and immediately communicated with the control room over the 1-MC.

"Conn, Sonar," Chief Parker said. "I have a contact Sierra One-one-fiver bearing two-three-zero. She's about six thousand meters away, sir."

Lieutenant Jeff Smith, the officer of the deck on watch, picked up the 1-MC and answered. "Sonar, this is the conn. What have you got?"

"It looks like we've found our contact, sir," Parker answered. "The sound track matches and she's following her estimated course and speed."

"Roger that, Sonar, begin your track," Smith said.

Captain Wilson had been in the control room while the sonar report came in. Putting his coffee cup to the side, he picked up the microphone to the 1-MC and switched the system to shipwide.

"This is the captain," he said, "Mr. Rockham, please report to the control room."

To the COB, Captain Wilson said, "Come about and make your course two-three-zero, full speed."

"Course two-three-zero, full speed," the COB repeated, then gave the same instructions to the diving officer and helmsman.

As the submarine came about, Lieutenant Rockham entered the control room from the aft passage. "Yes, Captain?" he said.

"Mr. Rockham," Wilson said, "we've found your little party right where she was expected. We'll slip up and take a look, then fall back and follow her in. I thought you might like to take a look."

"Thank you, sir," Rockham said, "I would indeed."

As the submarine closed in on the sonar target they'd been searching for, Captain Wilson brought the boat up to periscope depth. Using a periscope wasn't the common occurrence it had been in World War II. Modern submarines tracked their targets through their sonar suites and other sensor systems. Lifting even a small periscope mast above the surface of the water would raise a white wake behind it, which could be seen for a good distance by a sharp lookout.

Captain Wilson didn't think the lookouts on the *Pilgrim's Hope* were all that professional, but he hadn't gotten to where he was in the command structure by taking unnecessary chances. As the submarine came up to periscope depth, sixty feet, he had the *Oklahoma* change speed to one-third ahead, almost its slowest speed, to minimize the periscope wake.

The diving officer called out from his position, seated between the helmsman and the planesman, "Engine room answers slow ahead one-third, periscope depth."

The *Oklahoma City* carried two periscopes, mounted side by side. On the starboard side was the Kollmorgen Type 2D attack periscope, which had the smallest head, giving it only a slight wake in the water. It was a simple optical device that could be set to 1.5 power or 6 power magnification settings.

On the port side of the platform, the Kollmorgen Type 18 was one of the most sophisticated periscopes in the U.S. Navy. The Mark 18 was both an optical and electro-optical device with a variety of accessories. The optical power of the periscope was adjustable from 1.5 power, 6 power, 12 power, and 24 power magnifications. A low-light TV camera was part of the optical system, and it could send the picture seen through the periscope to a number of stations on the sub. A still-picture camera was also part of the periscope, and it included a motion compensation system to allow for sharp, clear pictures to be taken. Lastly, a radar warning head on top of the head of the Type 18 could detect a radar sweep of the area.

Now, standing up on the periscope pedestal behind the officer of the deck, who stood watch, Cap-

tain Wilson went to the Type 18 port-side periscope
and moved the control to raise the scope. The long
tube traveled up through the sail of the submarine,
extending up from a storage cylinder that went
most of the way to the keel of the boat. The upper
part of the periscopes were covered with a mottled
gray and green pattern to help break up their outline on the surface.

It was unlikely that even a sharp-eyed lookout on
board the *Pilgrim's Hope* would see anything
against the surface of the sea. But the Type 18 gave
the people on board the submarine a very good view
of the quarry they had been tracking for three days.

"There she is, Mr. Rockham," Captain Wilson
said, his hands on the black knurled handles on either side of the large flat control face of the big
cylinder. "A far from shipshape looking piece of
flotsam. But it isn't for me to judge. Care to take a
look?"

"Very much, Captain," Rockham replied, and
moved forward up onto the platform and leaned
into the rubber eyepiece protecting the lens. The
Swedish optics of the periscope brought the distant
ship into sharp focus. With the magnification and
view, Rockham could clearly see the streaks of rust
trailing down from the scuppers along the old
cargo ship's deck. The rigging on the cargo booms
looked serviceable enough to offload the cargo the
SEALs had been sent to search for.

While Rockham was looking through the
periscope, Captain Wilson engaged in quiet conversation with one of his officers at the side of the

periscope platform. The other officer quickly moved up forward and to the port side of the sub. But as Rockham continued to study the cargo ship, he was oblivious to the activity around him.

Within a few minutes the captain reminded Rockham that it was time to bring the periscope down and resume their speed for the chase. With a quick apology for his absorption in what he'd been looking at, Rockham stepped off the platform and back away toward the rear of the control room.

"Down scope," Captain Wilson said.

"Down scope," the COB repeated as he operated the controls to bring the big periscope back into the submarine.

"Make your depth one-five-zero feet," Captain Wilson said. "Ahead two-thirds."

As the crew repeated his commands and adjusted the speed and depth of the submarine, the captain walked over to Rockham and said, "I certainly hope you were as much impressed by the target as I was when I first saw her."

"She isn't much to look at, Captain," Rockham replied. "But we're a lot more interested in what she might have inside her than what she looks like."

"Ah," Wilson said with a smile. "Good looks aren't as important as a good heart in your book, are they?"

"Not really in this case, sir," Rockham said with a big grin of his own. "In this case we expect to find a pretty black heart on the inside of that ugly exterior. But only if she does what she's supposed to as far as anchoring tonight."

"Well, I can tell you that she's following the same course to reach Muhammad Qol that she set yesterday."

As the captain was talking, the officer he'd spoken to earlier came back holding a clipboard. Taking it from him, Wilson lifted the stiff, cardboard security cover over the sheets of paper it held. After glancing over the pages, he lowered the cover and said, "Accompany me to my stateroom, please, Mr. Rockham."

Rockham followed the captain down to the second deck until they were forward of the enlisted mess and just across from the officers' wardroom. The captain entered his stateroom and held the door open for Rockham. It was the only private quarters on the sub, and it allowed the two men to have a private conversation without having to clear out a compartment or the officers' wardroom.

The stateroom was roughly ten feet long and eight feet wide, but a combination closet/desk unit took up most of the compartment. On the outside bulkhead there were a pair of seats with a small table between them.

Sitting at the table, Captain Wilson set the clipboard down and invited Rockham to take the other seat. Folding the security cover back on the clipboard, the captain flipped the pages until he came to a specific one, then pushed the open clipboard toward the SEAL.

"It looks like your luck is holding, Mr. Rockham," he said. "While we had the periscope up, I had the communications shack put up the antenna and get us the most recent message traffic. This one specifically refers to you."

Rockham, who'd been reading, looked up. "This says that the play was successful and the game play should continue," he said.

"That tells me that the *Pilgrim's Hope* will be looking for an anchorage tonight because her pier is unavailable," Captain Wilson explained. "At our present course and speed, the *Pilgrim's Hope* will be pulling into the channel south of Dungunab Bay about 1840 hours local time. That should give any pilgrims on board plenty of time to take local transportation to the village for evening prayers at the mosque. Since it's the Muslim holy day now, they probably won't be coming back this evening."

"That follows the outline we were given during our briefing," Rockham said.

"So what time will you want to launch, Mr. Rockham?"

"We want to start our assault late in the midwatch, sir," Rockham said. "About 0300 hours local time. Part of our insertion plan will center around just where the target anchors. We've been told that the best anchorage is on the landward side of Mukawwar Island, so that's where we'll plan on the target being when we go in."

"That's not going to be something we can help you with, Mr. Rockham," Wilson said. "The hundred fathom line is about eighteen miles offshore in the Dungunab Bay area. The closest I can bring the *Oklahoma* in to shore is a point about two miles southeast of Angarosh Island. That will keep us clear of the reefs, but we'll be in less than three hundred feet of water. Not a very comfortable position for an attack submarine.

"The Sudanese navy is not exactly a major threat to us. From our intel, they have maybe four operational coastal patrol craft that they've received from the Iranians over the years. And they've been cannibalizing others for spares to keep at least a few of them running. The biggest ordnance they mount is a 20mm cannon, and their antisubmarine warfare equipment may consist of a box of hand grenades and a fish locator, so as I say, they aren't exactly much of a threat to us.

"Aircraft are more of a problem, but the nearest airfield is seventy-five miles to the south at Port Sudan. I don't intend for us to be on the surface long enough to be even a blip on anyone's radar. So we'll launch you and your men just off the Angarosh Reef. The depth across the reef averages eighty to one hundred and sixty feet, so you won't have any trouble with your boats. But the launch point still puts you and your men about twelve miles from the landward side of Mukawwar Island."

"That should still be fine, sir," Rockham said. "It would take our Zodiacs about an hour to cross the water from that launch point to the northern point of Mukawwar. I don't want to have my team swim more than a mile or so maximum if I don't have to. It would take us an estimated seventy minutes to

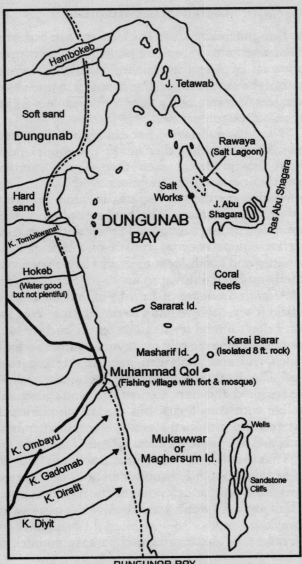

DUNGUNAB BAY

cover a mile across the reefs. If we had to swim much over about two miles, we would breathe down our rigs and use them up before we could complete a return trip. The problem is, we won't know exactly where the *Pilgrim* is anchored until we pass around the point of the island."

"That isn't something I can help you with either, I'm afraid, Mr. Rockham. There is no position where the *Oklahoma* will be able to get a sight line with the landward side of Mukawwar."

"I understand that, sir," Rockham said. "I've been going over the charts and I can't see any way around just going in and looking. Once we find the *Pilgrim*, we can move in to within a mile in relative safety. Our outboards are very quiet, and the Zodiacs have a low silhouette. The chance of our being spotted from the target is pretty slim. Our worst problem will be a chance encounter with a fishing boat."

"That shouldn't be much of a risk, Mr. Rockham. The government of Sudan is being overrun with Muslim zealots. Today is the beginning of their holy day, their day of worship. Most likely, any fishermen in the area wouldn't chance angering the local mullahs by working on the sabbath—no matter how much Sudan can use the food. No, the timing for the *Pilgrim's* arrival is one real stroke of luck."

"I hope it isn't the only one we have. But our plans don't call for luck."

"It's just a nice thing to have," Wilson said with a chuckle.

"Yes, sir," Rockham agreed. "But to go back to

your question about timing. Given a seventy minute swim, and about another hour to get to the dropoff point in the Zodiacs, means leaving the *Oklahoma* at 0050 hours. Add in an extra twenty minutes of traveling time to cover any contingencies and glitches in launching, and we should be good to go at 0030 hours."

"That gives you somewhere around eight hours to get ready, Mr. Rockham," Wilson said. "We expect the *Pilgrim* to anchor in between three and four hours for their people to make evening prayers. I'll put the antenna up at 2100 hours to see if we can't receive any updated intelligence on the target's location. Someone in D.C. wants you and your people aboard that cargo ship rather badly. I would not be surprised if they have additional assets assigned to this mission that we have no idea about.

"One advantage the distance from shore gives us, Mr. Rockham," Wilson went on. "We'll be over the horizon for anything less than fifty feet tall. Our sensors will tell us if there's any radar with a mast higher than that, but I wouldn't expect anything. The only ship we know of with radar is the *Pilgrim's Hope*, and we'll be screened from her by Mukawwar Island. So we'll be able to surface to launch you and your boats."

"That will simplify things quite a bit, sir," Rockham said. "It will not only keep us from having to use our breathing rigs to launch from under the surface, it will make things much faster since we won't have to use the escape locks."

"I thought it would meet with your approval, Mr. Rockham," Wilson said with a grin as he started to get up from his seat. As he stood, Rockham got to his feet too.

"I'll let you get back to your people, Mr. Rockham," the captain said. "I'm sure you'll want to discuss this new information. In the meantime, my people will make the *Oklahoma* a deep shadow in the water to that freighter."

"Thank you, Captain," Rockham said before leaving.

CHAPTER 19

★ ★ ★ ★

The *Oklahoma City* had been following the cargo ship for hours with little change. Now the target was entering the waters south of Dungunab Bay. The single channel leading through the reefs to the north of Mukawwar Island was a mile wide, tapering to a half mile on its landward end. As the *Pilgrim's Hope* passed through the channel, the *Oklahoma* lost the last of its sonar contact with her in the noise of the reef.

About twenty minutes later the sonar watch reported hearing heavy machinery noises, like the kind an anchor pulling a heavy chain from the chain locker would make. The sound was brief, but it was enough to tell the men aboard the *Oklahoma* that their target had come to rest for the evening.

The way the SEALs handled the wait until launching time reflected the quality of their training. The last few hours before going into a hazardous situation can be wearing on a man if he lets the tension build up and get to him. The SEALs all handled the wait in their own way, but they shared some of the same preaction habits.

The leadership of the unit, Rockham and Daugherty, as well as their leading NCOs, Monday and Ferber, spent the time going over the operational plan, making sure they hadn't missed a point while at the same time not picking the plan to death. Fine-detailing an operational plan didn't make much sense. It was an old military axiom that no plan survived contact with the enemy, and the leaders of the SMD didn't feel their plans were any different. Things such as emergency communications procedures, the breakdown of a breathing rig or a boat motor, or even early contact with a local, had all been covered in their training and emergency action drills. The points regarding primary and secondary emergency rendezvous locations, emergency escape and evasion provisions, and other details were discussed and studied.

The primary plan was flexible. The SEALs could even take their Zodiacs into the village of Muhammad Qol if they needed to. That would only increase their planned boat insertion from twelve miles to eighteen. But they couldn't finalize the insertion times until they had the location of the target. And they wouldn't get that until they got to the landward side of Mukawwar Island and saw whether the *Pilgrim's Hope* was anchored there. There would be only one freighter in the area; all they had to do was find it.

Then came a real break for the SEALs. At 2100 hours local time, when the *Oklahoma City* put up her radio mast past the surface, the intelligence download they received gave them the answers to the last questions in their puzzle, and some very good news. Sunset had been only a few minutes after 2000 hours local time, and the satellite pictures that had been taken and were later transmitted to the *Oklahoma* were done sometime between 1915 and 2000 hours.

The setting sun on the left side of the pictures cast long shadows of objects on the land and anything that was above the surface of the water. The black shadow following the oblong object to the west of Mukawwar Island made its image even easier to find: the image of a 440-foot cargo ship sitting at anchor. They now knew the location of the *Pilgrim's Hope*.

The SEALs had also received intel from a HUMINT source right there on site. They didn't know who the source of the human intelligence was, and didn't want to know. But eyes on the ground had reported that not only had eight pilgrims left the ship, but ten crew members had as well.

That left a skeleton crew on the ship—between five and ten people, according to the original intel estimates. That made the number of possible non-hostiles aboard the target a more manageable number for the SEALs to handle. Rotating watches would only have one or two people on the bridge and in the engine room. Rockham had known their chances for a successful operation were good, otherwise he wouldn't have accepted the op. As the commander on site, he could have aborted the operation if he felt, in the final analysis, that the odds against his men were just too great.

Rockham speculated that whoever was in higher command, whether Captain Moisen or someone else, must have realized the possibility of an abort when they issued the authorization to Captain Wilson to use a missile on the target. This was a significant operation against a strategically important target—too bad that no one outside of a very few would probably ever hear of it.

Not that the men of the Teams did their missions for glory and fame. The men did what they had to in order to support each other. And now Rockham was going to tell his men just what the final word on the op was. Gathering up the new intelligence, he headed back down to the torpedo room and his SEALs.

As Rockham expected, the men paid attention to what he told them about the target and examined the photos and marked charts. For most of the members of the unit, the new intelligence didn't tell them anything more that would change their part of the operation. The planning was done by Rockham and Daugherty, with input from their chief and leading petty officer. If anyone had an idea or input, they were free to speak their piece. In the

Teams, everyone's opinion mattered—it was experience and knowledge, not just a rank, that made an operator—and a good officer listened to the operators. And there wasn't any question in any of the men's minds that Rockham was a very good operator.

Rockham, Daugherty, Monday, and Ferber all went over the final details. The fine weather on the surface had given them an excellent satellite picture of the target area. Just a handful of clouds were scattered in a north to south line on the far eastern side of the picture. That fine weather made for great visibility for pictures—and great visibility for anyone looking out over the sea as the SEALs came in.

For the insertion, the SEALs would have preferred a dark, cold, and cloudy night, with a drizzly rain, the kind that makes those who stand watch try to take cover rather than keep a lookout. But they wouldn't be able to wait for the weather to change. There was a time crunch on this op, and it was either go tonight or abort completely.

The final order for the men going in on the op was decided upon. The only two men who would not be going into the target ship itself would be Ed Lopez and Henry Lutz. They would be the coxswains for the two Zodiacs. They knew surface navigation, and had been the coxswains during training ops. Now they would have to stay with the Zodiacs, to extract the SEALs after the operation had been completed.

Ed Lopez had plenty of training and experience conducting navigation problems both on the sur-

face and underwater back when he was in SEAL
Delivery Vehicle Team Two. If anything, running a
Zodiac would be a lot easier than driving a Mark 8
SDV, the eight-boat all the Team guys loved to hate.
With Henry Lutz, the situation was different, and
in a way even more important. As one of the unit's
communications men, Henry would have his full
loadout with him, as would Lopez. But Lutz would
be packing along an HST-4 satcom rig with a KY-
57 encryption set as well as his MX300-R Motorola UHF radio.

Lutz would be able to relay information back to
the submarine if everything went wrong aboard the
target; for example, if Sukov couldn't use his own
satcom as the communications man with the boarding team, or the Motorolas all crapped out. It would
be up to Lutz to call back to the sub, or even Special
Warfare Group Two back at the Creek, to tell them
what had gone down. Though he wouldn't think
about it, Lutz could easily be the man who had to
call for the Harpoon missile that would take out the
target, with or without his Teammates aboard.

That situation would be extreme. The Teams
planned on how to deal with a worst-case scenario,
but no one ever dwelled on them. But each man
knew that the mission came first. If it wasn't important enough to have the SEALs called out on it in
the first place, they would have just sent in the
Marines.

So Lopez and Lutz would be going on the op, but
not boarding the target. That made the assault force
sixteen men broken down into eight shooter pairs.

Each of the two squads could break down into a pair of fire teams, the smallest unit that would conduct a clearing operation. The unit broke down as follows:

| First Squad | | Second Squad | |
Fire Team One		Fire Team One	
1 Greg Rockham	OIC	1 Shaun Daugherty	
+		+	
2 Mike Bryant	Point/Lead climber	2 Ryan Marks	
3 Dan Able	Breacher	3 Roger Kurkowski	
+		+	
4 John Sukov (Commo)	Hook man	4 Sid Mainhart	

Fire Team Two		Fire Team Two	
1 Mike Ferber	Leading NCO	1 Frank Monday	
+		+	
2 Pete Wilkes	Point/Lead climber	2 Larry Stadt	
3 Wayne Alexander	Breacher	3 John Grant	
+		+	
4 Jack Tinsley	Corpsman	4 Henry Limbaugh	
Ed Lopez	Coxswain	Henry Lutz (Commo)	

Every odd-numbered man would have an even-numbered man as his shooting partner. The Zodiacs would each carry a single squad, with fire team one riding the port side and fire team two on the starboard side. Though there were two hook and pole men, the unit would try and gain the main deck of the ship with a single caving ladder. The backup pole man would put up his hook if the first was compromised or failed. The single ladder had turned out to be the best way to get the whole team on the deck and ready to go in a coordinated manner.

So they were ready—the plans made, the gear checked, double-checked, and then checked again.

Mainhart was going over his weapon for what seemed like the fifth time. But he was brand new at this, and whatever it took to keep his head straight was fine with the rest of them.

Wayne Alexander was probably one of the better examples of how some SEALs coped with the stress of waiting for the go signal. He'd gone over each piece of his equipment meticulously. Even a spot of rust on his sledgehammer would be immediately polished and treated with oil.

The breacher's load was the heaviest, so each of the four breachers in the unit also happened to be among the strongest individuals in the unit. In addition to the sledgehammer, hooligan tool, and crowbar, a large set of bolt cutters had been added. One of the two breachers in a squad carried explosives, and the other packed along a Dupont instantaneous cutting torch and several boxes of rods, as well as a pair of goggles. The cutting torch would immediately ignite when the single tank was turned on and oxygen started flowing through the special rods. It could quickly burn its way through fairly thick steel. For first squad, Alexander had the cutting torch slung alongside the tool holsters on his pack frame.

One piece of breaching equipment was carried by each man in the squad. That equipment was a short length of steel water pipe. In case the men had to go through a watertight hatch on a ship that was held closed by dogs—handles that turned and wedged the hatch shut—each man would slip his piece of pipe over the dog handle. The extra leverage of the pipe, and the fact that one man would be on each handle, could make going through a water-tight hatch as fast as breaching a normal door.

So Alexander checked the pressure of the oxygen tank on his cutting torch, his shotgun, ammunition, flash-crashes, and the dozens of items each man carried. He paid attention to the briefing, had no questions to ask or suggestions to make, and just lay back on one of the open mats that were laid out. Within a few moments he was snoring.

The noticeable snoring was funny to Alexander's teammates, though they were by now almost used to it. No one ever wanted to share a compartment with Alexander on a deployment because of the noise. But the rumbling roar meant that everything was fine, and the tension level went down a bit more.

When the announcement came down that the mess had chow ready for any SEAL who wanted it, all of the men went up to the mess deck. It would be a long, hard night no matter what happened. And the SEALs knew that some of the best chow in the Navy was served on board the nuclear submarines.

Besides the joking around, there was no animosity between the SEALs and the submariners. Sid Mainhart had been a "bubblehead"—the derogatory nickname for submariners—less than two years earlier. The crew on board the submarine felt that the SEALs had been assigned an almost impossible job, to swim from rubber boats and take over an enemy-held ship. For the SEALs, the idea of serving a Navy career aboard a steel pipe, only seeing the sun and smelling fresh air every few months or so, sounded like the hardest job there was. Each group felt sorry for the other in their own way.

Except for Alexander, who didn't feel sorry for anyone, not when they were served good chow like what he was eating in the mess that night. The steaks had been frozen, and the corn was from a can, but that didn't matter. The food was hot, good, and there was plenty of it. After the meal, Alexander joined the rest of his Teammates back in the torpedo room—and promptly fell asleep again.

2221 ZULU
20° 50' North, 37° 24' East
Southeast of Angarosh Island, off the reef
Sudan
Red Sea

This was it—game time. This was the moment that all the training, hardship, sweat, and not a little blood, was supposed to earn for every man in the Teams. In the peacetime Navy the opportunity to go on a hot op, to see if all of the training and study worked, didn't come along every day. Operations were few and far between, even for the men of the Teams who were on the very sharpest edge of the knife that was the U.S. military. Now, the men of the Special Materials Detachment had a hot op, the second in as many years for many of them, and it was time to launch.

They had spent the last hour moving their gear up from the torpedo room to stack it in the passageway outside the sonar room. After all the equipment had been moved, a final inventory was done of every piece of gear. They would climb the short ladder through the weapons loading hatch and out onto the deck of the submarine when it came time to launch. Much of the gear had been carefully placed in bags, to be donned when up on the deck, or in the Zodiac. The hatchways were just too narrow for some of the SEALs to get through when burdened by all of their equipment.

Several crewmen from the submarine stood ready to help the SEALs prep and launch the Zodiacs. The man in charge of the sub's deck crew was the COB himself, Master Chief Chase Bonner. Most of the SEALs wouldn't have even known his name if they hadn't seen it on his uniform. No one on the submarines had called him by name within their hearing, he was always referred to by his title, COB.

But the COB had brought the wrench necessary to open up the line locker on the outside deck. And with him directing the sub crew up on the deck, the SEALs would be in very competent hands indeed. Commanding officers moved on and off a nuclear submarine more often than the highest ranking enlisted man aboard. The chief of the boat was someone who knew everything that had to be known to run a nuke boat. Launching a rubber boat from the deck would be a simple task for someone of his experience.

With a half hour to go, the area was "rigged for red"—the lights in the passageway changed to red lights so the eyes of everyone going out on deck could adjust to the darkness they would find topside. While they were waiting, an air bottle was rigged up on the deck with a long length of flexible hose. In case the CO_2 bottles in the Zodiacs didn't inflate them to capacity, the air hose would be able to finish the job.

In the control room, Captain Wilson had the sub brought to dead slow speed and up to periscope depth. The low light camera on the Type 18 periscope showed the same thing that he'd seen through the eyepiece—a large expanse of empty ocean. Even more important, the sensor package on top of the periscope head didn't detect any radar emissions in the area. With the local sea clear, Captain Wilson ordered the *Oklahoma City* to the surface—slow and easy.

Ryan Marks accompanied the COB and a sub crewman through the control room and up through the sail. Opening the bridge access hatch, the three men climbed down the ladder built into the side of the sail to the deck of the sub. While the COB and others were climbing down the sail, the weapons loading hatch was being opened up forward.

With the line locker deck wrench, Marks and the sub crewman opened the stern line locker and recovered the outboard motor fuel bladders. While they were opening the line locker, lookouts climbed up and into position on top of the sail. Captain Wilson and the XO were both up on the sail bridge, along with Lieutenant (jg) Dave Jane, the sub's supply officer, who was the officer of the watch.

While securing the fuel bladders, Marks carefully bled out the seawater and any air in the fuel lines. His Teammates were moving the first Zodiac up and onto the deck behind the weapons loading hatch. Then they removed the hoisting lines and went back to the hatch to haul up the second Zodiac and move it back into position. With the two Zodiacs up, the rest of the gear packages could be quickly brought up and lined up on deck.

The Zodiacs were picked up, carried aft of the sail, and laid out on deck. Ryan Marks and Dan Able set to work preparing them, while the rest of the SEALs formed an equipment-handling chain to move their bags aft as quickly as practical. The lines holding the rolled-up Zodiacs were cut and the hulls unrolled with the bow of the boat pointing to the port side of the submarine. Captain Wilson had the *Oklahoma City* running with the night breeze coming in on her port quarter and the sub's speed down to only about four knots.

The sea was calm and smooth. The small wake kicked up by the bow of the sub was greater than the few ripples coming across the water. The moon was a waning crescent, a little less than a quarter moon showing. But the clear night air and absolute lack of lights anywhere around had the stars and moon shining down on the dark sea like it was black glass. Even the color of the stars could be seen clearly, the few red giants seeming like minuscule red spots in the white-dusted heavens. It was easy to see just how astronomy had been born millennia ago not far from where the submarine moved across the water.

It was under that incredible sky that the SEALs

toiled to launch their boats and get their mission under way. The Zodiacs were quickly inflating as their CO_2 systems were activated. The transoms were secured into the boats and the gear bags put into place.

At the weapons loading hatch, Henry Limbaugh called out "Last item" as the final gear bag was brought out on deck. Though he'd spoken quietly, his voice sounded loud in the still night air. Limbaugh climbed out of the weapons loading hatch and joined his Teammates behind the sail for launching. The outboard motors were secured in place on the rigid transoms. The fuel lines were attached, the motors primed, and Lopez and Lutz were in the ready positions on board.

At the command from Rockham, the two Zodiacs were picked up and slipped into the water stern first, over the starboard side of the submarine. As soon as the first boat hit the water, Lopez pulled on the line and started up the outboard. Lutz did the same, his motor also starting on the first pull of the line. The running outboards quickly settled down to a quiet burbling, the noise suppression around the engines and on the exhausts working as it should.

Now the only thing holding the Zodiacs to the submarine were the bow and stern lines of the boats in the hands of sub crewmen on the deck. The SEALs climbed on board, Rockham standing for a moment and turning to the sail.

"Good luck, SEALs," Captain Wilson called down. "We'll be waiting for you when you get back."

Rockham snapped off a salute, which was returned by the captain. Rockham then stepped down and took up his position at the port bow of the first Zodiac. The crewmen let go of the lines and cast the Zodiacs off. As the boats with the SEALs aboard moved out toward the black shore barely visible as a bumpy line along the western horizon, the sub crewmen moved quickly back and down the weapons loading hatch. The COB went down the hatch last and secured it in place. At Captain Wilson's order, the sub made ready to dive. From the first moment that the weapons loading hatch opened to the second the submarine rigged for dive took all of seven minutes.

The two Zodiacs moved out across the sea, both coxswains following their plotted headings of 277 degrees. That would take them to a point off the northern end of Mukawwar Island. There was nothing for most of the SEALs to do for the next hour but ride the tubes and think. Not even Alexander was going to be doing any sleeping on this trip.

There was nothing to see, and little enough to feel. The smooth water made the wakes of the SEALs' boats stand out more than they would have liked, but they were moving as slowly as practical right now. The clear night was also working in their favor, as it was easy for the SEALs to see that no one at all was on the water around them. The black boats moved out across a black sea, the silver reflection of the moon rippling as their wakes washed across it.

The distant shoreline, only visible as a black void

that blocked the stars, didn't seem to be drawing much closer as the Zodiacs cruised on. Off to the left a taller shadow seemed to be rising from the sea. That was the seaward-facing sandstone cliffs of Mukawwar Island. But for the whole of the island, and the mainland shore miles farther to the west, there were no lights to be seen, none at all.

This was the third world in front of the SEALs. In fact, it could be considered the downhill side of the third world in some respects. Sudan had been racked by famine, drought, and civil war. There almost wasn't a functioning infrastructure for the country. On this northern shore there was no electric power grid to speak of, and a very limited road system. The complete lack of visible lights from the shore, or on the sea around them, was no surprise to the SEALs.

2315 ZULU
20° 52' North, 37° 12' East
North of Mukawwar Island
Northern Sudan
Red Sea

Rockham was pleased to see that they were running about ten minutes ahead of schedule when they pulled around the northern point of Mukawwar Island and hove to when the *Pilgrim's Hope* came into sight. When he raised his clenched fist in the hand signal to halt, Lopez immediately took the outboard out of gear and allowed the Zodiac to coast to a stop.

Immediately behind and to the starboard of the

first boat, Lutz saw Lopez bring his boat to a slow halt. As Lutz cut his forward power, the two Zodiacs drifted close together. When they came abreast, Mike Ferber reached out and took hold of the 14mm black nylon lifeline woven through grommets on the buoyancy tube of the second Zodiac. Sid Mainhart, at the port-side stern of the second Zodiac, did the same thing as Ferber and grabbed the lifeline of the first boat. Floating there, the two boats rocked slowly while Rockham and Daugherty watched the *Pilgrim's Hope* through binoculars.

Held by the anchor chain dropped from the bow, the freighter slowly drifted in the tide and rotated about the anchor point. The crescent moon was the only source of light, and it shone down from the island side of the ship. There were a few running lights illuminating the deck of the target, but only about half the number of lights that a craft of her size would normally have. But the electric lights illuminated the deck well enough for the SEALs, and the extra shadows cast by the missing lights would be put to good use.

What the two officers were doing was watching and timing the rotation of the ship about its anchor chain. It took about ten minutes for the stern of the ship to swing south, stopping when it was pointing roughly southwest. Then it slowly started to drift back and point to the west. With its stern pointing southwest, the port side of the target ship was completely in shadow from the moonlight, and it stayed that way for about ten minutes. That would be the point where the team would board her.

They had remained in position for about twenty minutes while the target was observed. The rest of the SEALs maintained a watch, covering all points of the compass around them. Larry Stadt and John Grant, on the starboard side of the second Zodiac, could see a few warm yellow lights to the west. The color and location of the lights identified them as probably being kerosene lamps in the village of Muhammad Qol, some miles to the west.

Rockham had observed the target boat to his satisfaction. But he had used up the cushion of time they had, as well as dipping into the time scheduled for their swim in to the boat. The total lack of any movement on the *Pilgrim's Hope*, as well as there not being anything visible on the water or island around them, made his decision an easy one. Putting his hand over his head, then waving it down and pointing, told Lopez to move out in the direction of the target.

The lack of movement and probable observation told Rockham that it seemed safe enough to move closer to the target in the boats. The rally point would remain the same, a small rock off shore to the northwest of Mukawwar. Once the Zodiacs had dropped off the swimmers, that rock was where they would go and wait for a signal from the target. If there was no problem with the radios, the Zodiacs could be either called in all the way to the ships or wait at the rally point while the swimmers came in to them.

The backup signals in case the radios failed were

through the use of chem lights or flares. A red chem light was the signal for the boats to wait at the rally point. A green chem light meant that the ship was secure and the Zodiacs could come in for a pickup. A red Mark 13 flare meant the mission was compromised and the boats should pull back to the secondary rally point, Mayeteb Island, a small rock sticking up from the reefs to the east of Mukawwar Island.

The boats were now slowly moving in toward the target. The carefully maintained outboards made little noise, even to the SEALs in the boats. The fact that the running lights were on aboard the *Pilgrim's Hope* told Rockham that at least the generator had to be running, and even that much engine noise would completely block out any sounds that could be heard from the Zodiacs.

Finally, Rockham raised his clenched fist again and brought the Zodiacs to a stop. Turning back to the men behind him, Rockham sat up and brought his arms up and crossed them over his chest, beating his fists against the top of his chest twice. The men, who were already wearing their assault loadouts, would now don the rest of their diving gear.

With practiced motions, the men pulled up gear bags and brought out swim fins, masks, and other gear. They were already wearing their UDT life jackets, but would also put on Secumar life preservers that could act as buoyancy compensators. The nomex flight suits were worn in place of wet suits since the local waters were relatively warm. But all of the armor, weapons, ammunition, and other equipment they were carrying made the buoyancy compensators absolutely necessary. The breachers with their heavy loadouts particularly needed additional buoyancy to properly swim underwater.

The Draeger LAR V rebreathers went on over the chest of each SEAL. The pure oxygen rebreathers were closed-circuit systems. That meant they didn't release bubbles into the water. Instead, pure oxygen was breathed in by the operator. The carbon dioxide in the operator's exhalations was chemically absorbed, and the oxygen used was replaced from a small green tank at the bottom of the pack.

The Draegers resembled a square black turtle shell on each man's chest, two corrugated rubber hoses leading up from the top of the shell and ending in a mouthpiece. It had taken a lot of training to use the Draegers properly and safely. The oxygen in the system was poisonous if the operator went too deeply underwater. At a depth of fifty feet the Draegers were only safe to use for ten minutes. At twenty feet down, the normal depth for use, they were good for 240 minutes of breathable gas.

Fully geared up and ready for the swim, and starting at the stern of the Zodiac, each man squeezed the shoulder of the man to his left. That was the signal he was good to go. The signal wasn't passed farther up until the next man was also good to go. When Rockham was squeezed by both the man to his right and to his left, he knew the whole boat was ready to dive. Turning out his fists, thumbs pointing to the sides, he gave the signal to enter the water. Starting at the stern of the Zodiac, each SEAL softly rolled back and slid off the tube, entering the black water with hardly a splash.

CHAPTER 20

★ ★ ★ ★

Once they were underwater, the SEALs were in their element. During their basic training, almost a full third of the time was spent learning how to operate underwater. Each SEAL knew exactly what he was supposed to do, and there was no confusion and very little wasted motion.

Rotating in the water to get their bearings, each SEAL found his swim buddy and quickly oriented himself to the rest of the squad. Starting from the outside of the formation and working inward, each SEAL snapped a buddy line to his swim buddy, when he was set to begin the dive. The six-foot length of thousand-pound test line with a snap and ring at each end, snapped to the man's rig, was the signal between them. The SEALs were proficient at not getting tangled in their buddy lines, and the signal quickly ran along the formation to the men at the center. The lines didn't connect more than two men together, and the middle of each one had a ring attached by a plastic tie to each end so it would break away if the lines did get jammed or tangled.

During planning, Rockham had decided to do a pole dive rather than swim the SEALs together on a lizard (derigging) line. The pole formation was more flexible and moved the entire unit together, delivering them on the target at the same time with all of their equipment intact.

For the pole dive, the SEALs would swim abreast, each squad extending out from the center, the whole unit swimming in line together. That was the best way to guarantee hitting the target in dark water, the width of the formation making up for any inaccuracies in the compass bearing.

Lining up in the water after having left both of the boats, the two squads joined up with the officers in the center of the formation. Mike Bryant would be the lead compass man, with Greg Rockham as his swim buddy and timekeeper. First squad extended out to the left of Bryant and Rockham. Shaun Daugherty and Ryan Marks were, respectively, the timekeeper and compass man for second squad, which extended out from their right.

Mike Bryant was carrying the attack board, the lanyard attached to the neck strap of his Draeger, down flat in front of him. The Benz magnetic compass at the top of the board, with its illuminated face, showed the directions clearly. Also attached to the board were a depth gauge and timepiece. By holding the board down flat in front of him and facing down while he was reading the dials, Bryant could hold a steady depth and course over the three-quarters of a mile they had to swim to the target.

Greg Rockham also kept track of the elapsed time from when they started swimming. As the line formations extended out, John Sukov, the primary breacher/ladder man and hook man for first squad, was at the far left end. Dan Able, who swam next to him, had the coil of caving ladder secured to his equipment, while Sukov carried his painter's pole with the boarding hook attached at the top. On the far right side of the formation were Roger Kurkowski and Sid Mainhart, respectively, the primary ladder and hook man for second squad, with a mirror image of the gear Able and Sukov had.

The choreography of arranging the swimming formation came easily only because of constant drilling and training. Within a few moments of hitting the water, the whole unit was in line and started out on their swim. The compass heading of 205 degrees was set and followed closely by Bryant. The long, deep kicks of the SEALs' swim fins drove the men through the water at a rate that covered a hundred yards in four minutes. The fact that the tide was with them increased their speed, so they were moving at one knot and actually covering a hundred yards in about three minutes.

The water was dark but very clear. The depth for the swim was fifteen feet, kept steady by Bryant's eye on his depth gauge. The crescent moon projected enough silvery light down into the water so the SEALs could make out the shapes of some of the men next to them. They were swimming well above the bottom, which was the reef almost 40 meters below them, and the bioluminescence of some of the smaller sea creatures moving along with them revealed flashes and glows of blue and blue-white light.

The bioluminescence, also called phosphorescence, came from the millions of plankton and other tiny sea creatures that moved along in the water. Some of these creatures were big enough that a shape could be made out, outlined by the light they created. Others were merely tiny flashes, invisible save for the light they made. The large volume of almost microscopic animals and plants in the water made it seem that the SEALs were swimming along in thin soup.

Some of the SEALs looked about them as they swam along, enjoying the show the sea put on. Others just swam along, kicking rhythmically, doing their job and not getting any particular fascination from it. Mike Bryant only had eyes for the attack board he held flat out below him. It was his swim buddy, Greg Rockham, who was able to keep an eye on what was going on in the surrounding waters.

Except for the dancing lights of the plankton and other tiny creatures, the SEALs didn't see much as they swam. The pelagic fish that had been discussed during their initial briefing weren't apparent. And high above the reef, they didn't see any of the colorful marine life that populated tropical reefs.

The penetrating moonlight cut through the gloom, but the wavering lights could cause the shadows to move and flow. Anyone with a good imagination could see whatever shapes they wanted to in the flowing waters around them. The SEALs had spent untold hours in the water, however, and they didn't let their imaginations run away with them.

Suddenly, Rockham recoiled in shock. Coming out of the shadows in front of them was a mouth—a mouth attached to a head. But that head had to be over six feet wide! And the gaping mouth was the size of a car hood.

Holy mother of God! he thought. Just what the hell was it? Bryant felt the jerk and pull on the buddy line between himself and Rockham. The jerk felt almost strong enough to break the plastic ties holding the line to its central ring. Then Bryant looked up and he too saw the gaping huge mouth coming slowly toward them.

The rest of the SEALs also responded to their officer jerking to a stop. One of the men—though later no one would admit to having been the one—screamed through his mouthpiece. The sound came out more as a dolphin's squeak than a human scream, but it did point out how startled the SEALs were. There had never been a recorded fish attack against a SEAL or UDT man during a combat operation—not even during the bloody days of World War II. But it looked like the men of the SMD would be changing that statistic.

The huge head was moving very slowly as it came closer. The mouth was a huge black oval with the phosphorescence of the waters flowing into it. It seemed like the monster had dozens of light-colored eyes surrounding a gaping mouth, with huge fangs lining the front of the jaws. The SEALs hung motionless in the water now, their weapons and explosives useless against such a leviathan of the deep. One of the SEALs' combat knives might make a dent in such a massive creature, but the blade probably wouldn't be long enough to even get through the skin.

As the SEALs hovered there, the massive face came closer and closer, then tilted downward and started to pass below them. Whatever the hell this thing was, it was the size of a city bus! This sure as shit wasn't any whale going by, Rockham thought. Not with spotted markings and a dorsal fin like—

Then the identity of the great fish popped into Rockham's mind. It was a whale shark, the largest member of the shark family. This one was probably on the far end of fifty feet long. The body was wider than two men, and the dorsal fin alone was taller than the biggest man in the unit.

But for all of its huge size and fearsome relatives, the whale shark was truly a gentle giant. It didn't care about the SEALs, couldn't have eaten them if it wanted to. Though its mouth was huge, the throat was small, only a few inches across. The massive mouth gathered in water loaded with the whale shark's food, the microscopic plankton glowing all about them, which bloomed around the waters of

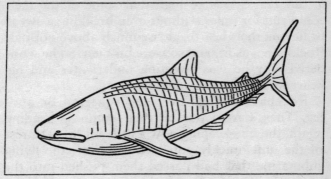

WHALE SHARK

the reefs and must have attracted the gigantic creature. The shark swam against the tide, the surge helping drive the plankton into its mouth.

As it slowly passed under them, the SEALs could see that the many "eyes" had actually been just the thousands of light-colored spots on the shark's skin. The mouth was just a smooth oval. The fangs had been nothing more than small fish darting about the giant's gaping maw.

Sport divers could spend their entire lives in the oceans of the world and never see the sight the SEALs just had. The monstrous tail of the whale shark, moved by muscles thicker than a human body, slowly stroked from side to side as the creature moved past the SEALs and on its way.

The Navy, it's not just a career, it's an adventure, Rockham thought.

SEALs trained for feats of physical endurance worthy of Olympic competitors. The level of fitness in the Teams was so high that some of the men could run for miles without even breaking a sweat or having their heartbeat rise much above normal. Rockham was fit, and so were his men. So he wondered why he was sweating underwater and his heart was racing like a trip-hammer.

Rockham reached over and squeezed Bryant's leg. They started out on their compass heading again, the timekeeping now a little bit off. The rest of the unit quickly got back into line, the living submarine that had passed them pushed into the back of their minds. Maybe it was a good thing that the missions of the SMD were so classified that none of the men could talk about them to outsiders. No one else would believe what had just happened anyway.

The kicking strokes continued, and the glowing particles in the water continued to move around. But now none of the SEALs were as complacent as they'd been earlier. There might have been a few more suspicious shadows flitting around in the gloom, and imaginations might have built a little more out of those shadows than before. One thing the swim had proven—imaginations had a hard time keeping up with reality when you were underwater.

They could hear the sounds of the sea around them. There were clicks, grunts, whistles, and burrs. All kinds of noises made by all kinds of critters. For the SEALs, the only sound they made was the rush of gas through the breathing hoses as they took in oxygen and breathed out carbon dioxide.

Then, faintly, there were other noises in the water. Faint mechanical noises.

The SEALs had already swum a half mile by Rockham's calculations. He now wanted to go up and take a tactical peek to see where they were in relation to the target. He touched Bryant's shoulder to get his attention. When Bryant looked up, Rockham held up a clenched fist, the signal to stop. Turning to his left, Rockham repeated the signal to Mike Ferber, the swimmer next to him. In turn, the signal was passed along down the left side of the formation.

On the right side, Bryant repeated the signal to Marks, who passed it along. Still in the water at a depth of fifteen feet, the entire unit held their position and waited. Tapping on Bryant's face mask with two of his fingers, Rockham gave the signal that he wanted to surface. This would be a combined effort between Rockham and Bryant, so the two men started to very slowly rise up toward the surface.

At about ten feet of depth, Rockham stopped and started to breathe down his rig. Taking a rapid series of short, shallow breaths, he was using up the oxygen in his Draeger breathing bag without actuating the demand valve that would have replaced the oxygen from the pressure tank. The Sofnolime CO_2 absorbent in the Draeger's scrubbing can took the moisture and the CO_2 out of Rockham's exhalations. The absorption of the CO_2, without the replacement of the O_2, caused the volume of gas, and buoyancy, of Rockham's Draeger to diminish.

Now the SEAL officer could very slowly rise up to within a few inches of the surface. He slowly turned, looking for the target or any sign of something that shouldn't be there. Off to the right a little he saw the glow of lights. Very slowly, Rockham barely broke the surface, just coming up enough so he could see the lights of the *Pilgrim's Hope*, not a hundred yards away to the right.

They were almost bang-on target. If they had continued swimming, the formation probably would have crossed under the shadow of the ship or come up to the anchor chain. Either way, they would have known they were there. Now Rockham watched the *Pilgrim's Hope* move in the tide and slowly rotate around her anchor chain. The ship was moving at the same rate he'd observed earlier, and the starboard side was slowly moving into shadow from the moonlight.

Breathing out through his face mask, Rockham let the bubbles rise as he emptied his lungs and made himself negatively buoyant. He slipped down with barely a ripple on the surface. Sinking, Rockham breathed his rig back up, letting the demand valve do its job and replacing the oxygen he had used. Coming back down to Bryant, he indicated the direction they had to go and held up two fingers—two minutes to go.

Moving down farther in the water, the two SEALs were back among their Teammates, passing the signal to go—a squeeze on the leg—down the line. Bryant set his course, and the SEALs set out swimming.

Only a few minutes later they all came to the shadow of the ship. They had arrived on target. The water got darker as they passed into the shadow cast by the old freighter. Slowly rising, the SEALs reached the bottom of the hull and could now make their way to the side. Slipping up to the starboard side, they made ready to remove their diving gear and begin the takedown.

When they reached the point where they would climb onto the ship, it was time to lay out the derigging line. At the far end of the formation, the two hook men, Sukov and Mainhart, reached into their equipment for bear-claw magnets. The powerful two-by-six-inch magnets would stick fast to the steel hull of the target. Before attaching them to the hull, a scraper was pulled from the men's gear to clean off a section. The barnacles, scum, and flaking paint made a cloud in the water as an area was cleared for the magnets.

Securing the end of the derigging line to one of the bear claws, the hook men swam along the formation toward the center. Once past the entire squad, the hook men attached another bear-claw magnet to the hull and secured the other end of the derigging line.

The painter's poles, with their hooks attached, hung down into the water from lanyards attached to the derigging line. Now each SEAL went through the gyrations of carefully removing his diving gear and attaching it to one of the loops in the derigging line. The two breachers who were carrying the caving ladders also moved to the center of the formation to derig and prepare to assist the hook man.

When the SEALs were all in position, the outside men unsnapped their buddy lines and passed them up to their swim buddies. Squeezing the arm of the next man in line conveyed that the men to the outside were ready to derig. When the signal reached Rockham and Daugherty, they sent two squeezes back down the line the signal to derig. The gloves each man wore made the removal of his equipment more clumsy than it could have been, but the protection the gloves gave the SEALs' hands from the cuts and abrasions they would otherwise suffer from the barnacles and sea life made it worth the trouble. The fact was, the *Pilgrim's Hope* seemed even rustier than the practice ship they had worked with back in Virginia, which rendered the hand protection even more welcome.

The lack of waves or surge in the water helped the SEALs when they removed their diving equipment underwater. They were only a few feet under the surface, and care was taken not to broach the water and break security. The last man in line sucked his Draeger empty of gas and secured it to the derigging line. As he headed for the surface, he grabbed the shoulder of the man in front of him, pulling him up. That way, from the outside in, all of the SEALs broke the surface together, all of them right up against the side of the ship.

Just before their heads came up out of the water, however, each SEAL pulled off his diving mask. No wet glass gleamed in the night, ruining the dull black camouflage paint each man had smeared on his face.

Rockham ran a quick head count, making certain that each man was ready and accounted for. Looking up along the hull of the ship, he led the SEALs to the designated climbing point, which was on the starboard side of the after well deck, just behind the superstructure in the center of the hull. The bulwark, a solid fence along the hull pierced only by small ports, surrounded most of the main deck and would have to be climbed to gain the after well deck. The eighteen feet of freeboard—the distance from the main deck to the waterline—could be easily covered by the painter's pole, without the pole even fully extended. When the SEALs practiced in the James River, the hook at the top of the pole had been checked to be certain it could slip over the top of the bulwark back.

At Rockham's signal, John Sukov, covered by Dan Able, moved away from the cover of the hull to set the hook and caving ladder in place. The ladder had been secured to the hook at the top of the painter's pole, and the pole extended far enough to reach the edge of the main deck. The locking mechanisms were secured and the pole was as rigid as it had to be.

With Able, his shotgun up, covering him, Sukov raised the pole and set the hook down on the edge of the deck. No noise followed the setting of the hook or pulling away of the pole. The two-pronged padded hook slipped out of the end of the pole, the rubber tubing securing it in place stretching and slipping off the pole.

Lowering the pole, Sukov secured it to the end of the caving ladder with a snaplink, then swam back to the side of the ship. Rockham and Bryant were slipping off their swim fins and securing the last of their gear before climbing the ladder. Holding onto the caving ladder with his left hand, Bryant did a quick touch check of the location of each of his weapons. It looked like a strange parody of a Catholic cross, as Bryant touched his slung MP5K-N, hip holster, knife, and ammunition pouches.

Pulling up his MP5K-N, Bryant made sure the suppressor was screwed firmly onto the muzzle. The folding stock that extended out along the right side of the weapon was in the closed position. This was a new, short version of the MP5 submachine gun, with a solid folding stock rather than the sliding stock the rest of the SEALs had. Later this version of the MP5 would become known as the MP5 PDW, or Personal Defense Weapon, but for now it was just the Navy K model with a folding stock.

Bryant pulled back the cocking knob of the submachine gun and let it slide forward. That stripped a fresh round from the magazine and chambered it. Pulling the bolt back to load a round helped drain the water from the weapon's barrel and suppressor. Any water still remaining in the suppressor would actually help lessen the sound of the first shot.

Bryant's experience handling an MP5 while also holding onto a rappeling rope during their certification operation had motivated him to look for a new sling. One of the chiefs who'd taught the unit how to do boat takedowns, a plank owner of SEAL

Team Six who had helped develop the technique, came up with a new sling design of his own that Bryant adopted. It consisted of a pair of shoulder straps with a cross strap around the chest and back. A special snaplink on the front of the sling attached to a small D ring strapped to the back of the MP5K-N. With the stock open or closed, the weapon could be easily operated with either hand. And if dropped, it just hung down on the chest, allowing both hands to be used for whatever had to be done.

It was a good system, and most of the SEALs were interested in picking up one for themselves. But at the time, they were being made only on a custom basis. In fact, for this operation only Bryant and second squad's lead climber, Ryan Marks, were armed with MP5K-Ns and the new slings.

Their weapons locked and loaded, Bryant and Rockham were ready to climb. There was no sign from the ship that they'd been spotted, or even much sign that there was anyone aboard the rusted hulk. But as the point man, it was Bryant's job to make sure the deck was clear before Rockham, the officer in charge, followed him to the deck.

Under the quarter moon off the northern coast of Sudan, the takedown and capture of the *Pilgrim's Hope* had just begun.

CHAPTER 21

★ ★ ★ ★

0054 ZULU
20° 54' North, 37° 12' East
After well deck, port side
Pilgrim's Hope
West of Mukawwar Island
Northern Sudan

Steadily climbing up the caving ladder, Mike Bryant kept his eyes on the railing only a dozen feet over his head. The rest of the unit waited at the bottom of the ladder. Greg Rockham held onto the ladder and waited for Bryant's signal for him to begin his climb. The other SEALs were tucked into the side of the ship, concealing themselves in the shadows.

The SEALs had all removed their swim fins and attached them to the bottom rungs of the caving ladder with snaplinks. Mainhart and Kurkowski had hooked their painter's pole and caving ladder to the derigging line as the last pieces of gear to be left underwater. With everyone against the skin of the ship, there was very little chance of being discovered. The one Teammate in harm's way was Bryant, who would be on the ship alone for several moments.

Speed was the key for this part of the takedown, which was why all of the SEALs had derigged and removed their swim fins. But the speed of climbing the caving ladder wouldn't come into play until Bryant had signaled Rockham to follow him. Once Rockham was on the deck and had made fast the hook, he would signal the rest of the SEALs to board.

Even though it wasn't a hot night, Bryant was sweating as he climbed up the last few rungs of the caving ladder. The tubular aluminum rungs felt slick against his wet glove in spite of the rough "no-slip" tape wrapped around each rung. The fingertips of the gloves had been cut away for sensitivity, but he wasn't worried about losing his grip or about the gloves slipping off. In addition to developing upper body strength for just this kind of exertion—climbing a caving ladder—the SEALs also built up hand strength through exercise. And Bryant had very strong hands.

Just short of exposing his head above the edge of the bulwark, Bryant stopped and pulled up his MP5K-N. In a rock-solid grip, he held the weapon with his right hand, snapped off the safety selector with his thumb and moved it two detents, switching the weapon to full auto fire. Long hours of practice and thousands of rounds fired downrange had made Bryant extremely competent with his weapons.

A squeeze and release of Bryant's finger would

send a single shot through the suppressor and into his target. A longer squeeze would keep the weapon firing at a cyclic rate of nine hundred rounds per minute, fifteen rounds a second. Anything on that deck that he saw, he could hit.

With the silver muzzle of the stainless steel suppressor following his line of sight, Bryant lifted his head up and reconned the deck. Nothing met his sight but a gray bulkhead to his left, pierced by an open oval hatchway and a round porthole. To his left front rose up the mechanical bulk of a deck winch used to power the boom rig that towered above it and extended out to the right. Directly in front was a wide expanse of mottled, rusted deck, a ladder leading up to the boat deck on the far side of the winch, and the raised platform of the number four hold hatch cover. To the right were a number of scattered oil drums, some crates, machinery, pipes, lines, and cables. This was not a neat ship.

But nothing moved. There wasn't much in the way of sound except for a low rumbling that was felt more than heard. The noise the SEALs had heard underwater during the approach was probably the generator running to keep the deck lights on. Except for the creaks and groans of a ship turning in the current, there was nothing to draw the attention of the SEAL, or the weapon in his hand.

After a minute had passed, Bryant continued his climb. He quickly negotiated the last few rungs of the caving ladder, slipped over the coaming of the bulwark and, at his most exposed, landed on the deck in a crouch. Bryant now stepped over to the side and knelt next to several oil drums that concealed him from the view of anyone at the stern of the ship. Again he made a slow, careful scan of the deck. The superstructure he faced was four decks tall above the main deck. Two sets of ladders were on both the port and starboard sides, each ladder leading up to another that continued on to the upper decks.

No light shone through any of the open hatchways or portholes Bryant could see. In the long moment that he knelt on the deck, he could feel his heart beating as fast as if he'd just completed a run. His mouth was dry. But nothing distracted the SEAL's attention from everything going on around him. He knew that the lives of his Teammates, and the success of the mission, depended on his noticing anyone on the ship before they could spot him.

Satisfied that his security check had shown the area to be clear, Bryant slipped back over to where the caving ladder hook was snagged on the edge of the bulwark—the raised wall that protected the edge of the deck. Looking over the side, he leaned out and waved up with his left hand, his right still holding out his weapon and pointing it out across the deck. Feeling tension on the caving ladder, Bryant knew that Rockham had begun his climb. Now Bryant's job was to provide 360 degree security while his officer climbed onto the target.

Bryant swept the deck with his eyes and the muzzle of his weapon as Rockham slipped over the bulwark to crouch beside him. Even with his finger carefully off the trigger, Bryant could have brought fire onto anything within his sight in less than half a second. He knew that because he'd proven it over and over again during practice drills.

Without a word spoken, Rockham looked about the deck quickly, then leaned over where the hook was secured, making sure it was solidly in place where it had snagged over the rail at the top of the bulwark. Though it appeared secure, Rockham slipped a short safety line around it and tied the hook off to a bulwark stanchion—an angled beam connecting the bulwark to the deck. So far, the fact that there was a solid bulwark instead of the fence-like lifeline was the only difference the SEALs had seen between the *Pilgrim's Hope* and the ship they'd practiced on back in the James River.

Rockham pulled up a red chem light strapped to his knife sheath. Tearing open the package, he bent the soft plastic tube until the glass vial inside shattered. Shaking the tube created a soft, red light. Waving that light over the side, down the bulwark enough to block it from any view of the decks, Rockham signaled the rest of his SEALs to board.

Quickly, the men climbed aboard, fanning out in a semicircle as they arrived on deck. Meanwhile, Bryant maintained a steady watch on the superstructure. The open hatches and portholes were the most likely place a crewman's face or body might appear. If someone did spot the SEALs getting aboard, the chances were good that Bryant could nail them with a suppressed shot before they could raise an alarm. His MP5K-N held tightly with both hands, the weapon pushed out against the securing sling, Bryant scanned the decks with his eyes and the muzzle of the suppressor.

The paint on the *Pilgrim's Hope* was even more splotched and rusted than the practice ship in Virginia. That pointed to a slovenly crew, one that probably wouldn't be very sharp at standing watch, if they didn't sleep through their watches. But that kind of assumption could kill people in the SEALs' line of work, and so as each man came on board, he added to the security perimeter being set up around the boarding point.

The first set point for the SEALs was at the corner of the ladder next to the number four cargo hatch. There, the SEALs would establish their perimeter and prep the remainder of the gear, removing the waterproofing from their communications while taking any rebriefing Rockham thought they would need.

Any rebriefing would be short, since the ship was like a ghost town. If it wasn't for the few running lights illuminating the deck, and the sound of the generator, the ship would have appeared an abandoned hulk. The SEALs didn't expect anyone to ambush them from the shadows, but they were prepared to shoot back if necessary at the first sign of danger.

With the team all in place and a final head count made by Rockham, it was time to split the assault elements. Rockham and his squad would go up the port ladders to the bridge deck. Daugherty would move to the starboard side of the ship and go down to take the engineering spaces. Once the two primary targets were secure, the ship couldn't send out a distress signal over the radio or start up her engines to run. Then, from the top and the bottom of the superstructure, the SEALs would sweep from deck to deck to fully secure the ship.

The primary target for the takedown was the bridge. That was the command center for the ship. Most likely they would find the ship's master either on the bridge or in his stateroom. If he wasn't on the bridge, they would secure the ship's controls and command of the vessel. On the starboard side toward the stern of the bridge would be the chart room. There, they would find most of the intelligence on the ship's route and probably the bulk of her papers.

Once the bridge was secure, Rockham would remain there with John Sukov and his commo gear. The rest of the squad would continue the clearance of the next deck down, the cabin deck, which was where the ship's officers slept.

On the boat deck, below the cabin deck, they would find the bulk of the ship's complement, probably a number of the guards, and crew for the missiles as well. The trouble was, if there were any pilgrims on board, they would most likely be in the boat deck as well. And the last thing Rockham wanted to deal with during a hostile takedown was a hostage situation.

So, for as long as possible, the SEALs would conduct a "soft assault." They would remain clandestine in their penetration of the ship's spaces, and try to retain the element of surprise for as long as possible. If they were compromised, the whole team would immediately go into the standard assault mode, in which they'd move through the ship quickly and deliberately. But with the chance of innocent bystanders being aboard—whether the ship's crew or the pilgrims—even a standard assault would be complicated. Targets would have to be chosen with care, and taken out as surgically as the SEALs were capable of doing.

First squad headed for the upper decks and the bridge. Second squad went over to the port side passage and prepared to take control of the engine room. The late hour and supposedly safe mooring point had combined to give the crew a sense of safety. There were no guards visible and only the normal running lights on to illuminate the deck, but the SEALs would not be taking anything for granted.

To help control prisoners, each man in the unit had learned a basic set of Arabic commands: "stop/halt"—*qiff*; "you are a prisoner"—*inta sajeen*; "quiet"—*haedi*; and "hands up"—*irfaa idak*. None of the SEALs felt their linguistic abilities were going to get them around town anytime soon. The simple fact that they were so heavily armed would no doubt make more of an impression on the crew of the *Pilgrim* than anything they said—no matter how badly. As for the guards, if they were armed, the chances were the SEALs wouldn't be doing much talking to them.

The practice on the James River was going to pay off now. The superstructure of the ship was confusing at the best of times, and the SEALs had no time to waste just looking around. The captain had his stateroom up on the cabin deck and not on the bridge deck above it. It was likely he was using the same cabin as on their practice ship—it was one of the only two aboard that had its own head facilities, and it was directly below the bridge.

The radio room was also on the cabin deck, on the port side of the ship at the center of the passageway. The upper deck housed the bridge and the chart room. The three locations that would have a watch stander in place were the bridge, the engine room, and the radio room. Those watch standers would probably be the only people awake on the ship at this hour of the morning.

To avoid contact for as long as possible, Rockham was going to take first squad up the outside accommodation ladders to the bridge deck. This left the SEALs exposed to observation by anyone out on deck, but it was also the fastest and safest route as far as being discovered by anyone inside the superstructure.

The ladders on the aft end of the superstructure were simply sets of steel stairs leading up one deck at a time. A ladder opened up on the open weather deck of the next higher deck. The next ladder leading up would be closer to the centerline of the ship. The final bridge deck was only about half the size of the deck below it—the cabin deck—and they would have to cross the long expanse of weather deck along one of the highest points of the ship.

Right now the SEALs were on the main deck.

The first ladder would lead them up to the boat deck, so named because of the lifeboats that lined each of the outboard sides. To the front left of the first ladder, the open maw of a main deck passageway gaped in front of them, a few dingy electric bulbs illuminating the long passageway.

This was the deck where the crew had their quarters. Over a dozen hatchways, closed with standard wooden doors that could be found in any old U.S. home, lined the sides of the passageway. But the SEALs were going to deal with the individual crew cabins now. The main target was the securing of the bridge deck.

As first squad set up their assault train to go up the ladder, Wayne Alexander and Jack Tinsley brought up the back of the formation and maintained rear security. While Alexander looked out across the main deck toward the stern of the ship, Tinsley looked forward and aimed his weapon down the passageway in front of them. They kept a careful watch to either side, forward down the port side main deck passageway, and especially behind the squad, covering their Teammate's "six."

Assaulting up a ladder was more complicated than moving down a passageway, but the technique was about the same. Mike Bryant was the point man in the number one position in the squad, and right behind him was his shooting partner, Lieutenant Rockham.

The ladder was only a dozen steps tall, so the eight men of the squad would cover its entire length. When all were set for the assault to the next level, the squeeze was passed up from Tinsley in the rear to Bryant. With a quick glance over his shoulder, Bryant quickly stepped up the length of the ladder, not quite at a run but moving quickly.

As they headed up the first ladder, the entire squad maintained body contact with each other. When Bryant came close to the top of the ladder, he slowed and moved aside so Rockham could come up next to him. As Bryant moved to the right at the top of the ladder, Rockham moved forward and to the left to cover the port side. Speed was everything in this kind of assault, but not at the expense of security.

Because of the layout of the deck, Bryant had to step back to go around the end of the next ladder before he could cover the rest of the weather deck on his side. The port side passageway of the boat deck opened up underneath the next ladder leading up. Only four cabin doors could be seen down the left side of the passageway, but several other passageways opened up along its right side.

Dan Able settled down in a crouch next to the end of the ladder and aimed his suppressor-equipped MP5-N down the left side of the passageway in front of them. John Sukov, Able's shooting partner, took the other side of the passageway, moving in behind Rockham and aiming his weapon down the right side.

The other four SEALs rapidly moved into position at the base of the ladder leading up to the next deck. Lining up the head of the train, the point man for the next deck would be Pete Wilkes, with Mike Ferber as his number two. The steel plates of the deck had long since radiated away the heat of the hot African summer sun. But despite the relative cool of the night, a number of SEALs were sweating from the tension of the assault.

Sweat beaded on dark-painted foreheads before gathering up in larger drops and running down the SEALs' faces. The men hardly registered the discomfort, however, since they were concentrating on their part of the task at hand. As the train assembled to go up the next ladder, it became Rockham's and Bryant's turns to be at the rear of the formation. Bringing up the back of the train meant that they were now responsible for their Teammates' rear security.

Not a word was spoken as the men continued with their mission. Once the train was stacked up, Rockham and Bryant took their places at the tail. Then they started the squeeze signal that went up the stack to Ferber and Wilkes. With Wilkes leading the way, the train started up the next ladder.

Moving up the ladder, Wilkes repeated Bryant's action as he slowed just below the lip of the ladder to let Ferber pull up alongside. The two SEALs looked out across a short open expanse of weather deck to the aft bulkhead of the cabin deck. The rest of the squad came up and immediately set up a perimeter security, covering both sides, behind them, and upward to the next deck. The deck they were on held one of the priority targets for the team. But it would be Rockham's decision whether to move on to the bridge and secure it first, or to move out and secure this deck.

Wilkes had moved up as soon as he'd reached the deck, going forward half a dozen steps before crouching down next to the ladder leading up to the bridge deck. The open passageway in front of him had only one hatchway on the right side. But on the left side there were four hatchways, also closed with regular wooden doors. The only difference in this passageway compared to those they had already passed was the line of light that could be seen glowing underneath the third door forward on the left.

As Ferber took up his position on the left side of the passageway entrance, Wilkes made the "enemy seen" signal by spreading his nonfiring hand over his face. Then he pointed to his eyes in the "I see" signal and pointed down the passageway.

Nodding his understanding to Wilkes, Ferber leaned out and looked down the passageway as the rest of the squad continued moving up and across to set up the train on the next ladder. Wayne Alexander and Jack Tinsley moved up behind Wilkes and Ferber to increase the security at the passageway. As Rockham and Bryant came up the ladder, Ferber repeated the "danger" and "I see" signal to Rockham, then pointed to Wilkes.

Rockham moved up behind Wilkes and followed the SEAL's pointing left hand to the line of light under the door halfway down the passageway, which was like a warning beacon. According to what they'd learned aboard their practice ship, that light was in the radio room—which was where they'd expected to find someone up on radio watch.

Now Rockham had to make a decision—to secure the bridge and come back down to take the radio room, or to secure the radio room first, and whoever had that light on, and then assault the bridge. There was no movement in the room that could be seen—no shadow crossed the line of light. Rockham decided to continue with the mission as they had planned, but to hedge his bet a little.

Lifting his nonfiring hand to his face, he held it vertically in the "set security" signal, looking like a very dangerous Curly of the Three Stooges blocking a finger poke. Then he pointed to the passageway in front of them and to Ferber and Wilkes. The two SEALs were to hold their position and set security on the passageway. Once the rest of the squad had set up their train and continued with the assault, Ferber and Wilkes could move to whatever situation suited them best. Both men nodded their understanding to Rockham.

This course of action split up Rockham's forces before they reached their first major objective. But with the sign that someone might be on watch in the radio room, leaving some security to watch the hatchway was the best thing to do. They had considered this possibility during their planning sessions back at the Creek. If the assault of the bridge went badly, Ferber and Wilkes could be told over the MX-300 radios to take down the radio room on their own. If the assault on the bridge went well,

Ferber and Wilkes could back up the assault on the radio room from their position.

There was supposed to be a ladder at the back of the bridge that ran down to the cabin deck, ending just aft of the captain's stateroom. The rest of first squad would continue with the takedown by coming down that ladder and taking the captain in his quarters if he hadn't been found on the bridge. Then the radio room would be secured.

Now it was Bryant back in the point position for the final ladder leading up to the bridge deck. The train lined up with Wayne Alexander and Jack Tinsley back in the rear guard position. Dan Able and John Sukov took up the number three and four positions behind Bryant and Rockham. Tinsley started the squeeze signal going up the train. When Bryant felt the squeeze on his shoulder from Rockham, he led off up the ladder.

The top of the ladder to the bridge ended on a wide and long section of weather deck. A raised ventilation casement in the center of the deck was about two feet tall and had six angled hatch covers on top of it. Several of the hatch covers were propped open for ventilation, but no light shone up from underneath them. In the center of each hatch was a circular scupper, also with its cover clamped down. The open hatches weren't a threat, just another reason for the SEALs to remain as stealthy as possible.

The raised area wasn't a concern at the moment. With all of the hatches closed, whatever was below couldn't reach the SEALs anyway. As soon as he reached the top of the ladder, Bryant moved forward and crouched down next to the raised platform, Rockham directly behind him.

Able and Sukov came up the ladder and immediately moved to the right side, crouching down behind the center of the ventilation casement. Able turned and aimed his weapon down the ladder that came up on the starboard side of the bridge deck, leading up from the opposite side of the cabin deck. Pushed up solidly on Able's back was his shooting partner, Sukov, who held his position as rear guard, aiming his weapon back down the ladder the SEALs had just cleared. Both men had a clear field of view back out across the stern deck of the ship, where nothing moved at all.

As per their original plans, fire team two was going to assault the bridge from the starboard side, while fire team one came in from the port side. Only Alexander and Tinsley were left from fire team two; Ferber and Wilkes were holding security on the cabin deck. But the tactics were to continue to follow the plan, so Alexander and Tinsley moved out to the starboard side of the raised ventilation casement. Alexander crouched low at the corner and aimed his weapon, while Tinsley aimed his weapon around the raised ventilation cowl on the forward part of the casement.

Reaching around behind him with his nonshooting hand, Alexander passed the squeeze signal, indicating to Tinsley that he was ready. In turn, Tinsley passed the silent squeeze signal back up the train. This would be the last communication between the two fire teams until after the bridge was taken.

When Rockham received the squeeze, he waved his hand, chopping down with the edge and pointing in the signal to go forward, then squeezed Bryant's shoulder to pass the same message along. Tinsley and Alexander began to move forward along the starboard side of the bridge deck. Able and Sukov fell in behind Rockham as Bryant went forward and crouched just behind the tall circular funnel that rose up in the center of the deck, just behind the bridge area itself. This was where the two teams would lose sight of each other. As the train built up behind Bryant, Alexander and Tinsley waited. The plan was that fire team one would initiate the takedown of the bridge, fire team two coming in after the initiation.

Just past the stack, right in front of Bryant, was the hatchway that opened up to the bridge deck wheelhouse. Alexander and Tinsley had to pass around the ladder that led up to the flying bridge to reach the hatchway that led into the wheelhouse itself. With Alexander being one of first squad's breachers, he would have no trouble getting through the hatchway on his side of the bridge. Bryant stepped to the right, out of the way, and let Dan Able come up to breach the hatchway on their side of the ship. The train was ready, and Rockham keyed his radio for transmission.

"First squad ready," he said quietly into his throat mike.

Over their earpieces, every member of the unit on board heard Daugherty answer, "Second squad ready."

"Execute . . . execute . . . execute," Rockham said quietly.

CHAPTER 22

★ ★ ★ ★

0106 ZULU
Bridge deck
Pilgrim's Hope
West of Mukawwar Island
Northern Sudan

With stealth still of primary importance, Able tried the direct approach to breaching the hatchway to the wheelhouse: he reached up and gently pulled on the handle. The hatch was unsecured and moved at his touch. Before fully opening it, he reached into a pocket of his vest and pulled out a squeeze bottle of oil. He squirted some on each of the hinges so the hatch would hopefully open without the squeal of rusted metal.

Bryant moved back to a position just behind Able. The squeeze signal was passed up, and Bryant initiated the breach. When Bryant squeezed his shoulder, Able pulled the hatch open and stepped to the side. Crouching, Able took up the rear guard position at the hatchway, covering the area they had just crossed with his suppressed MP5-N.

Bryant, Rockham, and Sukov immediately moved into the wheelhouse. A short distance inside from the hatch, a passageway led off to the right. As the rear man, Sukov stopped and covered that passageway as Bryant and Rockham continued on to the wheelhouse proper.

Covered in black clothing and equipment from head to toe, the two SEALs barged into the wheelhouse, taking in the situation in the compartment at a glance. The small black holes in the silver muzzles of the suppressors on their submachine guns held a silent promise of death for the crewman who stood in front of the brass compass binnacle, a forgotten cigarette dangling from his mouth. He'd been standing midwatch on the bridge.

Bryant moved in on the man, shoving him down to the deck. As the man squeaked in alarm and fear, Rockham said, "Quiet! You are a prisoner," in his badly accented Arabic.

The man struggled for another moment, while Bryant kneeled down on his back with his right knee. Shoving the muzzle of his suppressed MP5-K PDW into the man's ear, Bryant leaned forward and growled, "Quiet!" Poorly pronounced Arabic aside, the man settled at the sound of menace in Bryant's voice.

As Bryant secured the prisoner, Tinsley, quickly followed by Alexander, entered from the port side of the wheelhouse. Seeing that Bryant and Rockham had matters under control, Alexander and Tinsley moved to the left to secure the chart room.

The only other compartment on the bridge, the

MP 5-K PDW

chart room was directly behind the bridge on the port side. A small enclosed compartment, the starboard side of the chart room had a large wooden desk with a few charts laid out on it, a lamp, and the box to a manual radio direction finder/receiver in the far corner. On the port side of the compartment was a very worn and threadbare couch.

Stepping back into the wheelhouse, Alexander and Tinsley both said "Clear" in quiet voices. On the port side of the wheelhouse, Sukov had pulled back against the port bulkhead so he could still maintain a watch on the passageway in front of him while now able to see into the wheelhouse proper.

Bryant dropped his weapon, to dangle down on its sling, as Rockham covered the prisoner from the front. Without crossing into Rockham's line of fire, Bryant pulled the prisoner's hands behind his back and secured them with a double-looped tie-tie. Slipping the tie over the man's hands and pulling the tag end tight took all of the slack out of the loop, securing the hands solidly. The nylon plastic loops would cut through the man's wrists well before he could put enough pressure on them to break the straps.

From a pouch, Bryant pulled out a military triangular bandage, which he quickly unrolled. He put the thick center of the bandage over the man's mouth and tied the loose ends behind his head, effectively gagging the man. To make sure the prisoner could still breathe, Bryant pulled the man's head back and looked down to see that his nose wasn't covered by the bandage. Then he roughly patted the man down, searching him for any weapons or documents.

It was a thorough search, down one side of the man's body, then the other. Everything was checked out—the prisoner's pockets, shoes, socks, belt, and hair. And still Bryant never once moved between the prisoner and Rockham, who was holding his weapon on the man.

Once Bryant was satisfied that he'd checked the man's back and sides completely for anything that he might have in his pockets or taped to his body, he stepped to the side and rolled the prisoner over. The gagged man's eyes were huge as he looked first at Bryant, then at the muzzle of the suppressed submachine gun not more than three feet from his head.

Everything the man had on him had been tossed

to the floor to be examined after the search was complete. Each of the SEALs had several plastic bags and other waterproof containers to secure any documents or materials they found. Since none of them could read Arabic, they didn't bother examining documents, they just gathered up everything loose that was printed and stuffed it into their bags. Even the ship's log would be going back with them.

Any and all information was considered valuable. Later, it could be translated, analyzed, and correlated into an intelligence format by specialists. That wasn't the SEALs' job, which was just to gather the raw information. After the ship was secured, they would videotape and photograph everything they couldn't take back with them, including the faces of the prisoners.

With the bridge secured, the next priority target was the radio room back on the cabin deck. For the time being, the prisoner would remain trussed up on the deck in the wheelhouse with Rockham and Sukov. Sukov would run communications as Rockham established a C2—command and control—position in the wheelhouse. Bryant would join in with the balance of first squad as Able's shooting partner in place of Sukov.

The only change in standard procedure for the operation was the lack of a security element on the bridge. With Mike Ferber and Pete Wilkes back holding security on the cabin deck, there wasn't enough manpower to spare a security element for the bridge. Rockham decided that the best thing to do was send everyone back down to the cabin deck to not only take the radio room, but also to secure the ship's master. He and Sukov would just have to set their own security.

Behind the wheelhouse, a ladder led down to the cabin deck. It was normally used by the officers and captain to get on and off the bridge. If everything remained the same as it had been on the practice ship, the captain's stateroom would be directly across from the foot of the bridge ladder.

"Ferber," Rockham said quietly into his throat microphone, "squad coming down the bridge ladder."

No acknowledgment was necessary. It was simplest to just speak in the clear over their radios. They were miles from the nearest habitation, and their MX 300 radios were encrypted. No one could hear them, and if they did, it would be nothing more than a squeal of static.

With Bryant in the point position, Able, Alexander, and Tinsley stacked up behind him at the head of the ladder. As every man quickly got himself ready, the squeeze signal was passed forward, starting from Tinsley. In spite of the complexity of their actions, the SEALs were competently moving forward with the mission. Only a few minutes had passed since they had first boarded the *Pilgrim's Hope* and already they had control of the bridge. But their professionalism, and the dangerous situation they were still in, kept the SEALs from relaxing their guard for even a moment.

Noise and light discipline remained tight. The rubber soles of the Danner CT boots they all wore silenced their footsteps. Aside from Rockham's few verbal commands, not a word had been spoken by the rest of the unit. The SEALs moved silently through the dimly illuminated ship, communicating mostly by touch and hand signals. Body contact between shooting partners allowed each man to concentrate on the task he was assigned. No one even had to glance to the side to know that their partner was right there to back them up.

Going down the ladder as an assault train was much easier than going up. But the ladder wasn't wide enough to allow the squad to go down in a double column, which would have doubled the amount of fire that could have been immediately brought to bear on a target as it showed itself. So instead, Bryant went down first, closely followed by Able and the rest of the squad.

The foot of the ladder opened into a passageway that ran the width of the superstructure. The bulkhead on the forward side of the passageway had three hatchways with the same wooden doors as the rest of the cabins. On the practice ship, the cabin on the far right had been the captain's stateroom. There was no reason to believe the compartments had been changed, since the captain's stateroom was one of the few on the ship that had its own plumbing and head. The compartment directly in front of the ladder would likely be the captain's office.

Bryant made the decision to breech the starboard

side hatch first. That should be the captain's state-room. Moving into the passageway, Bryant turned to his right and headed up to the targeted hatch. Once there, he stood to the far right of the hatch-way as Able set up to breach the door. Reaching up, the SEAL breacher tried to turn the handle on the hatch. It wouldn't move; the room was secured.

Since these were wooden doors that opened out-ward, Able pulled his hooligan tool from the scab-bard on his back. In a hot breach, the breacher would have just blown the hinges off the door with rounds from his shotgun. But for a soft assault, the hooligan tool was the best approach, since they didn't know if the door was secured by just the knob lock or if there was a secondary lock on the inside. The fact that the ship's master felt it neces-sary to lock his cabin door said something about the level of morale on board the *Pilgrim's Hope*.

Squeeze signals were passed forward from Alexander and Tinsley to Able. Bryant was main-taining a security watch on both the starboard pas-sageway and the area behind Able and the rest of the squad. Able slipped the edge of the claw on the head of his hooligan tool into the space between the hatch and hatchway. The old wooden hatch hadn't been replaced since the ship was built back in World War II, and it had worn and warped a bit in its frame. The sharp edge of the slightly curved claw fit easily into the space, and with a pull of his strong arms, Able tore the wooden hatch open with a rending, tearing sound.

Instantly, Alexander and Tinsley penetrated into

the dark compartment. When the SEALs squeezed their hands down on the slim switches on the fore-grips of their weapons, the flashlights attached to the weapons lit up, shining a bright light into the compartment. On the starboard bulkhead was a wide, unkempt rack, no neater than the captain, who was trying to sit up in it.

As the first man in the door, Alexander was already moving to the right side of the compartment. Seeing that the area was clear, he continued moving to the side and went over to the bunk. The short, extremely strong SEAL grabbed the captain and effortlessly pulled him from his rack, dumping him onto the floor. Before the astonished captain could say a word, the air was driven from his body in a great whoosh as Alexander knelt down on his back.

"Quiet, you are a prisoner," Alexander said into the captain's ear, the muzzle of his shotgun pressed firmly into the center of the prostrate man's back.

Captain Fala of the *Pilgrim's Hope* was shocked and confused, but he recognized the feel of a gun barrel shoved into his back. And the way this black apparition had casually tossed him around told him that the demon could easily snap his spine if he didn't cooperate.

Pulling the captain's arms behind his back, Alexander secured the man's wrists with a tie-tie. The powerful SEAL wanted to physically dominate the captain to keep him off balance and from thinking about resisting, but he also didn't want to hurt the man so badly that he couldn't walk. The SEALs wanted the captain in a compliant state and uninjured so he might be of use during their takedown.

But the prisoner was also an unknown factor to the SEALs, so he was secured, gagged, and searched just as completely as anyone else they would have found. With the captain under control, the rest of the cabin was quickly examined for any other personnel. The captain's head and office were quickly inspected. The time for a detailed search for information would come later. Right now, what was important was speed and security in taking control of the ship. With the ship's master in the SEALs' hands, they knew they would have the upper hand over the crew of the *Pilgrim's Hope*. But any Iraqi forces on board would be an unknown factor.

Designated as one of the prisoner handlers before the operation began, Jack Tinsley took control of the captain after the search of his quarters was completed. Captain Fala was to be taken to the bridge as quickly as possible while still maintaining security. Alexander left the compartment first, while Tinsley brought up the rear, pushing the captain in front of him.

The SEALs had been maintaining as quiet a takedown as could be expected, until they breached the captain's stateroom. The wooden hatchway had cracked loudly when Able ripped it open with his hooligan tool. It didn't appear that the tearing wood had been detected by anyone else on the ship, or at least there was no reaction that the SEALs had noted. Right now, the priorities were to get the captain on the bridge and in Rockham's hands, then to secure the radio room.

Second Lieutenant Nawaz was pleased he'd been given the opportunity to demonstrate his leadership of the guard unit and weapon technicians assigned to the special weapons delivery. He was a *mulazim*, a very junior officer in the Republican Guard, and very conscious of appearances, which was why he had bumped the ship's chief mate from his quarters and taken them over for himself. Captain Fala protested, but a simple reminder of who was paying for the voyage—and who had the guns—kept the protests to a minimum. Besides, having the chief mate's quarters had given Nawaz control of the key locker, which was in the mate's compartment. It also put Nawaz directly under the bridge and next to the captain's office and stateroom.

The cracking of the wooden hatch during the breaching had awakened Nawaz from the first good night's sleep he'd had since coming aboard back in Jordan. Lieutenant Nawaz considered himself a soldier and not a seaman. His strong physical reaction to what the crew deemed a relatively calm voyage was a point of amusement to them all—all except Nawaz. The calm of the *Pilgrim's Hope* at anchor convinced him to stay aboard that night; that, and the fact that they hadn't been able to unload the missiles, which were his primary responsibility.

Nawaz didn't know what had wakened him, but the noise in the passageway a few minutes later left him wondering what was going on. The noises were slight, but at this time of night there shouldn't have been anything but the sounds of the ship. Even Nawaz had learned that a ship at anchor is relatively quiet. The sounds it made were regular enough that they soon blended into the background. Any unusual sounds stood out, and that was what he'd heard—an unusual sound.

Discipline in the Iraqi Army could be rough, and Nawaz had heard the sounds of struggle before. Perhaps some of the crewmen who were still on board had decided to deal with their captain in a way that Nawaz understood. Simple brutality was something he knew well; he had directed its use himself. The Makarov pistol he armed himself with was as much a badge of his authority as a weapon. It should be enough to deal with some unruly sailors.

Alexander was back at the foot of the ladder leading up to the bridge as Tinsley pushed the captain out of his stateroom and into the passageway. None of the SEALs saw the hatch start to open at the far end of the passageway. But the movement of the Iraqi soldier who stepped out into the passageway was something Able, Alexander, and Tinsley saw almost at the same time. And they all saw the weapon in the man's hand.

As the Iraqi's eyes widened in shock at the armed men in the passageway, he made the last mistake of his life, by starting to raise his weapon. Both Alexander and Able fired in almost the same instant. The Remington shotguns in both SEALs' hands were loaded with eight rounds of 00 buckshot. The nine pellets of Alexander's shotgun smashed into Nawaz's chest, blasting the man backward against the hatchway frame of the compartment he had just left. As he impacted against the bulkhead, Nawaz convulsed, almost wrapping himself around the wound in his chest.

As he was hit, Nawaz's hand clenched and the Makarov discharged. The round-nosed 9mm bullet flew up against the steel overhead and screamed off in a ricochet down and out the starboard side of the passageway. It left a bright silver smear of metal against the steel of the overhead, and the flattened metal ovoid passed within two inches of Bryant's left ear as he turned to face back toward where the shots had been fired.

The deformed bullet actually clipped the rubber tip of the antenna to Bryant's Motorola MX 300, which he'd strapped down behind his left shoulder.

Able didn't have as clear a shot as Alexander, though he did see Nawaz's arm come up with the Makarov in his hand. Able's full view of Nawaz was blocked by the wooden door of the hatch that had opened between Nawaz and Able. Having already breached one of the doors only a few moments before, Able knew just how flimsy they were, and he simply blasted through the door with his shotgun.

Moving at almost 1,200 feet per second, the nine .33 caliber hardened lead pellets in the shotgun used by the SEALs was intended to knock doors off their hinges. But those same pellets would just as easily punch through a simple wooden door, and the human flesh beyond. When the second shotgun blast struck the already dying Iraqi, it knocked him back away from the hatchway and onto the deck.

The mechanical racking sound of pump-action shotguns being reloaded sounded out even as the echoes of the thunderous booms of the twelve-gauges still rang out. Any possibility of maintaining a soft assault went off the ship with the sound of the shots.

"Bravo Leader, Bravo Two," Bryant said into his microphone. "Tango down, Tango down."

"Elements, Bravo Leader," Rockham ordered. "Hot . . . hot . . . hot."

There would be no more attempt to maintain a low profile by the SEALs. The shots had to have warned anyone on the ship, asleep or not. Now, the best weapon the SEALs had at their disposal was their training, and the speed at which they could conduct a takedown.

Tinsley had knocked his prisoner down to the deck when the shooting started. Now he stood above him as the wisps of powder smoke trailed through the air of the passageway. Alexander and Able immediately moved to the hatchway the Iraqi had stepped out of, to clear the compartment beyond. With Able on the far side of the hatchway, Alexander pulled back the wreckage of the door. A quick glance around told the SEALs that they had already dealt with the only occupant of the compartment—now they had to move quickly.

Tinsley dragged the groaning and sobbing captain up the ladder to the bridge deck as Bryant set up with Alexander and Able to take down the radio room. A quick circling of Bryant's nonshooting hand over his head followed by a pumping up and down motion of his closed fist was the signal to Mike Ferber and Pete Wilkes at the aft end of the passageway to close in with Bryant, and the SEALs with him.

Though Ferber had been able to see the far forward end of the passageway, all of the action had taken place just around the corner and out of his sight. What he'd seen was Able blast his shotgun down the port-starboard passageway. Now all of the SEALs were gathering in the center of the fore-aft passageway and preparing to breach the radio room.

The hatchways on either side of the radio room door were ignored for the moment. Alexander maintained a rear guard position where he could look down both passages. Wilkes maintained a rear guard looking aft along the main passageway. Bryant, Able, and Ferber quickly set up a train and breached the door to the radio room.

The breach was fast and dirty. Able blasted the hinges of the hatchway, and the wooden hatch fell out into the passageway. During the setup for the breach, Ferber had pulled a flash-crash from an equipment pouch and tore the grenade free of its waterproof plastic wrapper. As the hatch fell, Ferber shouted out, "Crash!" and threw the grenade into the compartment, while Bryant kept his weapon aimed at the hatchway.

Less than two seconds later the thunderous explosion of the flash-crash, combined with its brilliant flash and smoke, roared out. The noise and light were almost guaranteed to immobilize anyone in the compartment for at least several seconds—and that was seconds more than the SEALs needed. Immediately following the blast, Ferber and Bryant entered the radio room.

The radio man had been trying to hide in the foot well of the desk that held some of the ship's radio equipment. The blast of the flash-crash had caused him to dive forward in the cramped area, and he'd driven his head solidly into the steel bulkhead on the port side of the compartment. As a result, the SEALs had a limp, unconscious prisoner on their hands. By the looks of the blow he'd taken, he might have had a concussion.

The SEALs secured the limp prisoner and searched the compartment. The one Iraqi with a gun had been more than enough for the SEALs, and they weren't going to allow the situation to repeat itself. The radio room secured, they moved on to clear the rest of the compartments on the deck.

The five remaining compartments were breached, crashed, and quickly searched without incident. Tinsley had come back down from the bridge and rejoined the train. With all six SEALs working, securing the remaining cabins and the cabin deck only took a few minutes. No further personnel were found, and there wasn't time for a detailed search for anything of informational value. Now the SEALs knew they had an alerted ship to take down, and they still had two decks full of cabins to go through before the superstructure could be considered secured.

Normally, the first compartment searched and cleared would be designated the detainee staging area. The cabin deck had been cleared, and only two prisoners were taken down. With the ship alerted by the gunfire, they now had to move as fast as possible with as many men in the train as they could. Tinsley was designated as the prisoner handler, with his shooting partner Alexander as backup. But to speed things up, with their only prisoner right now being the radio watch stander, Tinsley took him over to the ladder leading up to the bridge and handed him over to Sukov at the top of the ladder.

Tinsley had told Rockham that they had run into one tango on the cabin deck, and he'd been eliminated when he brought up the captain. When the bound and gagged radio room watch stander was turned over to Sukov, Tinsley said that the cabin deck was cleared. Now the rest of first squad was going to continue clearing the boat deck.

Rockham knew they couldn't go through the rest of the alerted ship quietly, but it would help if they knew how many of the enemy there was, and knowing where they were wouldn't hurt either. Now, he turned to the only source of information he had available, the ship's captain, while Sukov kept a close watch on the other two prisoners.

His own and the SEALs' inability to speak Arabic was a problem, and Rockham swore that he wasn't going to let himself or his men be put in this situation again. Bending over to the captain, who was propped up against the aft bulkhead of the bridge, Rockham said, *"Tatakallam inglizi?"* asking the man if he spoke English.

Finally, after shouting the same question at the captain several times, the stunned man recovered enough to haltingly say, in a heavy accent, "Yes, I speak English."

"How many Iraqis on board?" Rockham asked, not more than a few inches from the man's face.

The loudness of Rockham's voice wasn't as impressive to Captain Fala as the muzzle of the huge, black submachine gun the SEAL was grinding into his neck. As far as Fala was concerned, his life depended on his answering this heavily armed madman's questions as quickly and truthfully as he could.

"Six," Fala said after a moment. "There are six. Four guards and two who watch the cargo."

"What cargo?" Rockham said. "Where is it?"

"N-Number three hold," Fala stuttered, his courage failing him along with his command of English. "T-Two containers."

Rockham could see that the badly frightened

man was about to either panic or collapse. But he still wanted to know more details.

"Pilgrims," Rockham said. "How many pilgrims are aboard?"

"N-None," Fala said weakly. "Mosque ashore . . ." and the man lapsed into muttered Arabic.

"Crew!" Rockham shouted. "How many crew are aboard?"

But Captain Fala continued muttering an Arabic prayer even more loudly.

Hitting his mike button, Rockham transmitted the information he had learned to his men throughout the ship.

"Elements, Bravo Leader," Rockham said. "Sitrep, hotels"—by which he meant hostages—"zero, uniform three secured, tangos six minimum. Repeat, tangos six minimum, bridge secure."

CHAPTER 23

★ ★ ★ ★

0102 ZULU
Entrance to engine room
Main deck
Pilgrim's Hope
West of Mukawwar Island
Northern Sudan

Second squad had separated from first squad as the takedown of the ship commenced. Rockham and his SEALs would be taking the command deck and as many of the personnel decks as they could, while second squad took down the engine room. Next to the holds themselves, the engine room was the largest single compartment on the ship, and also one of the most complicated. The engine room was two decks deep. There wasn't a third deck in the room, more a series of platforms and catwalks. The bulk of the engine room was taken up by two large oil-fired boilers and the steam turbine they powered.

Throughout the deck of the engine room there

was machinery and the control board for that machinery. Besides the boilers and engines, there was a DC electric generator, pumps, electrical panels, pipes, conduits, and the long shaft down the aft center of the compartment, leading off into the shaft alley.

Supported on bearing blocks the length of the alley, the shaft, usually spinning, extended over a third of the length of the ship from the engine room to the eighteen-foot bronze screw under the stern of the ship. With the ship at anchor and only an absolute minimum of machinery running, the SEALs would have a break in their favor. The chances were that only one sailor, or at most two, would be standing engine room watch. The SEALs didn't plan for "chances," however. Second squad was prepared to go through the entire engine room and the shaft alley before they called it secured.

But well before they could take down the engine room, second squad had to get into position. The passageway that led to the ladder down to the engine room was roughly in the center of the main deck. The port and starboard running passageway had a ladder leading down to it from the boat deck above. And it had two ladders leading aft that emptied onto the first catwalk in the aft area of the engine room. Several other ladders and catwalks led about the engine room, but one long ladder led down into the engine room proper, the foot of it ending close to the main panel. If there was a watch stander in the engine room, that's where he would be.

The main deck was also full of cabins, but second squad didn't have the time or the manpower to clear them all before they took the engine room down, the control of which was their priority.

As they had practiced, while first squad started up the aft superstructure ladders leading to the bridge deck, second squad began penetrating into the main deck. Originally, they had practiced splitting up into two fire teams, each making their way down the port or starboard passageway. But during the practice ops against their fellow SEALs acting the part of aggressors, it was found that the concentration of firepower in one full squad outweighed the flexibility of running two fire teams.

Second squad started out with Ryan Marks in the point position, closely followed by Shaun Daugherty. In rear guard position were John Grant and Henry Limbaugh. Daugherty felt lucky to have the experience of Chief Monday in his squad. But in fact this kind of hostile boat takedown hadn't been done by the Teams much before, so everything was a learning experience, no matter how much they'd practiced and trained for the op back at Little Creek.

It had been calculated that it would take a minimum of four men to take down the engine room, since the compartment was so large and crowded. The rest of the squad would establish security going into the compartment.

The squad passed the ship's galley and half a dozen smaller compartments as they moved down the passageway. There were four larger crew compartments on their port side as they reached the central passageway beneath the scattered overhead bulbs, but there wasn't a sound as the SEALs reached their first turning point.

At the central passageway, Roger Kurkowski and Sid Mainhart stayed behind as the rest of the squad moved on. Kurkowski and Mainhart would maintain a security watch on the passageway and deck, making sure that the way out would remain open for their Teammates—and that no one could sneak up on them from behind. Using the same techniques first squad had used when they traversed the ship's ladders, Shaun Daugherty followed his point man down the ladder to the first landing stage in the engine room, the remainder of the squad following close behind.

On the first platform, Frank Monday and Larry Stadt took up positions overlooking the engine room. The other four men of second squad would go down the port side ladder leading into the engine room, then split into a pair of two-man teams to sweep the room under the watchful eyes—and ready guns—of Monday and Stadt. Only a few lights were burning in the engine room, one of them directly over the main panel on the starboard side of the compartment. That would be the area of responsibility for John Grant and Henry Limbaugh. Daugherty and Marks would be clearing the port side.

Any noise the SEALs might have made on the ladders was swallowed by the steady rumble of the

DC generator. For the moment, no one could be seen by any of the SEALs, since the machinery blocked lines of sight. Second squad was on their target ahead of schedule for first squad, but if there was a problem with first squad securing the bridge or radio room, second squad could make sure that the ship was going to remain immobile by securing the engines. If it came to it, second squad could also cut the power to the radio room, though the radio room probably maintained an emergency power supply of its own.

As Marks reached the foot of the port-side ladder into the engine room, Daugherty looked up to Monday on the catwalk. The SEAL chief silently pointed to his eyes in the "I see" signal. Then he held his hand open in front of his face in the "enemy" signal, held up one finger and pointed. His message: "I see one enemy, there."

Pete Wilkes had been holding his suppressed MP5K-N PDW locked against his shoulder, the muzzle pointed unwaveringly at the same target Monday had just indicated.

Daugherty repeated the signals back to Monday, who then went back to watching over the rest of the engine room. The same signals were repeated by Daugherty to Grant, Limbaugh, and Marks, who acknowledged them by returning the gestures. The one known target would be dealt with by Grant and Limbaugh, as it was on the starboard side of the engine room. Daugherty and Marks would make sure there wasn't anyone else among the machinery on the port side of the compartment.

One thing was known for certain now—they had found at least one engine room watch stander.

Najm Elahi was a young man and still new to the deep sea. He was only on his second voyage on the *Pilgrim's Hope*, though he had served aboard the much smaller boats of his small fishing village in Djibouti at the narrow mouth of the Red Sea. The sea, and the shipping that traveled on it, had always been of great importance to the economy of Elahi's small country, and many of its young men spent time on the water.

Serving aboard the *Pilgrim's Hope* was a fairly good job on the whole, though he didn't have much experience elsewhere to compare the ship to. But since the Iraqis had come on board back in Aqabah, Jordan, the situation had worsened.

Captain Fala was an easygoing shipmaster; even the inexperienced Najm could see that. But the Iraqi soldiers bullied everyone on board, crewman and pilgrim alike—even Captain Fala. When you met any of them in a passageway, you had to quickly clear out of their path. Not doing so fast enough would gain you a hard shove at best, the butt of a rifle against your side at worst. At least, that was the worst they had done so far.

Even the Iraqi weapons technicians, strutting about in the blue uniforms they seemed so proud of, looked down on everyone aboard the ship, or just ignored everyone as being somehow beneath their notice. Or at least most of them did.

One Iraqi had approached Najm and sexually

propositioned him. The man wouldn't take no for an answer, and Najm had an increasingly hard time staying out of the man's way. The leader of the Iraqi guards didn't care about what one of the technicians was doing with the ship's crew. Still, the technician was an Iraqi, so the Iraqi officer had just told him to deal with it himself.

Chief Engineer Younis had taken to switching Najm's watch-standing schedule to keep him "unavailable" to the Iraqi. The irregular hours had cost Najm some sleep, but at least the Iraqis would be gone the next day, when the ship could finally dock and unload. The only problem right now for Najm was standing mid-watch in the engine room alone. That wasn't something that helped keep a man awake. In spite of his best intentions, Najm found himself lulled by the thrumming drone, and the young man was slipping off into sleep.

Since they couldn't move along a bulkhead as they would have gone into a normal compartment, Grant and Limbaugh switched their method of movement when they hit the bottom of the ladder. In a bounding overwatch pattern, they moved toward the starboard side of the engine room. As one SEAL covered his partner, the other quickly moved forward and took up a protected position behind the cover of one of the many pieces of machinery and panels. As soon as the moving SEAL had taken cover and had his weapon pointed ahead, his partner moved up and past him.

The bulky pieces of machinery in the engine

room kept the SEALs moving forward in short bursts. But this was something they knew well, and the sequence of actions came instinctively.

For a big man, John Grant not only moved quickly, he was absolutely silent. He and Limbaugh were soon at the side of the long starboard ladder that led back up to the catwalk. Crouching down, they could both see the engine room watch stander sitting on a stool in front of the main panel.

The slightly built sailor was slumped down with his back turned to the SEALs. Daugherty and Marks, in position on the far port side of the engine room, couldn't see the watch stander because of the engines in the center of the room. They weren't able to offer any covering fire to their Teammates, and so continued with the clearance of their side of the compartment.

Grant, in contrast, had a clear view of the man sitting at the panel. Aiming his suppressed MP5-N, he started moving forward. Holding the large submachine gun like a pistol in his hand, Grant maintained a rock-steady aim on the sailor while he crept forward. The sailor would never know what happened to him before the black shape of the deadly SEAL slipped up on him.

As Limbaugh and the other SEALs on the catwalk watched, Grant grew closer to his target. Then Grant let the submachine gun in his hand drop down to hang from its sling. Straightening up, he suddenly moved so fast that none of the SEALs watching could later say just exactly how he'd done it. One moment, Grant was behind the sitting sailor—the next, he'd slipped his left hand past the man's head and over his mouth while grabbing his belt with his right hand.

Picking the slight man up, Grant spun him to the side and slammed him down to the steel deck platings. If there was any cry of alarm attempted by the sailor, it never happened, since his breath was driven from his lungs with a whoosh.

Before the stunned man could move, Limbaugh stepped forward and stood watch over the sailor Grant had pinned to the deck with his knee. The weak struggles of the stunned man were ignored as the powerful SEAL pulled his prisoner's arms behind his back and secured them with a tie-tie. A bandage gag was slipped over the sailor's head, silencing any sounds the man could make.

With the prisoner secured and gagged, Grant quickly searched him thoroughly and roughly. Picking the prisoner up with no effort at all, Grant flipped him over and completed the search. By the time he was done, Daugherty and Marks were holding up their thumbs in the nonverbal signal for "clear" as they finished sweeping out the port side of the compartment.

As Grant covered his partner from where he stood over the prisoner, Limbaugh moved past him to check out the area behind the main panel. A few seconds later the two SEALs were also able to lift up their thumbs to signal "clear."

Normally, sleeping while standing watch was one of the more serious offenses a seaman could do. Men had been executed in time of war for such an

infraction of the rules. At other times, ships had
been lost as they ran aground or collided with
something that sank them. Najm Elahi would never
know that being asleep at his post probably saved
his life.

In fact, for the rest of his life Najm never fully realized that he had fallen asleep on watch—only
that a sudden thunderbolt in the form of a man had
driven him to the deck. John Grant had been ready
to kill the watch stander long before he could have
given an alarm—whether he had to shoot him or
crush the life out of him with his strong hands.
When he saw that the very young man was nodding
at his post, he hadn't even thought about what to
do, he just acted.

The engine room was now secure, but the harrowing part of clearing the compartment had to
take place. Even though they didn't think anyone
had detected them and taken cover, the SEALs now
had to clear the shaft alley leading aft from the engine room. As Grant and Limbaugh stood watch,
Daugherty and Marks stepped past the heavy mass
of the thrust bearing at the forward end of the propeller shaft and entered the long, dank passageway
leading to the stern of the ship.

The shaft alley was supposed to be well-lit from
the lights along the arched overhead. But only one
bulb was burning near the aft end of the alley. To
the SEALs' right was the huge steel shaft, its many
support bearings spaced out along its length. Anyone with a weapon could have fired a shot and hit

the SEALs, almost like shooting down a pipe. But no one did.

Using the lights on their submachine guns when they had to, in order to keep from tripping over anything scattered on the deck, Daugherty and Marks moved down the alley. Daugherty moved to the left side of the passageway as Marks moved down the right, closest to the still propeller shaft. Sweat built up on the men in spite of the dank coolness of the alley air. The smell of old oil, bilge, and rusting metal went unnoticed as they completed clearing the compartment.

Without speaking a word, the two SEALs reached the end of the shaft alley, having spotted nothing. They were able to turn and go back to a now secured engine room. As they approached, Daugherty said, "Coming out" in a clear voice.

"Come out," Grant answered back as he watched the hatchway leading to the shaft alley. As their Teammates had cleared the shaft alley, the other SEALs in the engine room had gone over the entire compartment, confirming again that their one trussed prisoner on the deck had been the only crew member on watch. Then the deep booms of a shotgun, followed by a pistol shot, echoed down to them from the decks overhead.

With Grant and Limbaugh holding security watch in the engine room, Daugherty and Marks raced up the ladder to the catwalk where Monday and Stadt stood. The radio crackled with the news from their Teammate that only a single tango had gone down. The answering message from Rockham to go hot meant that they were now going to clear the decks as quickly as possible.

After Rockham had announced the situation on the bridge, Daugherty keyed his mike and made his report.

"Bravo Leader, Echo Leader, engine room secure," Daugherty said over the radio. "Shaft alley secure."

That information would tell Rockham that the ship was now immobile. With his announcement that the bridge was secure, the most important objectives on board had been reached. Now it was a race to complete the securing of the ship before any crewmen or Iraqis could resist the SEALs.

The further securing of the decks had begun well, as Mike Ferber's voice came over the radio: "Bravo Leader, Bravo One, cabin deck secured. Going on to boat deck."

Second squad quickly rejoined with Kurkowski and Mainhart, who were securing the way into the engine room. Starting their sweep, the SEALs of second squad cleared the cabins and compartments of the main deck. Each compartment was breached, crashed, and entered. Speed and the sudden overwhelming application of force would be their main allies. During their savage action, they came across two stunned and terrified crewmen in two compartments. But before the prisoners could be moved to a single holding area, the thunderous blast of a high-order explosion rocked through the superstructure.

The echoes of the explosion were still ringing when the sound of automatic weapons fire broke out from overhead. This wasn't the sound of an unsuppressed MP5 in the hands of one of their Teammates. This was the unmistakable deep booming thunder of an AK-47. Once heard, the sound of that weapon couldn't be mistaken. And all of the SEALs had heard that sound before, either in training or in combat.

When they had been assigned to escort the technicians and weapons from Iraq to Sudan, Majd Amini suspected that it was a relatively unimportant mission. If it was as important as they were told, why was an inexperienced *mulazim* like Nawaz in charge of the mission? Who put such a junior officer in command? But as an experienced sergeant, Amini had seen the politics of the Republican Guard at work before. He knew he had to just follow the orders he was given.

A conscientious soldier, even for a member of the Republican Guard, Amini kept his equipment in good order and his weapons always loaded and near at hand. So far, this mission had been a simple one—only a tiny handful of pilgrims and the crew of the ship itself had to be watched. But beyond just bullying the crew members enough to keep them cowed, Amini also had to watch out for the technicians. They were a pain in the ass, but he'd been told just how important they were to Saddam's plans. So Amini just followed orders again.

One of the technicians had been a problem with

a member of the crew. The man's tastes would have choked a camel, but he was one of the trained specialists who came with the assignment. At least he hadn't had the chance to bother the young crewman yet, and they would be off-loading the missiles tomorrow. That would bring an end to the ocean-going part of the mission anyway.

As he lay in his bunk, the sound of gunshots woke Amini. His experiences on the combat lines in Iran were only a few years behind him, and his reflexes had not faded. Immediately alert, Amini was rolling off his bunk even as the unusual sounds of gunfire still rang in his ears. One of the shots was a small bark, like a pistol would make. But the deep booms that had sounded out together, what had they been?

Lieutenant Nawaz was in the cabins on the next deck up, and he had been armed with a pistol. But who had fired the other shots? The bigger, louder ones? There weren't any other weapons on the ship. His men had made certain of that the first day out of port. But before he checked what was going on overhead, he would have to look in on the technicians in the cabin next door.

Grabbing his folding stock AKMS-47, Amini snatched up his web gear with his other hand as he kicked Amr Raza to make sure he was awake. Even though he was a fellow Tikriti, Raza was an indolent asshole who depended on others to pick up the slack. Raza was one of those soldiers that intended to ride out his political connections to a better life, and was only serving in the Republican Guard as the first step on the ladder to power and influence.

Telling Raza to get his weapon and check on the lieutenant felt like a waste of time to Amini. But he could beat the bastard later if he didn't do as he was told. Now, his much higher priority was to make sure their important passengers were okay.

Pushing open the door to their cabin with the muzzle of his AKMS, Amini looked out into the passageway. There was nothing to be seen in either direction. Darting out quickly, he ducked into the cabin just next door to his own. There, much to his dismay, he saw only Musad Arif, one of the two technicians.

Arif was practically jabbering with fear as he cowered on his bunk. He couldn't tell Amini where Faris Gaffari, the other technician, had gone. But even before Amini could decide what to do with the cowardly technician, a sharp explosion sounded out above them. Within a few minutes, another blast rang out. Whatever was going on, someone was going room to room on the upper deck, apparently tossing grenades into the cabins. At least that's what it sounded like to Amini.

He decided to hold his ground. When the intruders came up to the door to the technician's cabin, he would be the one to give a surprise to whomever was on the opposite side. The steel walls of the ship would protect him and the technician from what Amini had in mind. As he dug through his ammunition pouches, Amini's hand closed on the smooth steel ovoid of a Soviet RGD-5 fragmentation grenade.

When the sound of an explosion rang out in the next cabin, Amini knew their cabin would be next. He pulled the pin on the RGD-5 grenade and waited. The smooth steel of the grenade body was slick in his sweating hand, and he slipped his fingers on the enameled steel body as he prepared to throw.

While second squad began clearing the main deck, first squad moved down to the boat deck to continue their part of the clearing operations. Moving down a port side external ladder, second squad set up their train to start clearing the boat deck at the forward cross passageway. The first cabin they came to on the forward side of the deck was breached and crashed without incident. The compartment was quickly cleared by Ferber and Wilkes, while the squad moved on to the next compartment.

Before they could reach the next compartment hatchway, the squad had to cross the port side fore-and-aft passageway. Looking back at Ferber for an instant, Bryant saw the signal for the squad to turn and clear the longer passageway. There were five cabins on the port side of the passageway, the first hatchway less than ten feet from the corner where the SEALs started.

With Bryant in his usual point position, the squad set up the train and the squeeze signal was

passed. Bryant went past the door and Able set up
for the breach. As Bryant watched down the passageway, Able breached the door and Wilkes tossed
in a crash. When the sound of the flash-crash
roared out, Ferber and Wilkes entered the compartment. The rest of the squad set up to continue
down the passageway as Ferber and Wilkes stepped
back out of the cleared compartment. The two
SEALs now fell in at the rear guard position for the
squad as they moved on.

The upcoming breach was going to be difficult. It
wasn't that the wooden hatches were any different,
but that the hatchways of the next two compartments were right next to each other. One hatch
opened from the right and the other from the left,
both sharing a central post where their hinges were
secured.

Rather than risk opening two hatches and having to clear both rooms simultaneously, Bryant
stepped past the second hatchway to keep watch
down the passageway. Able knelt to use his hooligan tool to pop the first hatch, while Alexander
stood ready with a crash in his hand.

The squeeze was passed, Able popped the hatch,
and Alexander tossed the crash in. Following the
flash and boom, Tinsley and Alexander moved into
the room, Tinsley to the left, Able to the right. Then
all hell broke loose.

The two SEALs ducked into the room and immediately moved a few feet away from the hatchway.
Tinsley was on a bulkhead, moving in the direction

he'd entered the compartment, while Alexander had to make a sideways turn to get his back up against the starboard bulkhead.

In the center of the compartment stood a man with an AK-47 dangling from his shoulder on a sling. He was swaying, stunned from the blast of the grenade. Even before either SEAL could say a word, Tinsley's eyes were drawn to a small ball on the ground at the man's feet. The smoke from the flash-crash almost obliterated the SEALs' view of the object, and his eyes bulged as he recognized it for what it was.

The shiny olive-drab sheet-metal body held a serrated fragmentation liner of steel surrounding a central charge of 110 grams of TNT. The long, silver-colored aluminum body of a UZRGM fuse stuck up from one rounded end of the ovoid. And the safety lever and pull ring of the fuse were missing.

"*Grenade*!" Tinsley bellowed as he turned to his Teammate.

Alexander was turning to the hatch as Tinsley started to run from the compartment. The steel walls of the cabin would turn it into a good rendition of a blender as the hundreds of fragments from the grenade bounced and rattled around in it. The fragments would ricochet until they were spent or had stopped in something yielding, such as a bunk, chair, or human flesh.

Alexander was short and powerful, but he wasn't fast. As Tinsley was reaching the compartment hatch, Alexander was just coming up to it.

Grabbing his Teammate's arm, Tinsley hauled at Alexander, shoving the smaller SEAL out ahead of him. Knocking Able away from the hatch, Alexander landed almost on top of him while Tinsley rolled the other way. As the three men sprawled in the passageway, the explosion of the grenade thundered out behind them—smoke and flame belching from the open hatchway.

Fragments screamed off the bulkheads, and Tinsley and Alexander ducked down their heads and crossed their ankles. The reaction was automatic and had been drilled into the SEALs since their first days at BUD/S. Whoever was inside the compartment had been holding a live grenade when the flash-crash went off, the SEALs realized. He must have dropped the grenade while stunned, and it had detonated at their feet.

As the squad lay stunned, a new danger roared out. Able was on the deck with Alexander partially on top of him, both SEALs lying across the hatchway of the next compartment. Without warning, an AK-47 inside the compartment opened fire on full automatic. The bullets ripped through the flimsy wooden hatch and screamed off down the passageway as they bounced off the steel bulkhead and overhead.

Rolling over on his side, Alexander brought his Remington shotgun up to bear on the splintering hatchway. As Able pulled his own shotgun up to his chest, the two SEALs opened fire, blowing chunks off the hatchway and into the compartment.

Without a direct target, the SEALs tracked their

weapons across the hatchway, covering most of the compartment inside with a buzzing hornet's nest of lead pellets. The *clack-clack* of the shotgun's pumping action was blotted out by the booming thunder of the two weapons being fired.

When they finally stopped, there was only the sound of a dull, wet thud that came from inside the compartment. The sound of a shredded body falling to the floor.

"Bravo Leader, Bravo One," Ferber said into his microphone a few moments later. "Three tangos down, three tangos down."

CHAPTER 24

★★★★

The superstructure of the *Pilgrim's Hope* had been cleared and each cabin searched. With the super-structure secured, the unit spread out over the ship to be certain they had located all the members of the ship's crew who were aboard, and that none of the Iraqis had escaped them.

Captain Fala hadn't changed his story after he'd come back around and continued to answer Rock-ham's questions. He still insisted that there weren't any pilgrims on board the ship—that they had all gone ashore. And that information matched what the SEALs had found in the cabins after they were searched.

During the clearing of the main and boat decks, more prisoners had been taken with little resis-

tance. The ship's cook and chief engineer had both
been on the boat deck when the Iraqi's grenade had
detonated. And they heard the violent and fierce
exchange of gunfire between the SEALs and the
Iraqi with the AK-47. Altogether, the sound of gunfire and explosions thundering through the passageways took any thought of resistance out of the
few crewmen who had yet to be located by the
SEALs.

Younis, the ship's burly chief engineer, gave up
without any resistance when the SEALs breached
his cabin. The loud noise of the flash-crash had the
engineer doing little more than shaking his head
and moaning after being captured.

The ship's cook, a short but rowdy Burmese who
had been known among the crew for having a
quick temper, surrendered meekly when the SEALs
entered his cabin, close to the chief engineer's. The
cleaver the cook had raised in his hand was frozen
in place from the stun of the flash-crash—and
stayed there as the awesome black holes in the muzzles of the unwavering submachine guns in the
hands of Mike Ferber and Pete Wilkes kept his attention. Scarcely breathing, the shocked Burmese
had quickly fallen to his face when directed by the
two SEALs.

None of the SEALs were in a frame of mind to
take the slightest chance with any of the captives.
Prisoners who had been secured were watched
through cold eyes. Those in the process of being
captured were quickly trussed, searched, and secured. Two additional crewmen, located in two

separate cabins down on the main deck, were taken and secured by second squad. The SEALs acted quickly, efficiently, and thoroughly—they were all in a dark mind-set, since one of their own had been hurt.

Wayne Alexander had been out of the cabin before the grenade dropped by Amini had detonated. The armor he was wearing protected his torso, but his legs were exposed to the blast and fragmentation. Jack Tinsley hadn't been more than a few feet from Alexander when he was wounded, and the SEAL corpsman had immediately set to work. While Mike Ferber told Greg Rockham the short form of what had happened on the boat deck, Tinsley treated the wounds in both of Alexander's legs.

Tinsley felt that the fragmentation had torn up a lot of muscle and skin, but hadn't severed any major blood vessels or ligaments. Alexander should recover without any loss of mobility or strength, but for the time being he wouldn't be going on any more swims. The SEALs wouldn't be able to extract underwater as their original plan had called for.

Rockham wasn't overly concerned with the extraction problems. The Zodiacs could be called in and would get to the ship fairly quickly. It would mean exposing the SEALs to a longer boat ride in the open waters around Mukawwar, but that couldn't be helped. It looked like the SEALs had moved fast enough to prevent any signal going out from the radio room. There were few enough working boats in the Sudanese navy that Rockham didn't think any local equivalent of a Coast Guard cutter would be showing up anytime soon.

But the SEALs had to pick up the pace of their operation, just to be sure that no one on shore had the time to get out to the *Pilgrim's Hope* in a fishing boat. The gunshots and grenade explosion had been contained inside the superstructure, but sound had a funny way of carrying across the water, especially at night. Muhammad Qol was about seven miles away, but the SEALs didn't need a night fisherman who was ignoring the Muslim sabbath to come nosing around the ship and possibly spread the alarm.

Rockham directed the second squad to clear the forward main deck of the ship. The first squad would consolidate the prisoners into a single holding area at the stern, where Alexander could easily watch them all. The high, flat circle of the old five-inch gun deck, rising above the fantail and with a single entrance through the bulwark surrounding the deck, would be a secure place to watch the prisoners. Since Tinsley had been trained to closely handle and examine the warhead of any missiles they located, he would have to go back to the superstructure with the rest of the squad. Dan Able with his ready shotgun would back up Alexander on prisoner watch.

Acting as the intelligence man for the detachment, Pete Wilkes was now videotaping the faces of every man in the crew of the *Pilgrim's Hope*. He did the same for the dead Iraqis in their cabins, though there was little enough left of two of them after the grenade had detonated. With the prisoners now gathered up on the main deck, they were herded back to the stern of the ship.

Second squad split into two fire teams as they went out onto the forward deck. Working as shooter pairs, the SEALs conducted a bounding overwatch, one pair covering while the other moved ahead. Frank Monday was leading fire team two on the starboard side of the deck, while Daugherty took fire team one up the port side.

The deck was a mass of ropes and cables, boxes and drums, scattered about, some loose, some in stacks secured with ropes. The main features of the forward deck were the huge, flat covers of the number two hold up forward and the number three hold just in front of the superstructure. The tall king posts and horizontal booms of the handling gear towered over the decks. At the base of each set of gear was the squat, heavy cube of a deck winch.

Up far forward, at the bow of the ship, was the raised deck of the forecastle. Very few lights were illuminating the forward deck, which kept the SEALs in fairly good concealment. It also prevented the SEALs from being able to see much in the way of detail as they moved forward from cover to cover. What could be seen immediately was that the cover of the number three hold was partly open. The canvas cover that had been pulled over the hatch to the hold, drawn forward, and just piled on the deck. The huge lump of dark canvas would have been poor cover, but a great place for concealment—which was just what one of the Iraqi guards and the other technician had thought.

When the sound of the first gunshots rang out from the superstructure, Towaab Zahed grabbed for his AKMS-47 that he'd laid on the canvas nearby. As a technician, Faris Gaffari felt he had no need for a weapon. His protection was the blue uniform of the technical staff of Saddam's Special Weapons program. But at that moment, in the dark of the night, Gaffari wished he had a weapon, even if he wasn't very good with one.

Taking cover, the two men watched the brilliant flashes of light coming from some of the cabin portholes as the dull booms of the flash-crash grenades detonated inside. The much louder and different explosion of the RGD-5 grenade was something Zahed recognized, but the loud explosion simply frightened Gaffari even more.

They had been in hiding for what had seemed an eternity when the explosions and light flashes finally stopped. They could see some movement through the portholes high up on the bridge, but the angle from where they were between the holds prevented them from actually seeing anyone through the round ports.

Deciding to pull back to the front of the ship, Zahed nudged Gaffari, then shoved him out from between the two holds. Crouching low, the two men crept along the port side of the deck to where the forecastle rose up. To the left of the ladder leading to the forecastle deck was the huge bulk of the ship's spare anchor. To the right of the ladder was a closed waterproof hatchway that led down inside of the forecastle and back through the cargo holds. That hatchway was where the two Iraqis were headed as the SEALs came out on deck.

Turning to speak to Zahed, Gaffari's eyes bulged as he saw the shadows toward the center of the ship move. Zahed saw Gaffari's reaction to something behind him and the frightened soldier spun on his heel, opening fire blindly.

The thunder of an AK-47 firing on full automatic was something all of the SEALs had heard far too much of. Kurkowski and Mainhart dove to the left and took cover on the far side of a stack of extra booms for the handling gear. Not having moved past the hatch cover of the number three hold, Daugherty and Marks were already under cover when the gunfire broke out. All they could see were the muzzle flashes coming from far up, forward on the main deck.

Even though he was a member of the Republican Guard, Zahed wasn't a very good soldier, especially not when compared to the competence and professionalism of the SEALs. But even an idiot can get lucky when he's spraying around with an automatic weapon. And Zahed wasn't a complete idiot, he was a trained soldier. Each time he fired, he moved to another position. The only view the SEALs had of him was when he rose and fired back at them. The Iraqi was dug in behind steel cover and he wasn't going to be easy to reach—and the SEALs had to stop him quickly before the sound of his gunfire reached someone off the ship.

Tapping Daugherty on the shoulder to get his attention, Marks pointed back up behind him to the upper decks of the superstructure.

Understanding showed in the young SEAL officer's eyes as he realized what Marks wanted to do. Nodding his permission, Daugherty went back to looking forward and covering his partner as Marks fell back to the superstructure. The big SEAL quickly turned into a passageway and was gone from the sight of anyone on the forward deck.

Kurkowski and Mainhart were in the best position to move up on the gunman. They didn't want to fire blindly at the muzzle flashes, for that would just draw fire, but they knew they had to take the man out.

As the gunman quit firing, the mechanical sounds from up forward told the SEALs that he was reloading. Monday and the other fire team were in a good position to move forward, but their line of sight to the gunman was even worse than Kurkowski's or Mainhart's. At the sound of the gunman reloading, Mainhart darted forward to a covered position behind the center king post's portside deck winch.

Zahed rose up and started firing again, spraying wildly. The 122-grain steel-cored 7.62mm slugs from his AK screamed off into the darkness as they ricocheted and bounced from the steel plates, bulkheads, and fittings on the deck. This was definitely not a great place to be, Mainhart thought as he prepared to rise and open fire on the gunman. Before the youngest member of the SMD could take his chances with the AK, there was a smacking sound, as if someone had hit a pumpkin with a hammer. The firing stopped, and a gun fell to the hard deck.

Up on the port side of the boat deck, the hard eyes of a trained SEAL sniper looked out through the four-power Hensoldt telescopic sight clamped to the top of his suppressed MP5-N. Ryan Marks kept his sights trained on the spot where the gunman had disappeared until his Teammates could move up and secure the position.

The higher vantage point of the boat deck had allowed Marks to see the muzzle flashes of the gunman's AK when he lifted it over the hatch of number two hold. Estimating what would be the distance from the muzzle to where the gunman should be leaning against the stock of the AK, Marks had squeezed off a single shot, the suppressor eliminating most of the noise. The rest of the sound had been masked by the gunman firing. All Mainhart had heard was a single M882 124-grain 9mm bullet striking the gunman's head.

The SEALs completed the securing of the deck under the watchful gaze of Marks and his submachine gun. When they reached the forecastle, each of them could see the gaping black shadow of the open waterproof hatchway to the right of the portside ladder.

"Echo Leader, this is Bravo Leader," Rockham said into his mike a few moments later, after he heard Daugherty's report. "Go in and complete your sweep. Bravo units will go in number three from here."

As second squad entered the forecastle decks, Mike Bryant, Ferber, Wilkes, and Tinsley moved down to the engine room deck where they could enter the forward part of the ship through waterproof hatchways. Going out into the tween deck area between the main deck and the bottom deck of the ship, the SEALs passed under the open area of the number three cargo hold hatch. In the dim light of the cargo hold, the dark bulk of a pair of large shipping containers dominated the cavernous interior. The little light coming in from the open hatch cover above let the SEALs see the two oversized shipping containers, resembling boxcars without the wheels, secured to the deck.

As the SEALs slipped silently into the cargo hold, the sounds of a metallic scratching and clicking could be heard. In addition to the metal sounds were the muffled, fear-filled sounds of a man's moans.

Squeezing the switches on the sides of their submachine guns, the SEALs illuminated the cargo containers with brilliant white light, the four flashlight beams stabbing out. They pinned the figure of an Iraqi in a blue coverall uniform scrabbling at the padlock securing the doors of one of the containers.

"*Stop!*" Wilkes shouted, as did Ferber and Bryant almost at the same moment. The whines of fear got louder as the man at the end of the container panicked. Tinsley knew that the missiles they were looking for were probably in those containers. And who knew what this panicked individual could do if he got in the container with them? He could blow the warheads, or even now trying to arm a booby-trap or destruct device. There could even be weapons in the containers that the SEALs knew nothing about. The risks were too great, and the man had used up his chance.

Tinsley opened fire an instant before his Teammates did.

Four suppressed submachine guns stuttered a short burp of death in the hold. Gaffari jerked and danced like a badly operated marionette with its strings tangled before he bounced off the end of the container and slumped to the deck. Each of the SEALs felt a moment's distaste at what they had done. The danger the Iraqi had represented was a very real one, but the act of firing had seemed more like an execution than a necessity of combat.

The SEALs now had the entire ship under their control, but that was only one part of the operation. As Tinsley began searching the body of the technician, Ferber called up to Rockham on the bridge.

"Bravo Leader, Bravo One," he said. "We have the target secured. Two packages. Send down Bravo Four."

"Bravo One, Bravo Leader, acknowledged," Rockham said back. "Bravo Four on the way."

As Bravo Four, John Sukov was the commo man for Rockham up on the bridge. He was also the most experienced explosive ordnance disposal man in the unit. The containers had been located and secured, but that did not mean the danger from their contents was over. The containers could be booby-trapped, or the missiles too contaminated to work around. It would take the skills of both the unit's best EOD technician as well as those of Tinsley and Limbaugh to be certain that the contents of the containers were safe and were properly examined.

The long steel containers could be lifted from the deck of the cargo hold and swung over to a pier to be set down on a truck bed. Whatever was in the long boxes would just look like another semitruck trailer, though those probably weren't common in northern Sudan. The steel boxes were plain and simple, and could be booby-trapped any number of ways.

As Tinsley gathered up the materials he found in the pockets of the dead technician, he came across the keys the man had dropped. Holding the centrally split end doors of the shipping container shut was a simple metal seal and a heavy duty padlock. Carefully examining the lock, Tinsley could see that it was just a loose padlock hanging from a locking hasp. After he tried several of the keys, one turned in the lock and the shackle popped open.

Sometime after Sukov had gone down into the number three hold, Rockham left his position on the bridge and headed down to check out the target for himself. From what the men had told him over the radio, they'd found two missiles and little else. Time was getting to be in short supply, and Rockham wanted to extract and get back to the submarine while it was still dark. He'd already called in the Zodiacs in preparation for extraction.

Going down into the engine room, Rockham

stepped through the hatchway into the cargo hold. He saw that the rear doors of the two shipping containers had been pulled shut loosely, with light spilling out around their edges. As the other WMD expert, Limbaugh had come down to join Tinsley and Sukov in their examination of the weapons. But neither they nor Pete Wilkes were in sight. Bryant and Ferber were standing watch alongside the containers, and both men turned at Rockham's approach.

"Everyone's inside checking out the prizes," Ferber said. The SEAL's voice sounded dull and lifeless in the huge compartment. They had been operating without speaking for so long that talking out loud seemed to take a special effort.

As Bryant pulled open one of the doors of the container on the right, bright light spilled out.

Rockham shielded his eyes from the sudden glare, and Ferber said, "I found a couple of work lights and ran them into the containers."

At least something had worked well on board the rough-kept ship. The closed doors of the containers had held the light inside, preventing it from shining out into the cargo hold and up through the partially open hatch cover.

Stepping inside the container, Rockham could see that almost the entire interior was filled by a large missile on a skeletonized wheeled trailer. The long, dull mustard-colored missile looked like it was almost three feet in diameter and over twenty-five feet long. Four short, thick tail fins were spaced evenly around the base. The exhaust nozzle of the rocket engine was almost directly in front of Rockham's face as he stepped into the container and pulled the door shut behind him.

Looking up the ass end of a Soviet missile was not the view Rockham preferred, but it did clearly show him the shiny dark gray forms of the graphite steering vanes that would direct the exhaust of the rocket motor. Looking over the missile body, he could see, deep inside the container, Sukov and Tinsley bent over the far end of the missile.

"We're running out of time here," Rockham said. "What have you got so far?"

Tinsley and Sukov leaned back from the missile and looked toward Rockham.

"Boss, I just don't know," Sukov said. "This is a Soviet Scud B, or at least it was."

"What do you mean 'was'?" Rockham asked.

"It's been highly modified," Tinsley answered.

"That's right," Sukov agreed. "There are weld marks where the body has been cut apart and new sections inserted. The damn thing is longer than a regular Scud. And that's not the strange thing."

"What is?" Rockham asked.

"The damn thing doesn't have a warhead," Sukov exclaimed. "It just has a flat end here. No nose cone or anything."

"What's odd about that?" Rockham asked.

"The Scud doesn't normally have a removable warhead," Sukov said. "Whatever this thing was intended to carry, it's just not aboard this ship."

"There's no fuel drums or any boxes around in any of the holds large enough to hold the warhead," Tinsley said. "The few containers that could hold one are empty—we checked everywhere. It looks like just the missiles were being delivered and the warheads would be coming separately."

"Okay," Rockham said. "But we still have to get moving. Check everything you can and photograph all of it. Pick up everything we can take with us, we're extracting in five minutes. These damn things are too big to take with us, that's for sure. So can you destroy them without sinking this ship?"

"Not a problem," Sukov said. "Wilkes and Limbaugh are in the other container photographing everything they can reach. We've already pretty much completed any field examination we can do of this bird. All we have to do is blow the engines and the guidance systems with some small charges, and these two boxes will be full of just very expensive scrap metal."

"Do it," Rockham ordered. "You have three minutes before I want everyone out of here."

The SEAL officer turned and left the cargo hold. Sukov started rigging some explosive charges, while Tinsley gathered every piece of paper in the container and stuffed it in a waterproof bag. The SEAL corpsman even bent down and tore off a data plate he found inside the guidance and flight control compartment at the front end of the missile.

Within only a few minutes, everything that could be taken was packed up. Sukov placed a single M112 block of C4 explosive inside the guidance compartment after arming it with five wraps of lightweight detonating cord. Having folded the cord in the middle, Sukov had two ends of the explosive detonating cord hanging from the block. The high explosive core of the cord would detonate the block of plastic explosive. It would also let Sukov connect several explosive charges together for simultaneous detonation.

The 1.25 pounds of C4 plastic explosive in the M112 block would completely destroy the front end of the missile, which included the very delicate and difficult-to-replace gyroscopes and other components of the guidance system.

After Tinsley left the container, Sukov ran the lengths of detonating cord back along the body of the missile to the back end. At the engine, Sukov prepped another M112 block of C4 explosive by wrapping it with the dual detonating cord. He placed the block of explosive well up inside the rocket engine, where its blast would destroy the combustion chamber and nozzle. Attaching two three-minute nonelectric firing assemblies to each end of the detonating cord, he completed rigging the missile for destruction.

All of the SEALs were competent with explosives. Wilkes had rigged the other missile exactly as Sukov had. Part of their training for this operation included knowing how to destroy the missiles, and they brought the materials they needed along with them. Using the two firing assemblies and doubled lengths of detonating cord came as close as was practical to guaranteeing that at least one of the lengths of cord would fire the explosive charges.

Looking up at Ferber, Sukov said, "Good to go."

"Clear the compartment!" Ferber called out, and he waved all of the men, including Wilkes, back out of the hold.

After all the other SEALs but Sukov had left, Ferber went over the container on the left and picked up the M60 fuse igniters on the end of the dual firing system. Looking over at Sukov, he nodded.

"Fire in the hole!" Sukov shouted, and he pulled the pins on the ends of the fuse igniters. Ferber did the same with his. Holding the fuses just long enough to ensure that both were burning, the two SEALs laid the fuses down and quickly left the hold. The explosive charges wouldn't be enough to destroy the steel shipping containers, but the number three cargo hold would soon be a very loud place to be in.

Withdrawing to the aft deck, all of the SEALs climbed down the caving ladder. As the men gathered aboard the Zodiacs, a heavy, dull explosion rocked the ship.

"Scratch one pair of missiles," Kurkowski said.

Sukov was glad that he'd heard the charges detonate. He would have hated to climb back onto the ship and rig them again.

The diving gear had already been lifted up and stowed aboard the Zodiacs while Ferber and Sukov were completing the demolition preparations. Now, the two Zodiacs pulled away from the *Pilgrim's Hope* and headed out into the night. Despite all that occurred on the ship, the SEALs had been on board for just over half an hour.

Still remaining low along the side tubes of the

Zodiacs, to limit their silhouette, the SEALs in the two black rubber boats sped through the night. With dawn only a few hours away, speed was essential. An early morning fisherman might be moving out to sea, even though it was still the Muslim sabbath. Lopez and Lutz turned up the throttles of their outboards and the two Zodiacs ran like black shadows across the water.

Almost ninety minutes later the two boats approached the rendezvous area with the *Oklahoma City*. They'd made much better time heading out to sea with minimum stealth than while heading in. Now, to help the submarine locate them, the SEALs turned on the SDU-5E strobe lights they had with them. Velcro patches on the strobes and the tops of their pro-tec helmets allowed them to slap the strobe lights in place on their heads. The infrared filters on the lights subdued them, so they were invisible to the naked eye only a few inches away.

As the men were rigging up their strobe lights, Lopez and Lutz moved the two Zodiacs close together. When the boats were almost touching, a line was passed from one to the other and secured to the towing bridles at the bow of each boat. With the strobe lights flashing unseen in the darkness, the two rubber boats spread apart, stretching out the line that connected them.

The infrared strobe lights may have been invisible to the naked eye, but they were easily visible to the Type 18 search periscope on board the *Oklahoma City*. Captain Wilson was standing periscope watch himself, and he clearly saw the two groupings of flashing lights through the low-light camera on the Type 18.

"All slow, come to course 257," Wilson ordered as he directed the big submarine toward the two lights. "Make your depth five zero feet."

As his orders were repeated and acted on, Wilson kept his eyes on the indicators on the big periscope as well as watching through the lens. Maneuvering the huge sub with careful precision, he seemed to be threading the eye of a needle. In fact, he was doing something similar—raising the periscope and passing the sail of the submarine between the two rubber boats. The periscope mast would catch the rope that was supposed to be stretched between the two boats and pull them in toward the sub aft of the sail. If he hit the line just right, the sub could surface and simply raise the boats up out of the water.

Captain Wilson was very good at maneuvering his boat. And his crew was well-drilled at their jobs. The sub hit the line exactly right and drew the two rubber boats in.

After the sudden rush forward that told them the sub had caught the rope, the SEALs on board the Zodiacs felt themselves rise up as if on an elevator as the submarine slowly surfaced underneath them. Within a minute there were crewmen on the deck to help the SEALs unload. The process was not the same as when the SEALs had first come aboard, since a lot of equipment would be abandoned, especially the two Zodiacs, their motors, and support gear.

As the SEALs and sub crewmen passed rucksacks filled with weapons and breathing gear down
into the submarine, Rockham ordered the scuttling
of the two Zodiacs. Grabbing safely lines from the
submarine, the two coxswains were held secure by
several crewmen and their teammates. Pulling out
sharp Mark III knives, Lopez and Lutz slit the rubber of the boats, puncturing all seven of the airtight
buoyancy chambers in each.

The tough-coated nylon of the buoyancy tube re-
sisted the knives, but then parted as the sharp,
pointed blades slipped through. Gaping holes released the gas inside with a whoosh. The weight of
the outboard motors pulled the deflated craft down
beneath the dark water. They sank quickly to the
bottom in almost three hundred feet of water. It
would be a long time, if ever, before the wrecked
boats were found.

Within minutes of pulling the SEALs up onto the
deck, the *Oklahoma City* was passing down beneath the waves herself. The mission had been
completed and the missiles destroyed. Even if warheads came in by another means, their delivery systems were now gone. And back aboard the
submarine, the SEALs were safe again.

CHAPTER 25

★ ★ ★ ★

0310 ZULU
20° 50' North, 37° 24' East
Oklahoma City
East of Angarosh Island
Northern Sudan
Red Sea

The well-lit interior of the *Oklahoma City* was a welcome sight to the SEALs after their time aboard the *Pilgrim's Hope*. The information they carried in their bags, on film, and in their heads would keep the intel people working for some time to come. But right now the SEALs just wanted their wounded Teammate Alexander looked after. After he was taken care of and they'd stowed their equipment, a hot shower and some chow would be very welcome.

As soon as the SEALs were aboard the *Oklahoma City*, the two corpsmen had taken their wounded Teammate to the officers' wardroom, which could be quickly converted into a sick bay.

The *Oklahoma*'s own corpsman was quick to respond to the SEALs' needs. The good news that their Teammate would be fine was conveyed to the SEALs as they stowed their gear in the torpedo room even before the ship's officers arrived in the compartment.

They were welcomed aboard by Captain Wilson and the crew of the submarine. This had been the first major takedown of a ship at sea for the new coalition forces during Desert Shield. It was going to be far from the last. But that would come later.

"Attention in the compartment," Mike Ferber said as the captain entered the torpedo room.

"As you were," Wilson said. "Welcome aboard, SEALs."

The men of the SMD were scattered about the compartment, shedding gear and repacking rucksacks. They had stopped what they were doing as Ferber called them to attention, but the captain's quick response set them back at their ease.

"Thank you, sir," Rockham said as he walked up to the captain. He had his flight suit pulled down off his chest and tied around his waist as he helped his men put away the detachment's gear.

The torpedo room had an aroma of its own at the best of times: a mixture of electrical smells, lubricants, and the materials that made up the weapons for the *Oklahoma City*. Right now, it was permeated with that unique odor that SEALs tended to bring with them after an operation—a mixture of wet cloth, skin, sweat, salt, and rubber.

The smell was referred to as "undersea and under-wear" in the Teams.

But Captain Wilson had expected to come into a locker-room scene when he entered the torpedo room, so the smell didn't surprise him. He knew the SEALs had exerted themselves on their operation as few men could. Just the effort of getting to and returning from such a clandestine operation was a great strain.

"I had the cook put on some hot chow and soup for you men when you're ready," Wilson said.

"As long as it's not fish chowder," Kurkowski said from somewhere in the compartment. "I don't think I could eat a fish for a while yet."

Remembering their run-in with the whale shark, a chuckle went through the SEALs at the thought of how close it seemed they'd come to being chowder themselves. The captain was puzzled at their amusement, but he would be made privy to a good SEAL fish story later.

"I'm sorry to say you'll not be able to sleep in as long as I would let you," Wilson said as he faced Rockham. "Seems the Navy really wants whatever you brought back from that ship. They aren't going to wait the eight hours of steaming it would take for us to rendezvous with the *Eisenhower*. A pair of Sea King helicopters is scheduled to lift off and meet us at sea. They'll pick you and your gear up right from the deck."

For the moment, the SEALs would have pre-ferred to have gotten some chow and rack time. But they knew the importance of a quick debriefing. They were to tell their stories to the intelligence people on the *Eisenhower* as soon as possible— while the details were still fresh in their minds. But right now the hospitality of the *Oklahoma City* looked real good to them.

The showers were declared open and the limits on the fresh hot water were suspended, by direction of the captain. That was some of the best news the SEALs had heard in hours. The chow was good, hot, and there was plenty of it. The sub's crew stayed away from the SEALs to give them their privacy while they were in the mess room. The crewmen still couldn't believe what some men would do, swimming out to take down an enemy ship while at sea. And at the moment, the SEALs couldn't believe how anyone could bitch about life on board a submarine when you got chow as good as they were getting then.

Within hours the stuttering roar of the five-bladed rotors on two Sikorsky SH-3H Sea King helicopters could be heard over the waters of the Red Sea. The two birds flew along at low altitude more than fifty miles off the shore of northern Sudan.

As the pilots and crews of the helicopters watched, the shadow of a nuclear submarine solidified, the big, black ship surfacing on the relatively smooth sea. The small figures of men appeared on the wet surface of the sub's deck as the helicopters came down to hover nearby.

As part of their search and rescue equipment, the Sea Kings were equipped with a rapid speed rescue winch above their starboard-side cabin doors. The inside of the birds had been stripped of their normal antisubmarine warfare gear and canvas seats fitted for the transport of troops or rescued aircraft crews. The SEALs were pulled up by the hoist, two men at a time.

As one bird picked up a pair of SEALs and started winching them in, it moved over to the side of the submarine to make room for the second bird to come in. Working in pairs, the two helicopters quickly extracted the SEALs and then pulled in their rucksacks and bags of equipment in bundles hooked onto the rescue hoist. In considerably noisier and less comfortable surroundings than aboard the *Oklahoma City*, the men of the SMD sat back in their canvas seats for the long ride to the *Eisenhower*.

Not long afterward, following the directions of the *Eisenhower* crewman waving two illuminated wands, the two big helicopters settled easily down onto the flight deck of the aircraft carrier. On this flight, the pain in Alexander's legs had kept him awake, in spite of the painkillers the corpsmen had given him. So this time, instead of sleeping, he watched his Teammates nod off to sleep. Even Greg Rockham was feeling the effects of a long night of high stress followed by a long flight with little comfort.

Within a short time, however, all of the SEALs were awake and in another pilot's briefing room. Here, they would undergo a debriefing, almost an interrogation, by officers from the intelligence department aboard the *Eisenhower*, while the memories of their op were still fresh.

The coffee urns at the back of the briefing room were a welcome sight to the SEALs as they filled cups and prepared for a long session of talking. The documents, maps, and papers they'd brought back were being examined by some of the intelligence people, while others spoke to the SEALs. Each man of the detachment told his observations of the operation from his point of view. Opinions weren't solicited; what the intel people wanted were facts and direct sightings.

The confusion was a result of the SEALs' inability to speak Arabic or to understand it was mentioned by several of the men. Fluency in the language certainly would have made interrogating the crewmen of the *Pilgrim's Hope* a lot easier.

Everyone examining the documents the SEALs had brought noticed that they were written in three languages. Part of the manuals and materials for the missiles were written in Russian. Other sections were in flowing Arabic script. And large parts were written in English. Most of the technical materials were in English, a more common international language than either Russian or Arabic. And most of the weapons sold for export by the Russians came with supporting documents in Russian and English. The Arabic portions of the materials seemed to refer to the modifications to the missiles that had been found.

The blue-uniformed individuals had probably been technicians for the missiles, Rockham told the intel officers. And from what they learned about the documents, the men had probably been able to read and speak English. That didn't explain the actions of the one technician in the hold who had refused to surrender to the SEALs. When the intelligence people seemed to suggest that Rockham's men might have been a bit quick on the trigger, they were blasted down by Rockham, who solidly stood by his men and the decisions they had to make on the spot. If the other officers thought that the decisions had been the wrong ones, then they were invited to come out on the next operation.

Rockham's anger at the suggestion that his men had made a mistake caused the intel officers to quickly back up and look at another subject. The one thing the interrogators had trouble believing was that the missiles didn't have warheads and that there hadn't been any sign of them on the ship.

Sukov, Tinsley, and Limbaugh, based on their training and experience, had been looking for something roughly the size of a household propane tank—more than two meters long and almost a meter in diameter. While they'd been going over the missiles, the other SEALs were checking the other holds and compartments. It had been harrowing, dark, and dangerous work. They had no idea what they might find, but in fact they hadn't found anything. If the Iraqis had biological or chemical warheads for their modified missiles, they were yet to make an appearance.

Still, the SEALs had given the intelligence people something extremely valuable—a first, detailed hands-on examination of an al-Hussein Scud. The information, photographs, and descriptions of the expert SEALs were carefully analyzed to find the flight parameters and capabilities of the weapon. A careful study of materials the SEALs had brought out from Sudan could now reveal the weaknesses of the design.

Knowing those weaknesses would be a big step in developing a defense against the Scud. With the new weapons technology being fielded by the U.S. forces, it could be possible for the first time to actually stop an incoming missile. With the proper programming of the U.S. defense missiles, the teeth of Saddam's new weapon might be pulled, or at least blunted.

1335 ZULU
Grid Zone NI 38-1, Coordinates NP614270
South of Salman Pak
Iraq

The Salman Pak biological warfare facility was built on a huge expanse of land, more than twenty square kilometers, at the tip of a peninsula formed by a curve in the Tigris River. The entire peninsula was fenced off and patrolled by armed Republican Guards. The reason for the loyal security not only centered on the type of work done at the facility, but also on the two opulent villas on the grounds. The larger one, rarely used by its owner, belonged to President Hussein, the smaller to his nephew, Abdul Talfaq.

When Talfaq wanted to impress his people during a meeting, he sometimes had them come to offices he maintained at Salman Pak. In spite of the surroundings of trees and flowering gardens, visitors would have noticed the heavy security they had to pass through to get into the site. It didn't take much imagination to realize that the facility was a very bright and gilded prison. If the occupant didn't want you to leave, you wouldn't.

Late in August 1990, Talfaq was holding a meeting for several people from his biological weapons development facilities. The invasion of Kuwait and its annexation as the nineteenth province of Iraq was already a success. But the coalition forces were building up strength. Saddam wanted more weapons of greater power to convince the coalition forces that conducting an offensive against him would be a mistake. Talfaq knew Saddam wanted a nuclear weapon. But technical problems were preventing him from giving Saddam what he wanted.

No matter how powerful you were in Iraq, Saddam Hussein was still above you. If he looked on you with favor, it was because you gave him what he wanted. Telling him he couldn't have it was a quick way to fall from grace, even if you were a blood relative. Abdul Talfaq well knew his position and how quickly he could fall from grace. Supplying a biological weapon of mass destruction could save him from Saddam's anger at the lack of a nuclear weapon.

Around the table of the conference room were some of Talfaq's best technicians and administrators from the biological weapons program. The Hushmand woman was pretty and easy to look at, but then, so was a colorful snake. You could admire them but be wary of their poison. She was ambitious and desired power, which was something Talfaq knew how to manipulate. Yes, Badra Hushmand bore watching for a number of reasons.

The woman's brother was a very competent scientist. The people around him called him "Dr. Germ" for his passion to develop more and more lethal strains of agents. But his practical application of the agents he developed was lacking. He liked power, was intelligent, and had ambitions of his own. Only the fact that he was willing to follow his sister's lead kept him from being the more dangerous of the siblings.

Right now, Talfaq was more interested in what Abu Waheed was able to say. The man was a fool as far as political intrigue went. He didn't seem to realize just how much the Hushmand woman needed him, and just how much she hated him because of that need. But his technical expertise had the best chance of making the project succeed, and that was all Talfaq was interested in—for the moment.

"We must have a production line for the weapons up and running as soon as possible," Talfaq said as he addressed the people in the room in a loud voice. "Saddam wants these weapons now. I don't care what it takes, the production program is to be given a maximum priority."

"If we had been given the facilities we needed

earlier," Badra Hushmand complained, "we would be much further ahead than we are now."

"Do not give me excuses," Talfaq said in a dangerous tone of voice. "You have a crash program priority now. If you can't give me what is necessary, I will find someone who can."

The woman sat back in her seat and her dusky skin blanched at the threat. It had been a while since someone had talked to her like that. She didn't like it, but a predator quickly recognizes a stronger predator—it was the only way to survive. And she realized just how fast her "retirement" from the program and her position could take place.

Dismissing Badra by turning away, Talfaq faced Abu Waheed and addressed him directly. "What is the situation," he said, "in regards to actually loading a series of the bombs, and especially the missile warheads?"

"The R-400 modifications of the Expal BR-250-WP bombs are not a problem," Abu said simply. "The problem comes from the limited production ability we have to produce the dried agents. We can load up a number of the bombs within ninety days or so."

"That long?" Talfaq asked.

"Even with all of our facilities running for just the three major agents," Abu said, "it takes time to grow and process the materials. It doesn't matter how much money or people we put on it, the bacteria will only grow so fast. For the R-400 bombs, we can use the wet slurry system already in place. That will speed things up once we have the bulk filler."

"A purification and filling technique developed and put in place by my brother," Badra said with a smile and a nod to her sibling, sitting next to her.

"Yes, I know all of that," Talfaq said with a dismissive wave of his hand. "If it takes that long, it must. But how many weapons can we have by say, December?"

"The R-400 bombs?" Abu said as he started to jot notes on the papers in front of him. The technician didn't notice the glares Badra sent his way. He was getting deep into his subject and not paying attention to the ramifications his successes might cause for him.

"By December," Abu said after a few moments, "we can field about 175 R-400 bombs. Because of the wet-slurry loading, they will need a more regulated storage environment, but we have the refrigerated bunkers in place."

"What loadings will those bombs have?" Talfaq asked.

Picking up his papers, Abu read out loud, "about one hundred botulinum toxin loadings, fifty anthrax, and maybe sixteen aflatoxin."

"Why the aflatoxin?" Talfaq asked.

"We have it available," Saeed Hushmand said, speaking up for the first time. "There is a small stockpile of it from the tests we conducted earlier. We didn't go further with it because the lethality of the agent is not as rapid or effective as we wanted. The aflatoxin comes from the growth of fungus aspergillus, but we've only done that on a laboratory scale. It causes liver cancer in humans but is not rapidly lethal. We were examining its potential as an agent in combination with other materials."

"Very well," Talfaq said. "Include it with the total loadings. But what is the problem with the missile warheads? Those are of primary importance to our president."

"Loading the warheads takes another type of processing for the agent," Abu explained. "We have to freeze-dry the materials for dissemination, and that takes time."

"Time which we do not have in abundance," Talfaq said.

"No, but the warheads will work," Abu said. "I only wish we had a better system to work with. The triple-explosive burster method we are using on the al-Hussein warheads is limiting. The explosive system was intended for a liquid agent, not the dry one that works."

Abu did not notice the vicious look Badra shot his way. Her brother had designed the warhead system for use with his filler systems. But the technician had been right and his dry agent loadings were the way to go. He had proven her brother wrong, and that wasn't something she was going to easily forgive.

"The three explosive burster wells are simultaneously detonated from a contact fuse," Abu continued. "That is not the best way to disburse a dry, powdered agent. If we could change the warhead design—"

"Nothing is going to be changed at this stage," Talfaq said loudly. His tone of voice startled even Abu. "Your wishes are unimportant. The warheads you are working with shall be what you have. There are no others.

"In anticipation of the success of this project," Talfaq went on in a softer and more reasonable tone, "delivery systems have already been put into place. The present warhead design has to be used. Any major changes in the design, and the new warheads might not match up with the delivery systems already in the field. Or worse still, they might not work correctly. If that was to happen—the repercussions could be very serious."

Startled glances went around the conference table. "Serious" could mean anything from being fired to being sent out to some unimportant rural site. Or it could mean that people would just disappear. One day they were there, the next day they were gone. And no one knew, or would say, what had happened to them. This had already happened to a number of scientists in the nuclear weapons project. That was the cost of their failure.

"And there has been an additional complication," Talfaq continued, as if he hadn't noticed the widespread reaction to his threat. "The UN has seen fit to pass another of their illegal proclamations. Their Resolution 665 now allows the ships of the coalition to use force to illegally stop Iraqi commerce with the rest of the world. Their navies are now little more than pirates and brigands on the high seas, stopping the flow of goods to and from Iraq.

"This means that it will be just a little harder to move the warheads and delivery systems into place. The American president is but a paper tiger, as he was called by the Vietnamese just a few years ago. The ill-equipped Viet Cong stopped the much-vaunted might of the U.S. military, and they will find Iraq a much harder enemy to defeat.

"The American president will do nothing directly against Iraq. And when our Muslim brothers who have been fooled into joining that poor mob of a coalition finally see the Americans' cowardice, the coalition will fall apart. If it doesn't fall quickly enough, the precautions our great leader is putting into place will still hand us the victory.

"And I intend this project to be a major contributor to that ultimate victory," Talfaq said loudly as he slammed his hand down on the table. "Does anyone here feel differently?"

Talfaq looked around the table, and no one's eyes would meet his directly. This was fine with him—they were simply acknowledging his leadership. And more important was the fact that they would build the bombs and missile warheads for him—they were too afraid not to.

EPILOGUE

★ ★ ★ ★

0537 ZULU
October 1990
Office of the Deputy Director of Operations
CIA Headquarters
Langley, Virginia

Dr. Sharon Taylor ran a hand through her hair as she read another in a stack of intelligence reports on her desk. There was no question in her mind that the Iraqis were pushing forward with their biological weapons program. In spite of the embargo against shipping to or from Iraq, she knew that they had gathered enough supplies and materials over the years to run a massive bioweapons program for months to come.

The problem was not in suspecting that the Iraqis had such a program, but in locating the laboratories, production, and storage facilities that were necessary to make a disease a military weapon. In spite of the secrecy surrounding Saddam's bioweapons program, locating the facilities and the personnel who manned them would be a much easier proposition than trying to stop the weapons once they got to the field.

Putting down the documents, Dr. Taylor picked up the cup of coffee on her desk and held it in both hands. She leaned back, looked at the materials scattered across the desktop and reflected on the knowledge they contained.

The idea of biological weapons in the hands of terrorists and military dictators was one that had haunted her for years. It had taken major work on her part to convince the higher commands in the CIA, the Pentagon, and the politicians up on the Hill in D.C., that the threat was a real one. The Navy had been the first to respond to her arguments.

She looked at the speed-dial buttons to the left of the handset on the phone on her desk. The button second from the top would ring at a desk in the Pentagon. Answering that phone would be a Navy captain who knew just what she meant by a biological threat and what some of the responses to that threat could be. He was the first in the direct line of command of a tiny, elite military unit in Virginia Beach, a unit Dr. Taylor knew very well.

As she moved back to the work on her desk, Dr. Taylor knew that the SEALs of the Special Materials Detachment would be ready to go after any target she identified. They were very good at what they did and had proven that to her more than once, the last time only two months earlier.

She knew that the SEALs were there, at the other end of a phone line. And that gave her a very good feeling indeed.

The
TV SI
24